All Hallows' Eve

The Moon's Harvest

KEN CAROLL

BOOK 1

Published by GoPublish, a division of Visual Adjectives.
Delray Beach, Florida.
www.VisualAdjectives.com
info@VisAdj.com

ISBN-13: 978-1-941901-03-8 (paperback)
ISBN-10: 1-941901-03-4 (paperback)
ISBN-13: 978-1-941901-49-6 (e-book)
ISBN-10: 1-941901-49-2 (e-book)

Library of Congress Control Number: 2016959668

First American Paperback Edition

Art by Ken Caroli
Book design and layout by Universal Designers

Dedicated to
Dark Shadows, for inspiring me
and
John Reid, for encouragement over the years.

BOOK 1
THE MOON'S HARVEST

TABLE OF CONTENTS

9 | **Chapter 1**
"A Signpost up Ahead"
Sunday, September 12, 1982

19 | **Chapter 2**
"Falcon's Aerie"
Sunday, September 12, 1982

31 | **Chapter 3**
"Homecoming"
Sunday, September 12, 1982

41 | **Chapter 4**
"First Impressions"
Sunday, September 12, 1982

53 | **Chapter 5**
"A Little Dinner Conversation"
September 12, 1982

61 | **Chapter 6**
"The Legend of the Curse"
September 12, 1982

69 | **Chapter 7**
"Colin's Story"
September 12, 1982

79 | **Chapter 8**
"The end of the Beginning"
September 12, 1982

85 | **Chapter 9**
"Music of the Night"
September 13, 1982

95 | **Chapter 10**
"Old News"
Thursday September 16, 1982

105 | **Chapter 11**
"An Afternoon Swim"
September 17, 1982

117 | **Chapter 12**
"Someone is Watching You"
September 17, 1982

125 | **Chapter 13**
"Reminiscing"
September 18, 1982

185 | **Chapter 14**
"A Morning Ride"
September 18, 1982

145 | **Chapter 15**
"Brownies"
September 18, 1982

TABLE OF CONTENTS

157 | **Chapter 16**
"A Chill in the Air"
September 18, 1982

167 | **Chapter 17**
"Conflicting Messages"
September 21, 1982

177 | **Chapter 18**
"The Pentacle"
Friday, September 24, 1982

185 | **Chapter 19**
"Contrary Appearances"
Saturday, October 2, 1982

193 | **Chapter 20**
"Oktoberfest"
Sunday, October 3, 1982

203 | **Chapter 21**
"Interrupted Journeys"
October 3, 1982

211 | **Chapter 22**
"The Wolf Man Cometh"
October 3, 1982

219 | **Chapter 23**
"Beauty and the Beast"
October 3, 1982

227 | **Chapter 24**
"The Morning After"
October 4, 1982

287 | **Chapter 25**
"Moon Rise"
Monday, October 4, 1982

247 | **Chapter 26**
"Creatures on the Loose"
October 4, 1982

259 | **Chapter 27**
"A Howling in the Woods"
October 4, 1982

267 | **Chapter 28**
"The Beast Must Die!"
October 4, 1982

275 | **Chapter 29**
"Awakenings"
Tuesday, October 5, 1982

285 | **Chapter 30**
"Truth or Consequences"
Tuesday, October 5, 1982

CHAPTER 1

A SIGNPOST UP AHEAD
SUNDAY, SEPTEMBER 12, 1982

Lighting flashed. The thunder cracked simultaneously. "Whew!" Cynthia jumped slightly. "That was a close one," she whispered to herself, her wary gaze darting about uneasily. She gripped the steering wheel tighter, peering into the murkiness beyond her windshield. Cynthia brushed aside a strand of her long blond hair that had fallen, unbidden, in front of her turquoise eyes.

Thick angry clouds hid what remained of the late afternoon sun. Rain came down in gray sheets, so heavy that she could scarcely see through it. Her windshield wipers couldn't swish the water away fast enough. Outside, Cynthia could hear the repeated splashes of her tires as they went through the puddles on this lonely stretch of Route 9. She could barely catch a glimpse of the Hudson to the west. The Mercury's headlights were able to reveal little of the road ahead.

Cynthia prayed that she wouldn't miss the turn onto the estate's private access road in this blasted downpour. It just had to pick tonight of all nights to come down like this, didn't it? Cynthia sighed in resignation, receiving no answer to her unvoiced question...Not that she'd expected one.

It was her first visit to the home of her new employers, the wealthy Blackthorne family. She recently passed the state exams to obtain her license as a child psychologist. "Dr. Cynthia Akers." How proud she'd been the day she got that coveted license. What a naive idiot she had been! After all those years of education, a doctoral thesis and two years of internship, it never occurred to her that she would have trouble finding a job. It had been just her luck to get her license during a damned recession.

In the months since she received her license, nobody would hire her. A few claimed that the positions that she applied for were already filled. One told her outright that she was too 'green'. Another said they were cutting jobs, not adding them, due to tight budgets, but most never responded at all.

Then an unexpected phone call promised to change her life. One of her favorite professors from Columbia, where she'd gotten her degrees, went to an old acquaintance, another alumnus, Dr. Richard Marsden. He ran his own sanitarium in the Hudson valley about two hours north of Manhattan, out in the country. Marsden offered

Cynthia a job, though a rather unusual one.

Marsden requested that she take a freelance job first then she could work for him at the sanitarium afterward. He didn't make it a condition of the job at the sanitarium, yet asked her to consider it. His godson, a retired musician, owned an estate a few miles from the sanitarium. Marsden's godson had just regained custody of his fourteen-year-old son after years of separation, due to a divorce. The boy, who was to be her patient if she accepted, had been troubled since before his parents divorced in 1976, mostly because of a family tragedy a few months earlier.

Dr. Marsden felt the boy needed personal care from a therapist focused solely on him. That meant living at the estate. Later, if her charge required less intensive therapy, Cynthia could move to the staff quarters at the sanitarium until she could find a place of her own.

Though the request sounded a little odd, it was not unheard of amongst the wealthy; though it was more common to have live-in nurses or medical doctors than psychologists.

After an appropriate pause, Cynthia accepted the offer, trying not to sound as desperate as she really was. It wasn't as though anyone else was beating down her door with job offers. She had to pay off her student loans somehow.

Marsden gave her directions to the estate over the phone, promising to meet her there for dinner, where he'd introduce her to the family. The estate, called Falcon's Aerie, lay on a bluff overlooking the Hudson in Putnam County, south of Peekskill. West Point was a bit further to the north, across the river. Somewhat beyond that was the bridge between Beacon and Newburgh.

The town nearest the state was a tiny unincorporated village called Corchester-on-Hudson. It was just a couple of miles from the estate, between Route 9 and the river. Although it was less than fifty miles from the Big Apple, Corchester might well have been on a different planet. It was a quaint little town, Marsden told her, yet slowly dying of attrition as the younger locals moved elsewhere for work and excitement.

Not much had changed in Corchester for decades. The place saw a few tourists during the summer months and later to observe the fall colors, but the town virtually closed up during the winters; the people where on the clannish side, and not particularly welcoming to outsiders as more than short-term visitors. Cynthia laughed that it sounded charming. But she wasn't going there for the scintillating social life.

The Blackthornes had bought the estate less than a decade earlier. The place had been built by one of the Victorian era's fabled robber barons. The last member of the original family to dwell there was the son of the builder. He passed away in the mid '40s. A surviving cousin inherited the estate, yet did not live there. He had let the place become derelict, so it was relatively cheap by the time Blackthorne purchased it in 1973.

The original owner was an investor in the railroads. The estate had once been served by a private spur line, as well as steamboats at its docks. Little remained visible of the spur, save for the ruined depot, which was abandoned during the Great Depression, cars having rendered it obsolete.

The mansion resembled the Gilded Age cottages of other fashionable havens of the rich such as Newport, the Berkshires, the Hamptons, Bar Harbor in Maine, and Long Island's North Shore. But the Hudson Valley was the oldest enclave due to its proximity to New York City, via the railways and steamboats.

The builder's family had owned the estate since the 1820s, although the current house wasn't built until about sixty years later. It was a family seat rather than a vacation cottage. Cynthia hypothesized it had been constructed where it was because it had already been the family home for a long time. At the time, Newport and the other colonies of the rich had yet to crystallize.

Dr. Marsden suggested the place was chosen out of a desire for privacy, and though it still seemed a trifle excessive to Cynthia, it did make sense for a retired rock star trying to get out of the limelight. Fans or reporters would not have an easy time finding the place.

Hopefully, Cynthia wouldn't get lost once off the main highway. What she'd viewed of the scenery before the rain set in was gorgeously bucolic. She could understand why someone might choose to live here. It was beautiful and quiet. Yet, for a suburban girl like Cynthia, it was too different from what she was used to. She found it daunting... too wild and isolated for her taste.

Intellectually, Cynthia knew that she was in greater danger at home in Queens than out here in the open country and small towns of the valley, but in the city she knew what to expect; if not always when to expect it. Here, surrounded by fenced-off meadows and woods with houses few and far between, she felt out of her element. Driving out here alone in the storm, Cynthia found the comparative wilderness disconcerting.

If anything were to happen to her out here, on a night like this... Cynthia shook herself forcefully. She could not afford to start thinking like that. It was just the apprehension about her new job and the weather. At least, so she kept telling herself.

Cynthia kept an eye out for the run-off to the estate. If anyone mentioned to her that there was a signpost up ahead, she felt sure she'd jump out of her skin, even if it wasn't Rod Serling. It all seemed too much like the Twilight Zone to her, as if she was leaving the normal workday world behind for some strange alternate universe.

The uncanny resemblance to a gothic novel wasn't lost on her either. The question was, once she went down this road, would she ever return to the world she knew? Laughing at her own foolishness, Cynthia shook her head wryly and drove on.

Cynthia turned off onto the estate's service road. The rain was still heavy, the thunder now grumbling off in the distance instead of right overhead. Periodic flashes of lighting illuminated the sky. Glancing up at her rear view mirror, Cynthia jumped, startled by what she saw there.

In the back seat was a young woman, soaked to the bone, her expression sad and her skin deathly pale. Her long dark hair was bedraggled. She appeared to be in her late teens or early twenties. From what Cynthia could tell, the girl was slim and not very tall. Although pretty, she made a distinctly eerie impression. She didn't speak and her luminous violet eyes, rimmed in shadow, never blinked. There was no malevolence about her, only an oppressive sorrow.

Cynthia screamed, accidentally jerking the steering wheel to one side. Her car whirled out of control, the tires screeching through the nearest puddles. She slammed her foot on the brakes, but the wheels found no purchase on the wet road. The Cougar was half off the pavement before it careened to a stop, with a jolt.

Once the car ceased to shudder, Cynthia checked the mirror again. She saw nothing. The backseat was empty. There was nowhere in the backseat big enough to hide. Cynthia hadn't stopped since the rain began. She must've imagined it. That was the only possible explanation. Too much morbid rumination...

Since it had to have been a hallucination, why that particular image now? Who could the girl have been? Cynthia couldn't recall ever meeting her or seeing a photograph of her. Yet, she must have without realizing it. Was it just the rain and the lonely road?

"They need you," said an unfamiliar voice — that of a young woman. It was full of sadness and Cynthia noted the hint of a British accent. "They're waiting. I tried to save them. I failed. You may be able to. You stopped him once before. Please — please help them..."

Searching for the source of the voice, Cynthia checked the mirror again. It remained empty. She felt a chill, like the breeze off a glacier, beside her. Turning, she gasped, stunned. The hollow-eyed girl sat in the passenger's seat next to her. Cynthia stifled a scream, nearly going off the road once more before correcting herself.

"Beware. He waits there, too. He caused all this with his hatred. He will try to stop you. Please don't let him...or they will all die.... on the Blood Moon."

Almost before she finished speaking, the strange girl was gone, as though she'd never been there. Maybe she hadn't. It had to be an illusion, Cynthia kept repeating to herself over and over. There was no other possibility. She must've been mesmerized by the road, preoccupied by the storm and nervous about her upcoming job. That was all it could be.

Curiosity aroused, Cynthia ran her hand along the passenger seat. Quickly, she pulled it away as if stung. To her surprise, the seat was wet, almost slimy, like something from the bottom of the sea had sat there. The dampness was icy-cold to the touch...

The window must've been open a crack, letting the rain in without her noticing it, Cynthia surmised. She'd been so preoccupied it could easily have happened and yet, the wind was blowing from the opposite side of the car, so it shouldn't have seeped in. Feeling the passenger-side window, Cynthia noted that there was no trace of moisture, not even a veneer of condensation. There was no drip outside....

Cynthia checked the headliner in case the moisture had come through the car's roof. It was a twelve-year-old car, after all. Maybe it had rusted through beneath the vinyl and she hadn't noticed before. The headliner was dry...

Cynthia shivered. She didn't know how to explain what had just occurred. It made no sense. The girl couldn't have been in there, yet Cynthia had heard her speak, felt the wet seat, with nothing to dampen it. The seat had a somewhat briny odor to it. It had not been quite like the smell of the sea, yet she'd noticed it. So all her senses had been involved, or else they were all fooled.

She didn't believe in ghosts. It wasn't as though she had just read a Gothic novel or watched a horror movie. It was a while since Cynthia had read an entire novel of any kind or seen a movie in the theatre. She'd been too busy with her internship. So, where had the image of that girl come from? It baffled her.

And who was she supposed to save, and from what and whom? Given its dubious source, Cynthia probably ought to ignore the warning, but that was far easier said than done. She was not about to back off if somebody needed her. She prayed she wasn't going crazy.

Cynthia wasn't stupid. She hadn't received any "ghostly" visitations until she was well on her way to the estate. The warning almost had to be related to the Blackthornes in some way, if there was anything to it at all. It was a fair bet that her new patient was one of those she was asked to help. Who were the others? Was it the entire family, or only some of them? And who was the "he", whose hatred had caused everything?

Since she was not far from the estate, Cynthia guessed that she would soon learn the answers to the questions swirling through her brain. Was she up to the challenge? Should she turn back now, while she still could? Cynthia continued driving, the answer never seriously in doubt. She'd just have to wait and see if the ominous warning was born out or if it really was just all in her head...

About a mile up the service road, Cynthia came to a wall of stone with high wrought-iron gates between tall piers. Those were topped by weather-stained marble urns. Above the gate, amidst the florid iron tracery was a bronze oval incised with the name Falcon's Aerie in old English script. Eight feet up was a pair of decorative brass lanterns. Though obscured by the rain, they glowed softly in the darkness. A small lamp rested atop the oval, aimed down to illuminate the name.

She had arrived at last. She wondered what she would find here. A new chapter in her life was about to begin...

CHAPTER 2

FALCON'S AERIE
SUNDAY, SEPTEMBER 12, 1982

A few feet from the gates, there was a metallic box about two feet in height. On its raised, beveled surface, there was a speaker and several buttons. Just beneath the lanterns, Cynthia spied a couple of cameras angled down at incoming vehicles. Reluctantly, she rolled down her window. Since the mercury was facing westwards, the rain primarily struck her windshield rather than soaking her. She was grateful for small favors, though her hand and arm got drenched.

Cynthia pressed the button, signaling that she was there, and then waited impatiently. For a moment she wondered why the gates were even closed. She'd been told that they expected her. Then she reprimanded herself. Why have gates at all, unless you used them? The estate was out of the way and the Blackthornes were wealthy. That made them a tempting target for criminals...or the press. They couldn't just let anyone wander in without warning...could they?

"Is anyone there?" Cynthia asked, thrumming her fingers on the steering wheel, with an annoyed sigh. "My name is Dr. Cynthia Akers...I'm expected.

"Hold on, Doc...I'm gettin' there," answered a male voice. "We expected yuh. We just didn't know when yuh'd get here," the speaker sounded relatively young.

The gates slowly swung inward. Relieved, Cynthia put her window up. She wiped off her hand and arm then took her car out of park. She drove through the gates, and heard them clank shut behind her. It was a faintly ominous sound, given her mood.

A head of her lay a two-story, L-shaped building with a turreted round tower where the wings came together. On the ground level was a series of Romanesque arches. Cynthia guessed that they must be the former stables and carriage house, which had since become the garages.

Cynthia pulled towards the entrance where she saw a sliver of light. It was a set of double doors parting, a tall figure silhouetted against the light in the opening. She drove into the garage and put the car in park, then switched off the ignition. Taking out the keys, she thrust them into her purse. Then she pushed a button to pop her trunk and, grabbing her purse, got out of the car.

Closing the door of her car, Cynthia didn't bother to lock it. If it wasn't safe in a garage behind locked gates and walls, her car's lock would do little good. She headed for the back of the car to retrieve her luggage. Only then did she get her first clear look at the man who'd admitted her.

Tall and athletically built, he had longish wavy auburn hair and a full beard, with warm hazel eyes and a broad smile. He wore a flannel shirt over a t-shirt and faded jeans. Beneath the frayed cuffs was an old pair of Dr. Martins work boots. His hair and shirt were damp from having just shut the garage doors against the storm.

"Hi, Doc...sorry it took me a coupla' minutes. I just got back from the main house. I had a' bring Mrs. Jeffers some groceries for tuhnight's dinner an' help her put 'em in the pantry. It's a bit of a drive tuh the nearest store, in Garrison, 'specially in this mess. All they got in town's a damn convenience store. I'd a' been down sooner, but I was dryin' off upstairs. I'm Mat, by the way, Matthew Hunter. I work here as a sorta' jack-of-all-trades, groundskeeper, chauffeur, handyman, sometimes even a mechanic. Harlon-he's gettin' on in years-ain't up tuh as much as he used tuh be, but don't tell 'im I told yuh so."

"I won't," Cynthia giggled. "It's nice to meet you, Mr. Hunter." Cynthia offered him her hand which he shook. "Then you're the security here, too?"

"For now," Mat grinned in self-deprecation. "We're between companies at the moment. The last one raised its prices. So, Mr. Seth fired em' last week. Besides, Mr. Holderness wanted tuh upgrade the system now that his kid's here. Mr. Blackthorne and Leese-Lisa Ramirez, the secretary, are gonna be interviewin' new companies in a few days. I gotta handle the gates till they hire somebody."

"Do they really need the walls, gates, cameras and the rest?" Cynthia had wondered about that since she drove up to the entrance.

"Not so much these days," Mat chuckled good-naturedly. "But Mr. Holderness likes his privacy. So does Mr. Blackthorne. They especially don't want reporters gettin' in. Mr. Holderness don't tour no more, but he still sold millions a' records. People're nosey 'bout celebrities, even retired ones. The walls and gates' a been here since the place was built, but the Blackthornes put in all the ground lamps, cameras and motion detectors. They had a bad break in here years back; long time before I was hired. There was a lotta reporter's nosin' around here in them days, from what I heard. It was a real mess. It did take a while for the cops tuh get out here if we needed 'em. Corchester don' have its own force."

"The owner is the Ian Holderness of Odyssey? I knew the owner was a retired British musician, but I never guessed it was him. I assumed his last name was Blackthorne, like the family."

"I didn't know myself when I got hired," Mat nodded knowingly. "Heard his real dad was an American that died over there in World War II. I'm not sure o' his name. Mr. Holderness was about two or three when his mom married Mr. Blackthorne's dad. Mr. Blackthorne's Mr. Holderness' stepbrother. They was raised tuhgether. Dr. Marsden was the buddy of Mr. Holderness' real dad an' later Mr. Blackthorne's father. Doc Marsden helped 'em get their green cards. Since Mr. Blackthorne's dad didn't approve a' rock n' roll, Mr. Holderness used the name a his hometown so's not tuh embarrass the family."

"I never knew about that," Cynthia commented honestly. "My brother, Danny, used to have some Odyssey albums before he went into the Marines."

"Jar-head, huh?" Mat raised an eyebrow, his tone cryptic.

"Danny was in the Marines from '71 to '73," Cynthia stated off-handedly.

"I was in the service '74 tuh '76," Mat shared, his face unreadable. "Army. Couldn't wait tuh get out. Too much crawlin' round in the mud-getting' yelled at all the fuckin' time- too much nit-pickin' for me, thank you."

"Danny's a detective down in the Bronx." Cynthia ignored what Mat had said about his stint in the military. He had the right to his opinion. It wasn't her place to disapprove of it, though Danny was proud of his time in the Corps. "My family lives in Queens," she added.

"So he's a pi...a cop," Mat corrected himself mid-word.

"Yes." Cynthia pretended not to notice Mat's slip of the tongue. It wasn't the first time she's heard the police called pigs. She doubted it would be the last. Both she and Danny had heard far less polite terms. Cynthia had been called a shrink, or worse.. sometimes even by Danny, but at least he'd been joking. Not everybody was. "Do you have an umbrella?" She changed the subject. "I should've brought a raincoat, but it wasn't raining when I left the city. So, I didn't think of it." She hadn't wanted to over-pack. They'd fire her if they saw a U-Haul pull up with all her things.

Cynthia started to reach into her trunk to unload her suitcases, but Mat gestured her to one side.

"Let me help yuh, Doc," he offered, grasping one and lifting it out for her. "Then I'll get yuh an umbrella when I get my raincoat. I'll carry your bags up tuh the house for yuh." He took out the other two suitcases and set them on the ground. Cynthia closed the trunk, grateful that Mat had removed the luggage for her. Despite her best intentions, she'd still over-packed. Danny had had to help her put them in the trunk for the drive up to the estate.

"Thanks," Cynthia replied with genuine gratitude. "Sorry they're so heavy." She blushed slightly.

"Don't sweat it, Doc." Mat laughed. "They're not that bad. Heavy work's what I'm here for." He winced slightly but sought to hide it. Cynthia could barely budge them on her own. Maybe she ought to have brought fewer shoes.

"Let's get goin," Mat said as he took a raincoat and put it on. "They're expectin' yuh up at the main house. Sooner we get through this fuckin' rain, the better."

Cynthia nodded, sighing internally. She dreaded the walk, certain she'd look a fright before reaching the house, but there was nothing for it, and no other way to get there. Wordlessly, Mat handed her the umbrella he'd promised. Steeling herself, Cynthia opened it and raised it above her head, striding out onto the cobblestone drive. The rain continued relentlessly.

The main drive ran relatively straight from the gates for about a hundred yards, with a modest curve as it approached the house. It was perhaps twenty-feet wide, capable of handling cars going in either direction at the same time. Tangled oaks overshadowed it, their twisted branches interlacing above them.

They'd been specially planted almost a century before to line the drive, obscuring the view of the mansion like a natural curtain. The canopy shielded them somewhat from the rain, though the dripping from the trees themselves was nearly as bad. The wind tugged at the umbrella, threatening to pull it from her grip as they walked.

Cynthia turned up the collar of her brown suede coat against the damp cold. It was chilly for a late summer evening. She wished that she'd worn gloves, her fingers feeling like ice. Her boots clattered on the cobblestone. Cynthia winced subtly when passing through the unavoidable puddles. The boots weren't cheap.

Wind whistled through the trees, rustling the leaves just on the edge of the turning, and causing the branches to groan in protest. Thunder added to the eerie atmosphere. Danny would've loved to have been there to rag on her for being affected by it, as he had when they were kids.

As the branches thinned out, the great mansion loomed ahead of them. Cynthia caught her breath at the first sight of it. Falcon's Aerie was a vast Victorian confection, combining Gothic, Tudor, Chateauesque, and Scottish baronial styles. It appeared as if it would be more at home in England or perhaps Newport, than in the rural Hudson valley.

A phalanx of chimneys reared up against the roiling sky, occasionally illuminated by dramatic arcs of lightning. Pointed iron combs ran along the ridges of the high-peaked slate roofs, with their carved dormers. Turreted drumlins, out of a Scottish castle, were at each corner where smooth Ashlar masonry gave way to rusticated quoins. Ivy climbed up the gray walls, surrounding mullioned windows set with myriad panes of leaded glass. Most of the upper windows were dark, though those of the main block on the ground floor were brilliantly lit. Flanking each of the hyphens to either side of the main block were peaked round towers, soaring into the night.

A massive rectangular tower raised its crenelated parapets sixty feet above the drive at the middle of the main block. A large porte cochere crouched at the tower's base, protecting the principal doors from the elements. The Tudor arches of the porte cochere were high enough to admit a horse and carriage, with plenty of room to spare. In front of that was a three-tiered marble fountain, whose gurgling was temporarily lost in the staccato beat of the rain.

To either side of the main block were equal hyphens that had Tudor half-timbering beneath the eaves. A lower, more symmetrical wing, was to the north, while a one-and-a- half story extension opened south, via French doors onto the wraparound terrace.

A pair of brass lamps glowed beside the polished oak main doors, inlaid with gothic tracery in aged green bronze. The door knobs were of polished brass, as were the knockers in the shape of rings grasped by birds of prey. They gleamed like gold in the lamplight. A great gilded lantern on a draped chain hung from the wooden roof of the porte cochere'. Three broad low steps lead up to the doors.

"Wow!" Cynthia gushed in amazement. "When Dr. Marsden mentioned an estate I never expected anything this spectacular. It's right out of an old movie."

"Yeah," Mat agreed, chuckling. "The house of Frankenstein or Castle Dracula..." he rolled his eyes theatrically "Leese says it gives her the creeps, but it's just a big old house tuh me; more tuh take care of. That's why I'm here. Harlan and his wife, Aida, the housekeeper, are both in their sixties. They've been the caretakers here for years, since the last of the original family died. Mr. Holderness kept 'em on when he bought the place. They had no place else tuh go after so long, but they could never handle this place on their own anymore. Even with me here, they got half the house locked off. The family don't need that much space and there ain't no other full-time servants, 'cept Mr. Blackthorne's attendant, Hutchinson, and Leese, Mr. Holderness's secretary. Crazy, huh? Must be fifty rooms in this damn place."

"Fifty? Really?" Cynthia was fascinated, gazing up at the mansion in unconcealed wonder.

"That's what I heard," Mat shrugged. "Not that I ever bothered tuh count 'em."

"That's the family like?" Cynthia asked, trying not to sound as curious as she was.

"They're okay, I guess," Mat replied, uneasy at her question and trying to be diplomatic. "Mr. Blackthorne runs this place, even if he is in that wheelchair. You heard he was in a car accident not long after they moved here. He's nice enough, I suppose, but that chair creeps me out, though I shouldn't admit it. Mr. Holderness is usually friendly. He can be a cool dude. He's got his own studio over the garages, and he lets me ride his Harley sometimes. I'd love tuh own one o' those babies. But he...ain't around much an' he gets moody."

"What about Mr. Holderness' son?" Cynthia interjected, hoping to learn more about her patient.

"Don' really know the kid," Hunter shook his head negatively. "Mr. Holderness an' his wife split up a long time ago. She took the kid back tuh England with her. Leese said she's gettin' married again, so she pawned the kid off on us. Poor kid's afraid a his own frickin' shadow; been to a dozen doctors over there. He's only been here three weeks an' the bullies are already pickin' on 'im cause he's different. Kids can be brutal, know what I mean?"

"I know what you mean!" Cynthia answered guardedly, remembering her own childhood. She'd had...problems, terrible repeated nightmares. 'Crybaby', they'd called her... 'Freak'... 'Fraidy Cat'... Danny used to defend her from the other kids. Still, once in a while, he lipped and hurled the same insults at her when he got mad. But he always apologized later. Not everyone did. In fact, few did. Danny had his own bad dreams, yet was too stoic, even as a boy, to let on about it, except to her. "It must be hard on him. That has to be why Dr. Marsden asked me to drive up here tonight."

"Yep," Mat nodded. "That'd be why. If it keeps up, they're talkin' about bringin' in a tutor for him."

"So, Doc, ready tuh make the grand entrance?" Mat asked, winking at her wryly.

"Ready as I'll ever be." Cynthia inhaled deeply in preparation. "Let's get it over with...."

CHAPTER 3

HOMECOMING
SUNDAY, SEPTEMBER 12, 1982

Colin stared out his window forlornly. It was a nice enough room, his old one, in fact, but he hated it. This place could never be home to him again. Rain pelted the window, leaving beads and rivulets behind. He had turned off his bedside lamp so that the water cast weird shadows on the wall of his room. Thunder grumbled outside. At fourteen, he was too old for a night lamp, or so he tried to tell himself. He wasn't a bloody baby anymore, no matter what his taunters called him. A mere night light could not make him feel safe. Nothing could. What he feared could never be deterred by any lamp, since bullets had failed to stop it. He ought to be excited. He was with his father again, after almost seven years apart. Most kids would love to live in a mansion like Falcon's Aerie, with a rock star as a father, but they were idiots. Colin barely knew his father, not seeing him often even before he was taken to England by his mother. As for the estate itself, too much had occurred here; too many things he could never forget.

Colin hadn't forgotten a detail since that dreadful night...not a single ruddy one. He had been seven at the time. Ever since they told him things hadn't happened the way he remembered it. They were wrong. Colin knew better. He still lived the terror that began then.

Colin's father was always away touring or recording in those days. After he split from his group, he'd been home a little more often yet he became even more distant, if that was possible. His mother had been no better. Colin's grandparents and Aunt Jennifer tried to make up for his parents' neglect, but it just wasn't enough.

When they'd first moved to the estate, the place fascinated him. It had seemed like a fairytale castle to him then, but there was nobody his own age here. The kids from town weren't allowed to visit. Their parents disapproved of the new foreign owners, whom they saw as "dirty hippies". They resented the Blackthornes' wealth. That left Colin nobody to play with. He didn't go in town much, because they shunned or bullied him there. Nothing had changed.

The locals insisted the place was haunted. Before long, Colin came to believe them. The house had been closed up; virtually derelict for over thirty years, and the restoration went slowly. Much of the great mansion remained empty, musty and full of cobwebs. The heavy antique furniture, that he had to be so careful not to damage-the brooding portraits of people dead for decades, oppressed him. It added to the sense of unreality.

The woods filled Colin with foreboding; the eerie creaking of the tree limbs, the rustling of the leaves, the whistling and moaning of the wind, even the dappled shadows cast by the trees canopy. The fog rolled in off the Hudson, and when there was a storm it was worse...and there were lots of storms. Alone in this room after dark, the calls of the night birds chilled him, evoking all his childhood fears.

The estate started to feel less like a bright fairytale castle and more the haunted mansion the townsfolk said it was. Colin became increasingly convinced there was something there that had been there all along, though the adults denied it; something evil, waiting. Tragically, he'd been right. That horrible night had proven it.

Colin attempted to shove the memories away. He wanted to forget, even if he never could. His mother was preoccupied with her wedding plans....pretending that she didn't recall what had put her in the hospital for a ruddy month. She'd never been quite the same again.

She had put Colin into therapy and on all sorts of drugs. Yet, it hadn't worked any better for him than her attempts at self-medicating via alcohol, pills, and cocaine had. Kathryn acted as if she didn't realize that he knew what she was doing. But they both knew the truth. He acknowledged it, though afraid of it. Kate hid from the memory, pretending it didn't exist.

Colin's problem had gotten to be too much for her...too time-consuming and emotionally-draining. Now that she'd met somebody new, she needed a break from it all. Time for herself, she called it. Kathryn had carried the burden for seven years alone. Now, it was his father's turn.

Colin sensed that her fiancé, Phil something-or-other, was just his mother's latest attempt at distraction. Her fiancé would doubtless succeed as well as the drugs and booze had. Although angry at her for denying the truth, Colin couldn't hate his mother.

She wasn't a bad person, just wounded, though she refused to admit it.

Once she remarried, the alimony and child support stopped. Her fiancé refused to foot the bill for another man's troubled son. She couldn't afford all the doctors and drugs on her own without child support. Given her expensive tastes, they'd barely made it, even with alimony and child support. Kathryn claimed that she couldn't work because of him. Yet, she did love him in her own selfish, distracted way. As she never tired of saying, his dad was rich. She wasn't. It was time for Colin's father to share the responsibility.

Kate also insisted it was time Colin faced his fears and dealt with them, or he'd never lead a normal life. This was all for his own good. "Normal!" Colin thought bitterly. "What a joke." None of them would ever be normal again, no matter what they did or how many drugs they took. Kathryn couldn't bear to see the truth staring back at her though his eyes. That was the real reason he was back; so that she could go on pretending.

It was all Colin could do not to toss up the lunch he'd eaten a few hours before. His stomach was queasy, all roiled up. The terror this place evoked in him grew every minute...every bloody second that he was here. His head hurt and his heart pounded far too fast. Sweat beaded on his forehead. If he did throw up, it wouldn't be the first time since he'd found out he was coming back here...

Outside, the rain finally ceased and the clouds began to dissipate. The moon peeked out from behind the clouds at last. Colin stared at the slender crescent, where it hung over the estate like the scythe of the angel of death. It seemed to mock him. "Welcome home," it said. "I've been waiting for you."

Tears on his cheeks, Colin yanked the curtains shut, though he knew that the moon was still out there. Fighting a despairing sob, he crawled into bed and buried his head beneath the covers. It helped a little, but there was no escape for him there or any place else. No one could help and nowhere was really safe; just as he'd always known. He hadn't gotten away. He'd merely postponed the inevitable.

ALL HALLOWS' EVE
THE MOON'S HARVEST

Mat opened the double doors, and motioned for Cynthia to enter. She followed him in, and closed the dripping umbrella as she crossed the marble threshold. He turned and shut the outer doors behind them, cutting off the waft of cold, damp night air. Taking her umbrella and removing his raincoat, Mat hung them over a small metal grate that collected run-off via a drain. It was beneath the coat rack and umbrella stand, in a niche beside the outer doors.

They entered the foyer. It had a very high ceiling and polished marble tile floors. They were of gray, black, and white in an Arabic geometric pattern. Here and there, antique Persian rugs covered the tiles. At the center was a grand staircase to the second floor, with red velvet carpeting and elaborately carved mahogany balustrades. At the base of the banisters were two classically-inspired statues in bronze of a man and woman holding lit globes. Beside the stairs to the north was an old-fashioned Victorian wrought- iron elevator. On the other side of the stairs were the doors to the formal dining room. Next to the main doors was a pair of small marble-topped tables on which sat vases bearing freshly cut flowers. Above each table, there were matching mirrors in gilt baroque frames.

On the south side of the foyer a short hallway led to the library. The doors to the study were on the north wall next to what she guessed to be Seth Blackthorne's room. Between Seth's door and that of the study was another antique table, upon which sat an elegant vintage 1920s phone.

The paneling of the foyer was in a lighter, warmer-hued wood than the mahogany banisters. Beyond the elevator was a corridor to the room of the housekeeper and her husband. High above them glittered the impressive chandelier that brilliantly lit the foyer. Once again, Cynthia was awestruck. The interior was as incredible as the exterior.

"This place is unbelievable!" Cynthia whispered softly under her breath. "How do you take care of all this without an army to help you?"

"Ain't easy, Doc," Mat sighed with a weary grin. 'Takes a goddamned ladder tuh keep that thing clean." He pointed up at the chandelier. "It's too fuckin' dangerous for Aida tuh do it; she might fall, so I do it now."

"What's too dangerous Matthew?" asked a male voice from behind them, in a British accent. Neither of them had heard anyone approach. "And who is our lovely guest? You must introduce me."

Turning, Cynthia saw a middle-aged man in a wheelchair, coming toward them. She guessed that it must be Seth Blackthorne, stepbrother of the owner, uncle of her future patient. At the sight of Seth, Mat fought a frown.......

Blackthorne appeared to be in his forties, though his condition might've made him look older than he was. His moderately long brown hair was swept back from his forehead, with gray at the temples. He wore a brown jacket with patches at the elbows over a deep-green sweater vest. A blanket covered his legs.

Blackthorne must've been quite handsome when he was younger and healthy. He had grown pale from being indoors most of the time, and was gaunt as well. Fine lines radiated from his eyes and on his forehead. His eyes were an extraordinarily brilliant amber.

"This is Dr. Akers, Mr. Blackthorne," Mat replied stiffly, as if caught unawares. "I was just explainin' how I use a ladder tuh clean the chandelier."

"Yes...it is a bit of nuisance, I suppose," Seth mused. "I'm grateful to Matthew for maintaining it. It's such a stunning piece; all hand-cut Austrian crystal. The builder of this house, Jared Nicholson, brought it home from Vienna where he and his bride visited on their honeymoon a hundred years ago. I'm pleased to finally meet you at last. Dear Richard, Dr. Marsden, has spoken glowingly of you." Blackthorne smiled broadly, extending his hand in greeting. Cynthia reciprocated. "We've been eagerly awaiting you. Richard neglected to mention how attractive you are."

"Thanks for the compliment, Mr. Blackthorne," Cynthia blushed slightly. "With the way the weather's been, I was afraid I'd be a total mess by the time I got here," she demurred with a wary smile. She had been told at times that she was pretty, but she assumed they were just being polite.

When she looked in the mirror, she saw a hair a little straighter than she wished it was, lips that could be fuller, and skin in need of a deeper tan. Yet, maybe she was just too critical or too vain. Seth struck Cynthia as an inveterate flatterer. So, she took his effusive greeting with a proverbial grain of salt.

"You look fine, Doctor," Seth chuckled in mild amusement. "The weather had been atrocious tonight. It does remind me of home, though. Inclement weather is cliché there, but in season we can compete with England for rain and fog. Perhaps that's one reason Ian chose this place...all the "comforts" of home with better wine and lower taxes." Seth winked at her mischievously.

"If it rains like this normally here, I guess you're right. It's been a while since I've seen a storm like this. You don't have to call me 'Doctor'. I don't have a medical degree, like a psychiatrist. If I'm a doctor, it's only because I had to do a doctoral thesis. I don't want to be pretentious," Cynthia demurred, though she was proud of having earned the right to the title.

"That's alright, my dear. No need to downplay what you've achieved. While we don't stand on ceremony here, we have been known to have our own pretensions — occasionally," Seth's lips curled into a sardonic grin. "If we don't trumpet ourselves, who will?"

Cynthia knew he was making fun of her, yet it seemed a gentle mockery, meant with good humor. At least, she hoped so. Regardless, objecting to it would be too thin skinned of her. If Blackthorne was insulting her intentionally with his sarcasm, she refused to give him the satisfaction of getting visibly upset over it. She didn't know him yet. Best to give him the benefit of the doubt. "Is Mr. Holderness here?" Cynthia changed the subject.

"Yes." Seth frowned for a moment before he caught himself and forced an artificial smile. "He's upstairs. I'm sure he assumed you'd arrive a trifle later. Ian sometimes gets preoccupied and forgets the time."

"I was just curious," Cynthia fumbled, noticing that Blackthorne seemed to resent her question. It was an obvious one; she wondered why it bothered him.

"That's alright, Dr. Akers. It's a natural question. He is Colin's father. If I appeared to take it oddly, it's just that people are always asking for...or about my dear brother and he's rarely here to answer for himself. So, it's left to me to do it." Though his tone was polite, Seth's frustration with and jealousy of his brother was plain to see. She was in no position to criticize him for it, especially since she'd never met her employer. Maybe he'd earned the resentment.

"I understand that your nephew's having trouble at school," Cynthia shifted the subject yet again. If Blackthorne ran the household, it behooved her to not antagonize him on her first night here. It might be tempting to psychoanalyze the entire family and the staff, but they were not her patients.

"Yes, poor boy," Seth answered with apparent disinterest. "We all expected Kate to do something with him, maybe send him to boarding school. Instead, she fobbed him off on us."

CHAPTER 4

FIRST IMPRESSIONS
SUNDAY, SEPTEMBER 12, 1982

"Then you don't approve of his coming here?" Cynthia inquired warily.

"Nothing against the boy," Blackthorne waved one hand dismissively, shrugging. "His problems are understandable. Ian was always too busy and his marriage was shaky well before he and Kate got a divorce, but Colin only has two parents. So, what are you going to do? Given what happened here seven years ago, it's no wonder the boy is troubled."

"What did happen?" Cynthia's ears pricked up, not aware of any special incident at that time, unless it was the break-in Mat had mentioned earlier.

"I'd assumed you knew," Seth responded in a bored tone. "There was a deadly break-in here in the fall of '75, just before a party celebrating the release of Ian's solo album. Tragically, our security was inadequate at the time. They...whoever it was, broke into my stepmother's room, perhaps looking for jewelry. We never found out who. My late father shot at him but was ...stabbed before the man jumped through the window to escape. My father ...didn't make it and my stepmother had a heart attack when she found him. One of Ian's band mates, who was here to work on his solo album, was on the terrace at the time. He was thrown down the stairs to the garden. He died, too. My younger sister drowned just off our private dock, we assume, trying to escape the assailant. Ian nearly drowned trying to rescue her, but it was too late. Jen...she couldn't swim. Richard found poor Colin hiding in the boat house. He couldn't talk for weeks. How much he saw, we're not sure. He has vivid memories of that night, but there's no way to tell how accurate they are. He was only seven years old then, after all."

"That's terrible," Cynthia brought her hand to her throat in surprise. She'd never thought it was so bad. She was startled at the mention that her employer's sister had drowned at the estate. Could that be a coincidence? Possibly, but it was definitely an odd one.

"It would help if I had his files to study," Cynthia returned to the reason she'd come, avoiding family politics as much as possible, though she could see that wasn't going to be easy.

"Richard said they should be here tomorrow, perhaps Tuesday, if the post is timely," Seth sounded bored. "I do hope you'll have better luck than the doctors Kate took him to. They've had him on anti-anxiety and anti-depressant drugs for years, without success. It's sad really. Poor boy still wakes up screaming in the night. He just can't get over what occurred, not that any of us truly have." It didn't seem to trouble him much.

"I'll do my best to help him, Mr. Blackthorne," Cynthia promised earnestly.

"I'm sure you will, my dear," Seth sighed. "Of all the candidates, Richard spoke to us about he felt that you were the most promising, despite your lack of experience. You're young-sympathetic...focused only on him. That should help. You ought to be less threatening than...someone older." He was mildly baiting her and she knew it, implying that she was too young for the job.

"Thank you," Cynthia said sweetly, deciding not to take the bait. "This job means a lot to me. I've worked towards it all my life. I shouldn't admit it, but I really need this opportunity. I chose this career because of my own childhood. So, I'm not just saying it when I claim I'll do my best. I've been where he is now. I know what it feels like."

"How interesting," Seth perked up, his interest piqued. "You've been in therapy yourself? If it's not prying too much, may I ask the circumstances? You needn't answer if you don't want to.

"I don't mind," Cynthia replied calmly. "I had to go to psychologists and psychiatrists back when I was a girl, until I was about seven or eight, when we moved to New York. I used to have really bad dreams, the same one over and over. So, I woke up screaming, too. It's been more than twenty years....I can still remember how afraid they made me. I tried my best to forget them. My parents didn't know what to do for me. They tried to be sympathetic. They forbade me to watch scary movies, made my brother, Danny, stop picking on me, experimented with my diet, but none of it helped. I was always exhausted because I was too terrified to fall asleep. They took me to doctors, then psychiatrists. Some were nice enough, I suppose, but still threatening to a kid as young as I was then. Others were cold...too clinical, as if I was a lab specimen under a microscope. Just a problem to be solved; not a person. They put me on various drugs, too, to try to keep me quiet. It didn't do any good. They were less interested in what caused my dreams or making me feel better than in making me manageable. Eventually, the nightmares faded on their own as I got more involved in school and things, but I promised myself then that I would become a psychologist and treat my patients better than I was treated. You and your brother are giving me the chance to do that. I am grateful to you."

"It sounds like you're the perfect choice, Miss Akers....just what Colin needs," Seth smiled smugly.

Mat said nothing during their exchange, yet seemed distinctly uncomfortable. He looked around the room, trying not to focus on Cynthia or Seth. He felt out of his depth listening to them converse. Now that he'd brought her up to the house, he was the proverbial third wheel.

"Uh, if yuh don't mind, Doc...Mr. Blackthorne, I'll go take Dr. Akers luggage up tuh her rooms. I can get a fire started, since I'm already here now, an' I gotta take her bags up anyhow..."

"That would be great," Cynthia beamed at Mat with gratitude. "I need to warm up and dry off before dinner. I'll want to change, too. Is dinner formal, Mr. Blackthorne?"

"No," Seth chuckled. "You must be tired after your long drive up. Go relax a while, my dear. Dinner is at eight," he winked at her mischievously. "I'm sure you'll look lovely in whatever you choose to wear."

Cynthia forced a smile. Hopefully, the rest of the family would not prove as challenging as Seth. Besides, she didn't mind a bit of flattery, even if it did border on sarcasm. It would take more than that to scare Cynthia, if that's what Seth intended.

Dinner was served at 8:00 pm, as Cynthia was told that it would be. She chose a simple turquoise dress to match her eyes and a pair of open-toed high heels of the same color. The dress fell just above the knee, flattering without being exceedingly formal. Too tired to completely unpack, Cynthia did take out her makeup and brushes, along with her blow-dryer. While not as bad as she feared, her hair definitely needed some drying and a good brushing before she set it up for the evening.

Long hair could be wonderful, but it required a lot of work to maintain. She wished hers had more wave to it, on its own. At least she didn't have to dye it, since she was a natural blonde. Her twin, Danny's hair was even lighter than Cynthia's because he was outside more often than she was. He had a better tan, too, damn him! It annoyed Danny when people assumed he bleached his hair. He looked more like a stereotypical Californian than a Chicagoan or New Yorker.

When she got to the dining room, Seth was there, seated close to the head of the table. He wore a deep-blue jacket, over a pale-blue shirt, with an ascot in place of a tie. He grinned and waved for her to enter. "Do come in, my dear."

At the head of the table sat Ian Holderness. Though Cynthia hadn't previously known which member of the band he was in the old photos from Danny's Odyssey albums, she recognized him immediately. His hair was shorter than in those pictures. It was raven black with blue highlights. Parted on the left, it cascaded over his forehead and the collar of his russet turtleneck in unruly waves. Not a single gray hair was visible.

His skin was flawless, with a light tan. He had a mustache and a Vandyke goatee that gave him a rakish air. He was fine-featured, with a square jaw, though it was not as heavy as in some athletes. His smile was blindingly bright. She could easily drown in his silver-gray eyes. She remembered now why she'd though him cute back in her late teens.

Those almost-glowing eyes were difficult to look away from, though she noted shadows beneath them as if he hadn't slept well in a long time. She wondered what caused his sleepless nights. Maybe he was nervous about his son's recent return.

Holderness stood up when she entered the room. Although tall, he was less so than Mat or Dr. Marsden. He walked over to Cynthia. "Good evening, Dr. Akers," he said in the same deep rich voice familiar from his Odyssey vocals. "It's nice to meet you at last. I apologize for not being downstairs when you arrived. I was preoccupied, but that's no excuse." He held out his hand as if to shake hers. Cynthia held out her own, in turn.

She was surprised when, instead of shaking it, he bent his head and briefly kissed it instead, in a courtly manner. It was not what she'd expected, but Cynthia was quite willing to get used to it. He wordlessly pulled out her chair for her. "Welcome," he finally added with a wry grin. Once she sat down, Ian helped her to adjust her chair until she was comfortable. Then he went back and resumed his own seat.

Seth watched the proceedings with a broader-than-usual

Cheshire cat grin. He winked at Cynthia without immediately speaking, though clearly bursting with commentary. No one spoke.

"Wonderful to see you again, Doctor," Seth was unable to contain himself any longer. "You look as lovely as I said you would."

"Thank you, Mr. Blackthorne," Cynthia replied politely.

Holderness seemed about to say something; he gazed at Cynthia intently, but he did not speak, as if deciding against it. She wondered what he had been about to say, and then put the question aside as fruitless. She'd probably never know the answer, so why waste time on it?

Next to Seth sat a short girl, whose long, dark hair was pulled back by a scarf in a loose pony tail at the base of the neck. She had a heart-shaped face, her skin a soft golden brown. Her intelligent eyes were veiled by long lashes. Cynthia guessed the girl to be Lisa Ramirez. She looked even younger than the twenty-three years Mat had ascribed to her.

Opposite Lisa, was a lanky young black man, whom Cynthia estimated to be in his late twenties. His skin was a deep caramel color, his hair cropped short. He wore a coat and tie but did not seem comfortable in either, or maybe it was the occasion that made him ill at ease. He must be Jeremy Hutchinson, Seth's attendant.

Beside Lisa was Dr. Marsden. Cynthia had met him before, when she'd agreed to take the job. Then he'd reminded her of pictures she'd seen of Freud, though she thought Marsden to be better looking. A tall slim man, his hair was now white and he sported a full, yet trimmed, beard. His suit was dark blue, with a gray vest and wine-red tie. He remained vigorous even at sixty-eight.

Across the table sat an adolescent boy in a mint-green button-down shirt, his expression sullen, and his eyes downcast. He did not glance up when she entered the room. His medium-length hair was an odd, almost matte black that looked artificial to her. It could only be Colin. Cynthia couldn't tell what color the boy's eyes were.

The dining room was darkly paneled with antique eighteenth-century boards and a large marble fireplace at one end. Its style and motif was Neoclassical, rather than Gothic. Seascapes hung on the walls in elaborate frames. The table was long and rectangular,

covered by a silken cloth. When fully opened, it could seat twenty-six guests, but tonight the leaves had been removed for a more intimate setting of eight, but only seven places were filled.

There were seven high-backed chairs of dark carved wood, with red velvet upholstery. One was set aside, so Seth could roll his wheelchair up to the table. A bowl of flowers sat to either side of silver candelabra, above which glinted another chandelier, though a smaller one than in the foyer. Its electric candles illuminated the room. Curtained French doors dominated the west side of the room, facing the terrace and the garden. Beyond that, lay the river.

Dr. Marsden greeted Cynthia then made introductions to those she hadn't met formally yet. "You've met Seth and now Ian. Beside Seth is Miss Ramirez, his secretary. Next to me is Jeremy Hutchinson, Seth's attendant."

Lisa smiled warmly, blushing a little. "Hi," she greeted in a friendly manner. Jeremy nodded in acknowledgment, yet could only manage a wary half-smile. "Good Evening, Doctor."

"This is Colin," Marsden indicated the boy. Colin did not even look up, just made an unenthusiastic partial wave.

"Colin, you should say hello to Dr. Akers. You're being impolite," Ian's tone was soft but there was an edge underneath. "She drove a long way just to be here for you. The least you can do is look up and greet her."

"Hello, Doctor," Colin repeated his father's words dully, glancing up for a moment, yet still not looking directly at her. She saw that his eyes were a vivid brown. Ian sighed, shaking his head in frustration, but didn't press his son further. It was too soon to make a scene over minor infractions. He wasn't used to being a father again, and Colin wasn't used to having one.

"I'm happy to meet you all," Cynthia responded, concluding the awkward process as deftly as she could. While by no means terminally shy, Cynthia did not enjoy being the center of attention. She was more comfortable watching and listening than being the focus.

CHAPTER 5

A LITTLE DINNER CONVERSATION
SEPTEMBER 12, 1982

The dinner was roast beef, boiled potatoes, green beans, carrots, and soft, warm, buttered rolls, the fragrance of which filled the air. It made Cynthia's mouth water, reminding her of home. It was simple traditional fare, not gourmet, but it was delicious. Mrs. Jeffers was an excellent cook, and was rightly proud of it.

She had come to work at Falcon's Aerie as an assistant cook a few years before the builder's son had passed away. She met Harlan then and they'd married. When the owner died, the couple was hired to stay on as caretakers, though it was really too big a task for them alone.

Aida was a plump woman in her sixties, with short, wavy white hair and friendly blue eyes. Harlan couldn't have been more a contrast. He was a few years older, closer to seventy. Nearly as tall as Dr. Marsden, his back was slightly stooped. Harlan was a taciturn man with what seemed to be a perpetual frown. He'd begun as the grounds-keeper in the late '30s.

Harlan eyed Cynthia with a hint of suspicion, yet did not speak. She got the impression that took some effort on his part. He and Aida had dwelled alone at the estate for almost thirty years. Harlan was used to being his own boss. He still acted as if he were most of the time. Ian indulged the old man, which seemed to annoy Seth, but Blackthorne grudgingly deferred to his stepbrother. Jeffers did not appear especially grateful for Ian's indulgence, if he even noticed it.

Once the main course was cleared away, the seven of them remained in the dining room, to let their meals settle while waiting for dessert. They'd conversed little during the meal itself. Afterwards, there was an awkward silence for a time until Mr. Marsden took it upon himself to break the ice.

"Seth tells me you suffered a problem similar to Colin, when you were young. I wasn't aware of that," Richard observed. "Can you tell us more?"

"It's true," Cynthia answered. She wished Seth hadn't told anyone what she'd revealed to him, but she'd never asked him to keep it in confidence. It had been risky to tell him; she couldn't castigate him for it. "Unlike Colin, while I had dreams, I never knew what caused them. They began before I could talk. They finally stopped when I was seven or eight. I remember because we moved from Chicago to Queens, between second and third grade."

"They'd started taking me to doctors in kindergarten or first grade. Unfortunately, the doctors seemed more interested in sedating me...than 'curing' me."

"You're lucky she's come here to help you, Colin," Lisa said to the boy, encouragingly. "She knows what it's like."

"Yeah, I suppose," Colin glanced away with pointed disinterest. "If you say so."

"Do you remember any of your dreams?" Lisa inquired, riveted.

"Not much," Cynthia shrugged, answering guardedly. "It's been a long time and I tried my best to forget them. I can only remember a few things. I recall it was very cold; freezing and windy. I can still hear that wind in my head sometimes. It howled like a living thing; a really angry one." Her gaze was far away, remembering the nightmares. "I saw weird, almost greenish, lighting. There was no rain, but there was thunder. The clouds all swirled inwards, like a tornado or a mini hurricane forming. I could still see the moon at the center, in the eye of the storm. It was full and red, as if dipped in fresh blood. I couldn't move, like I was paralyzed or even tied up. It was terrible.

There was a man there, too; oddly dressed. I think it might've been Victorian or Edwardian. He carried a long, wavy bladed knife that looked almost silver. I knew he was going to kill me with it. I mainly recall this much, because I managed to get hold of records of my old sessions. The man wasn't familiar to me. So, I don't know where his image came from. I presume the dream symbolized something. I'm just not sure what."

Lisa looked shocked, which she made no effort to hide. Dr. Marsden appeared interested, from a clinical perspective. Both Ian and Jeremy seemed sympathetic. Seth had a strange conflicted expression, which he quickly sought to conceal. It was as if he'd heard something familiar, yet wanted to pretend otherwise. Colin was visibly interested now, both shaken and excited.

"I'll bet all the doctors told you to just forget it, that you were safe and it was only hurting you to keep bringing it up…" Colin's words tumbled out in a hurried rush. "That it was just a dream… that you only imagined the whole thing…"

"Pretty much," Cynthia responded. "It used to confuse me, why they refused to pay attention to the dream itself. I think they just wanted me to stop waking everybody up when I screamed…to quit bothering them by talking about it. It made them uncomfortable. My parents wanted me to sleep normally, so I could do better in school. The doctors couldn't understand how scared those dreams made me. They didn't want to. I'm not sure they cared. It hurt me as a kid, but it made me mad, too."

"That's how I feel," Colin nodded vigorously, excited. "They never really listen. They think they know everything."

"We'll talk more about it tomorrow, then," Cynthia smiled, "or later tonight if you want, after dinner. The difference is that nobody knew of anything that could've inspired my dream. I was too young then. I couldn't even find a movie I might've seen, but you actually went through a very real trauma. I think that's probably why it lingers for you. It happened, and it left real consequences."

"That dream would certainly scare me," Lisa chimed in, rubbing her arms with a visible shudder. "It sounds like something out of Lovecraft; maybe a sacrifice to open a rift between dimensions. Those stories always had that sort of thing going on."

"It does sound rather Lovecraftian…perhaps the Dunwich Horror," Seth agreed. "He was a master story teller; creating a unique atmosphere of dread, just as Poe did a century before. He rarely gets the credit he's due because his work appeared in the old pulps and more recently paperbacks."

"I vaguely know the name Lovecraft," Cynthia commented, "but I didn't read anything of his. I avoided horror for years, though my brother, Danny, used to watch the movies as kid."

"It's been reprinted in book form in the last ten or twenty years. Interestingly enough, Jared Nicholson, the man who built this house, was an occultist. He included grimoires in the library, and wrote commentaries on them. He bought all sorts of strange artifacts from his travels. He was even a member of the Golden Dawn. I've heard that he hosted Aleister Crowley himself, in this very house, around 1900. They'd met in England a few years earlier."

"Really?" Lisa was fascinated. "Crowley? That's freaky. He got into some pretty dark stuff, I've read."

"Indeed, he did," Seth nodded in agreement. "He was a genius in his own way, though drugs and hedonism did him in the end; such a waste."

"The bloody bastard was just a charlatan," snapped Ian in disgust. "The creep died alone, and broke. I guess he got what he deserved. A lot of people glamorized him, but if he had any real power, it didn't do him any good."

"You have to admit he was an interesting character," Seth interjected.

"I don't HAVE to admit anything," Ian huffed, shaking his head. "But it doesn't really matter. Can we change the subject?"

"Fine, Ian. I don't mind," Seth shrugged nonchalantly. "I don't know why you were getting so upset."

"Moira was the one who told me about him," Lisa commented. "She's read all about the occult and paranormal. I think it's neat, even though it scares me."

"Who's Moira?" Cynthia wondered aloud.

"She's a friend; an old high school teacher of mine. She and her husband, Irv, let me stay in an extra room of theirs while I went to secretarial school. I worked at their shop to make some extra cash, too."

"The Sorensons are good people," Ian agreed. "They recommended both Lisa and Mat to me, and I'm grateful they did."

"Is it true they're witches?" Colin asked eagerly. "Mat said they were."

"Yes," Lisa answered without a blink. "They are Wiccan. So am I."

"Really?" Cynthia was curious.

"My dad's not very religious," Lisa explained, "unless the sermon comes in a bottle. My mother left us when I was three. So I don't know about her. Wicca's not really like most people think or in the movies; no human sacrifices or orgies," she giggled lightly, blushing.

"How interesting," Seth mused, rubbing his chin. "I didn't know that. I admire your independence of thought, my dear.”

“I’ve never met a wiccan before,” Cynthia clarified, “at least none that I know of. My parents are Methodists, but they’re not fanatical about it. Danny and I have sort of fallen away; too busy at school and work I guess.”

“My late father was high church Anglican,” Seth chimed in, “and so was Rachel.”

Cynthia noticed that he hadn’t included Ian in his comment and used Holderness’ mother’s first name instead of ‘Mom’ or ‘Mother’. That was suggestive.

“We used to go to church every Sunday,” Ian sighed. “It bored the bloody hell out of me.”

“Once we settled here, we couldn’t find a conveniently located congregation. So, I’m afraid we lapsed,” Seth eyed his stepbrother to gauge Ian’s reaction. Holderness didn’t take the bait. Blackthorne seemed mildly disappointed.

“How about you, Jeremy?” Lisa smiled sweetly, genuinely curious.

“My mamma-my mother…” he corrected himself, “was Catholic. She got sick when I was a kid an’ my daddy left. We went to live with gran’ma. She never missed a service…till she died a few years ago, ’bout when I came here…” Hutchinson fell quiet, remembering.

“You don’t have any family?” Cynthia inquired conversationally. “No siblings?”

“No, ma’am,” Jeremy shook his head. “My mother lost a child, my lil’ sister, but then after Daddy left she took sick. She passed on when I was fourteen.” It was clear that Jeremy was uncomfortable being the center of attention. Cynthia sympathized with him.

“That’s too bad,” Cynthia tried to sound reassuring. “I don’t know what I’d do without my parents or Danny.”

“Mat said he was a cop…I mean a police officer,” Lisa corrected herself, with a chuckle.

“He is,” Cynthia nodded. “He’s a detective in the Bronx, in the 54th precinct.”

“My dad and I lived in the Bronx, until I was twelve and he got a job in Newburgh,” Lisa observed.

“Mom never liked church,” Colin half-whispered. “She didn’t take me there, not even for the holidays. She wouldn't even look at 'em when we passed by."

"Kate's father, Henry Baine, doesn't hold much with religion," Ian explained. "I'm not sure if he's agnostic or atheist. His god is business; money. That's how he raised Kate."

Ah yes...the great god, Mammon," Seth grinned wryly. "The principal deity of the modern world, it seems, but he's a relatively young god, as gods go. Doubtless he'll be replaced in time like all the others."

"What god do you serve, Mr. Blackthorne?" Cynthia couldn't resist the question, since Seth was acting so smugly.

"None, Miss Akers," Seth's lips curled again. "I may acknowledge the powers of a few, perhaps even ally myself with one or another, but I bow before none of them. I am my own master.'

"That's very...self-sufficient," Cynthia commented uneasily.

"Yes...so it is," Seth chortled softly.

"Enough talk about religion," Ian snorted in annoyance. "Seth just loves to be provocative. Like the old adage says, never discuss politics or religion in polite company."

"Or it doesn't remain polite for long," Seth's eyes twinkled wickedly. "But you've been so serious the past few years Ian. You used to have a sense of humor. Everything sets you off these days."

"I've had...plenty of reasons to become serious...so have you, Seth. It's not my fault you don't take anything seriously," Ian snapped.

"To change the subject," Seth ignored his stepbrother, "it's a perfect night for ghost stories. Why don't I tell the local legend about the curse of Falcon's Aerie? I'm sure Colin hasn't heard it, and Miss Akers may find it interesting."

"A curse?" Cynthia asked skeptically. "You're kidding, right? Curses aren't real..."

"No," Seth responded smugly. 'I'm not insisting there really is a curse, only that there was, and there may still be a local belief in one."

"Okay," Cynthia replied, "I'll bite. You might as well tell your story. It is a good night for it," she eyed Seth expectantly.

"I'd be interested, too," Lisa sat forward, attentively.

CHAPTER 6

THE LEGEND OF THE CURSE
SEPTEMBER 12, 1982

"There's really a curse?" Colin piped up excitedly. "I knew it! I just knew it!"

"Go ahead, Seth," Ian rolled his eyes. "Just make it short and sweet, alright? I'd rather not be up till dawn just so you can tell some bloody ghost story."

"As all of you know, this house was built by Jared Nicholson, son of the robber baron Samuel Nicholson, though it was not the original house on the estate. The previous one was built by Samuel's father, Geoffrey, in the 1820s. That house burned down in 1881. I'll reveal more of that later."

"Since Jared was not Samuel's oldest son, he indulged his interests in subjects Nicholson viewed as frivolous. He did so in large part to please his wife, who shared similar interests. Jared attended Harvard from 1870 to 1874. After that, Samuel reluctantly let him continue his education at Oxford."

"At Oxford, Jared met his mentor, Professor Aaron Stuart, and the latter's niece and ward, Meredith Sinclair. Nicholson obtained his master's degree there in 1878. Over the following year, he traveled in Europe with his mentor and another of Stuart's prodigies. The next year, Jared and Meredith were formally betrothed, despite some objections from Samuel. To him, the ward of a mere academic wasn't worthy of his son but, as usual, his wife mediated between them..."

"Hurry it up, Seth," Ian tapped his fingers on the table, growing frustrated. "We don't need their whole bloody biographies."

"I still don't see any ghosts or curses either," Cynthia observed skeptically.

"Just keep listening," Seth cocked an eyebrow. "Becoming fascinated by the aristocratic lifestyle he experienced in England, Jared commissioned Falcon's Aerie from an architect he met at Oxford. Samuel refused to pay for so palatial a mansion, as he made a point of appearing pious and frugal. So, once again they argued bitterly and Jared was nearly disinherited. Amanda prevented that, but the relationship of father and son remained strained."

"Jared and Meredith wed in 1881, here at the estate. After the ceremony, most of the guests soon departed for the city. Yet, before the couple could leave on their honeymoon, a fire broke out in the night. Samuel, Jared, and his elder brother did their best to get everyone out of the house safely."

"Tragically, in trying to rescue one of the guests, Samuel and Jared's older brother were trapped by a falling beam, and unable to escape. Jared failed to save them. All three men perished in the fire. The original house was destroyed. The whispers began then, saying that Jared had not really tried to rescue his father and brother; that he wanted to be rid of them."

"Jared inherited the fortune and the estate. He postponed his honeymoon for a suitable period of mourning, but still ordered the building of Falcon's Aerie to replace the original mansion. That exacerbated the rumors that he must have set the fire. The townsfolk disapproved of Jared's lavish lifestyle and unorthodox interests. He knew, but didn't care. It may even have amused him."

"One of the servants went missing after the fire. The locals became convinced that either he set the fire for Jared, or that Nicholson killed him or paid him off to say nothing. There was never any real investigation. The fire was ruled accidental."

"It didn't end then, however. In 1887, Meredith, her uncle, and Jared's brother-in-law all died in a relatively short period of time. Officially, Meredith suffered a fatal miscarriage, her uncle succumbed to a heart attack, and the brother-in-law to a recurrence of a fever he caught in the Sudan. He was British, you see, the second son of the Earl of Grantham."

"The townsfolk were certain that the tragedies were God's wrath on Jared, for the sin he committed to build his beloved castle. They used to say that this house oozed the blood of those who'd died so that it could be built."

"Nicholson's fascination for the occult only made matters worse. He was a member of the Theosophical Society, and supported the American and British societies for psychical research. After the passing of his wife in the 1890s, he joined the Hermetic Society of the Golden Dawn, the premier occult organization of the era. He met Aleister Crowley through it, in 1898, in England. None of that sat well with the piously provincial inhabitants of Corchester."

"They started to call Jared a warlock behind his back. They now claimed that he caused the fire with black magic, and sacrificed his own wife as part of some Devil's pact. They thought he'd murdered his mentor and brother-in-law for trying to stop him. They varied on whether the pact gave him greater wealth, more power, or extended youth, because he remained relatively well-preserved until he died at sixty-five in 1917."

"From those who worked on the estate, the locals knew that he had books on magic and quite a few strange, "heathen" objects brought back from his frequent travels abroad. Everything became grist for legend."

"Any especially fierce storms, odd diseases, disappearances, or unexplained deaths came to be laid at his door, much as was done with witches in the sixteenth and seventeenth centuries. To be fair to the tale spinners, there were quite a few weird occurrences."

"People heard strange noises in the night. They claimed to see unexplained lights and frightening apparitions. There were a number of unsolved disappearances. More than a few locals became ill, with doctors being unable to diagnose them. Others were found dead or catatonic in the morning for reasons unknown, or went crazy without warning."

"I realize it's easy to scoff now, with all our modern conveniences and the city less than two hours away, but if this area seems isolated now, imagine it fifty or a hundred years ago. Many of the locals were virtual fundamentalists here, then. Despite the trains and, later, cars, most never went as far as the city, living their whole lives here. Not until the highway came through, and television, did that begin to change. Similarly, medicine was less advanced in those days, and Corchester was always a backwater. They were very superstitious then. Some still are."

"The most feared of our local ghostly bestiary was a hooded and robed specter dubbed, appropriately enough, the Black Monk. It sounds medieval, like something one would expect back home in England, but in those days, what is now Richard's sanitarium was a monastic retreat and winery. It was abandoned due to Prohibition or so I've heard."

"This...entity it was said came in the night. No doors or locks could keep it out. Its eyes glowed like hell-fire, but otherwise it had no face beneath the hood. Reputedly, it drained the very life from its victims, leaving them weak, insane, or dead. Rumor whispered that it was the angel of death himself, or some demon summoned by Nicholson, if it was not an emanation of the warlock himself."

It was first reported in the 1880s around, when Nicholson's wife, mentor, and brother-in-law died. It was last seen about when Nicholson died himself, sixty-five years ago, seemingly confirming the connection to him. It was never been forgotten. The same day Jared died, his daughter-in-law and grandson did as well, in childbirth. His son, Dylan, never fully recovered and became a recluse. He never remarried, as neither his father nor aunt ever did. It became something of a family tradition, I suppose. Marcus Howarth, Jared's nephew and Dylan's cousin, from whom Ian bought this place, was no better. He was a widower for more than forty years. Because Marcus lived to such a great age, some said he renewed Jared's satanic pact."

"While most believe the curse ended with Dylan's death, a few old-timers keep the stories alive. They attributed Marcus' death and our...troubles to a revival of the curse, because we came here and sought to restore the estate. My own accident and the tragedy seven years ago have played into that."

"They disapprove of Ian the way their ancestors did of Jared. To them, Rock is subversive, if not outright satanic. They claim that Ian must've made a pact of his own to obtain success, just like the crossroads legend of blues guitarist, Robert Johnson, cited in the Eric Clapton tune a few years back. They whispered that the tragedy must've been because he tried to renege on the pact. Colorful, eh?"

"Obviously, every family and location has its share of tragedies. Still, it is odd how they've tended to cluster here. Most took place within a few days of Halloween, a rather appropriate holiday. That may sound silly, but it's true, nevertheless. Nicholson's wife, teacher, and brother-in-law died at that time of year in 1887. Jared's mother did in 1898. Jared, his daughter-in-law and grandson did in 1917. So did Dylan in 1944. Then, of course, there was what happened to us seven years ago. Doubtless it's all coincidental, but it is evocative."

"That's quite a tale," Cynthia inhaled sharply. "Are you sure of all the facts?"

"I've had lots of time to read…as you can imagine," Seth indicated his chair with distaste. "As best I can tell, everything I said is true. Naturally, I haven't done a poll to determine how widely the tales were or are believed, but they have been told here for years."

"I bet it is true!" Colin interjected vehemently.

Ian, who had clearly been biting his tongue throughout the story, shot Seth a sour look as if to say, "Thanks for nothing".

"There's one more piece of the puzzle," Seth raised an eyebrow once more. "Jeremy and I were down at the garages the other day, while Matthew was cleaning them out for the use by the new security company. We discovered an old portrait there, wrapped in sackcloth. I sent it out to be cleaned; it came back yesterday. We couldn't believe it. You won't, either, once you see it. Jeremy, please bring it from my room, will you?"

Hutchinson nodded, his expression sad. He got up and left the dining room. Ian appeared on edge. "What've you got up your sleeve, Seth?"

"You'll see, dear brother," Seth grinned. "You'll see. If you recall, we always wondered why there were no photos or portraits of Jared Nicholson here. It seemed off, since he built the house…"

"Marcus Howarth hated his uncle," Ian snapped. "He had plenty of time to get rid of any pictures of Nicholson and the motive to do it."

"Well, he missed one," Seth said proudly. "It was commissioned in England, in 1887." As he spoke, Jeremy returned, bearing a large picture covered by a cloth. He brought it over to Seth, so that his employer could unveil it for dramatic effect. Turning it to face the others, Seth pulled away the cloth.

Everyone gasped. There, on the canvas, was the image of a handsome young man with black hair and a goatee, dressed in a Victorian smoking jacket. It was the face that held their attention. It was Ian's face. The name on the plaque below the painting read, "Jared Nicholson: 1887".

"That's impossible!" Richard almost shouted, stunned by the likeness.

"You must've faked it," Ian grimaced in annoyance. "Why, Seth? Did you think it would be funny? Who painted it for you? Tell me!" Holderness was genuinely angry this time.

"I didn't fake it," Seth insisted. "Cross my heart and hope to die." He made the sign of the cross with his fingers, his face serious. "Take it to an art expert if you don't believe me."

"Why did you show it here, now?" Ian tried to control his temper, only half succeeding. "Are you that anxious to embarrass me? You go into detail about how Nicholson was a ruddy warlock, and inspired a curse on this house, and then you drag that damn thing out!"

"Oh come on, Ian!" Seth snorted derisively. "I wasn't trying to insult you. I just thought it was intriguing. That's why I told the story. If I wanted to insult you, I didn't need to go to so much trouble. You know how much I love to take credit. So you really think I wouldn't take it if I could? It's an uncanny resemblance. That's all. Did I say the curse was real, that Nicholson was actually to blame for it? In fact, I think he was unfairly maligned."

"Whatever you say," Ian hissed, clearly not satisfied. He looked away from his stepbrother, his emotions barely contained. "Let's just drop the subject, alright?" Then he stood and stalked from the room.

Richard followed Ian from the room. Holderness stormed into the library, where he went over to stand beside the great fireplace. He leaned against the mantle, and glared intently into the flames. He ignored his godfather's arrival.

Cynthia was tempted to go after them, but she'd just met Holderness and he was her employer. His problems with his stepbrother were not her business, unless he asked her to become involved. It might anger both him and Seth if she chased after him into the library. Marsden was family. She wasn't, but clearly the problem ran deeper than the portrait.

Cynthia excused herself, saying that she was tired, and headed for her room. Nobody objected, the tension still hanging in the air. Seth had already indicated that he was going to bed himself. As she got up to leave, Seth grinned at her. "Welcome to Falcon's Aerie, Miss Akers...pleasant dreams," he winked at her.

Jared Nicholson
1887

CHAPTER 7

COLIN'S STORY
SEPTEMBER 12, 1982

Cynthia went upstairs a few minutes later, after saying her goodnights to Seth, Jeremy, Colin, and Lisa. At the top of the stairs, she met Colin. He had hurried from the dining room to get to her before she reached her room.

"Were you telling the truth before?" he asked pointedly, eying her with mild suspicion. "That entire story about the dreams wasn't just some trick to get me trust you, was it?"

"I wasn't lying," Cynthia answered with a shrug. "But I don't know how to convince you of it. You can believe me…or not. That's up to you. I can understand why you'd be suspicious. I would be, too, in your place. I want to help you, Colin, but nobody can unless you let them."

"You still don't believe me, though," he looked away with a frown; so like his father, even at fourteen. "Why should I believe you? You weren't here that night. You didn't see what I saw, but you'll accept their word that I just made it up or couldn't tell the difference between a monster…and a man in a bloody mask; they think I'm lying crazy or fuckin' stupid! I'm sick of it! That thing was real. The police dredged the river for it, but never found it."

"What was it?" Cynthia inquired, her curiosity aroused. "They say it was a thief. What did you see, Colin?

"It was a werewolf," Colin replied without hesitation. "I just don't know who it is."

"A werewolf?" Cynthia raised her hands in denial. "I slipped up. This is all new to me. They haven't given me your file yet. Why don't you tell me what happened that night?"

"Okay," Colin answered, "but you won't believe me. No one ever does…"

"Try me," Cynthia persisted.

October 31, 1975

An unearthly howl echoed through the night. It was so close that it sounded as if it came from inside the house. Colin wondered what could possibly howl like that. There were no dogs at the estate. It sounded more like a wolf, but as far as he knew, they'd been extinct in the region for decades, maybe longer.

Then he heard gunshots, yelling...footsteps running in the hall. Colin's heart pounded painfully in his chest. He was supposed to stay in his room during the party downstairs, but he had to find out what was going on. It all felt like a bad dream. Yet, he knew deep down it was real.

Glass shattered only a few rooms away. He couldn't ignore that. With great trepidation, Colin crept from his room, glancing nervously each way as he entered the dimly-lit corridor. His grandparents' room lay at the end of the hall.

The door to their room hung half open. Though he'd heard running in the hall, he saw nobody as he'd neared his grandparents' door. The only light visible was that of the flames flickering in their fireplace. It was strange that they'd left their door ajar. They never did that. Colin realized that something was very, very wrong.

Looking in, he saw that the carpet was all crumpled up, a lamp lying broken on the floor. The dank chill of the autumn night wafted in through the shattered window. That had been the glass he heard breaking. The curtain billowed ever so slightly, despite the relative stillness of the night. He heard no sound from within the room.

His grandfather lay collapsed on the floor. Colin gasped in shock, his eyes widening. All the color drained from his face. His grandmother had fallen nearby, her eyes closed. She wore the gown she'd chosen for the party. Colin couldn't tell if she was breathing or not. He was too panicked to check her pulse, as he'd seen done on TV. There was a pained expression on her face, which he'd always seen smiling before.

His grandfather was sprawled awkwardly on the carpet, a pistol nearby. Roderick's eyes remained open, if just barely. Colin saw tears in them. The front of his tuxedo was torn in long ugly gashes, blood staining his white shirt. He moved fitfully, his breathing irregular.

"Grandpa, what happened?" he recalled crying, the tears stinging his eyes.

"I was...too slow," he croaked out, with difficulty. "I...waited too long...didn't believe what they...told me...didn't want it to be true.

He…it's out there…he…tried to…warn me…you've got to…hide, Colin…don't let it find you…"

Roderick groaned in agony. With immense effort, he reached inside his coat pocket, taking out a small chain with a silver medallion at one end…a pentagram. "This was for your grandmother. I never… got to…give it to her. It's too late now. I should've…worn mine, but I didn't believe. Wear it, Colin. It will keep you safe…hold it at bay…"

Then he couldn't speak anymore. He dropped back to the carpet, eyes open and staring. They were frozen, already turning glassy. There was no life left in them. His grandfather was gone…dead. Colin had sensed that without having to check.

Fighting back his tears, Colin tried not to hyperventilate. What had done this, the boy wondered. Colin backed away from his grandfather, out of the room. He had to find help. He didn't understand what his grandfather meant about the necklace protecting him. Whatever shattered the window had done it from within…the shots came from his grandfather's gun. Donning the necklace, Colin headed down the corridor.

Going to his father's room, he found it empty and dark. Then he tried his mother's door. It was locked. Colin knocked vigorously, yet received no answer. He thought he heard water running beyond the door. Maybe she was showering for the party. She probably couldn't hear him knocking.

Colin ran to the main stairs. The foyer was brilliantly lit for the party, but he saw nobody downstairs. He went to his Uncle Seth's door and knocked, but again, as at his mother's room, there was no answer. Listening carefully at the door, Colin heard nothing on the other side. Frantic and increasingly terrified, he tested the door knob, only to find that it, too, was locked.

Suddenly the lights around him started to flicker. Several bulbs popped. Colin felt an icy chill. The sickly-sweet odor of stale flowers pervaded the foyer, so strong that he nearly gagged. What looked like smoke oozed out from beneath his uncle's door; yet he didn't smell anything burning, nor had the door been hot to the touch. It baffled him, but he sensed that it was malevolent; that it was one form of the evil he'd long felt in the house.

The black fog rolled and billowed like a miniature thunder cloud. Tiny arcs of what resembled greenish lightning flickered within it. The mist flowed at him, rearing up as if to envelop him. The cold was like being trapped in a freezer.

Though he didn't know what, if anything, the mist could do to him, Colin did his best to avoid it. He backed slowly away from it, fearing to turn his back lest it catch up to him. The pentagram fell from inside his shirt when he moved, catching the light from the chandelier.

The cloud seemed to recoil as if stung, moving away from Colin as swiftly as it had approached. It went instead toward the main stairs, and began to ascend them as no natural fog would do, turning at the second floor. Then it moved off down the corridor, in the direction of his parents' rooms. It acted as if it were a sentient thing.

For tense moments, Colin was frozen to the spot, in fear and anticipation. Then a high-pitched scream of terror pierced the night... his mother's scream. It could be no one else's. What happened to her? Was it the sinister fog?

There had to be somebody to help. Maybe Dr. Marsden, the servants, or one of his father's friends, and where was his father? Where was his Aunt Jennifer? The scream broke him from his paralysis. He hurried to the kitchen. It was empty. The door to the outside swung open.

Colin wondered where everyone was. He was afraid that they might all be dead. Was he alone? Desperate, he ran through the kitchen door onto the terrace. There was no one visible on the terrace. His panic continued to grow. Beneath his grandparents' window his shoes crunched on myriad shards of broken glass.

At the base of the stairs from the terrace, down to the garden, was a nightmare. Paul Harrel, the former keyboardist from his father's band, was crumpled below the stairs, crimson gashes scoring his chest and neck. Blood pooled around his head. He lay in a twisted posture, as if he'd been thrown down the steps. Shock froze Colin in place. He couldn't even cry out.

Beside Harrel's prone body was a tall figure. It walked on two legs like a man, yet was decidedly not human. It looked gigantic even at a distance, well over six-feet tall. The thing was covered in dark fur, with long, curved, talon-like claws on both hands and feet. It wore torn black trousers, a ripped white shirt, and a vest; remnants of a tuxedo.

It had pointed ears, and ivory fangs rimmed its red maw. Saliva dripped from its jaws, while its eyes glowed like emerald flames beneath heavy brows. Those eyes bore into Colin. The face was neither simian nor bear-like but rather an uncanny mixture of canine and human. He recognized what it was…werewolf!

It reared its shaggy head and howled again, long and loud. The clouds had parted to reveal a bright crescent moon. Colin thought that it should've been full. Didn't the moon have to be full for there to be a werewolf? But it couldn't be anything else.

Colin covered his ears against the sound, clenching his eyes shut in shock, too frightened to move. He wanted to blot out the sight as well as the sound, but it was useless. He could still see the thing in his mind's eye. It would be seared into his brain for life. Nothing could block out that reverberating howl.

When he opened his eyes again, the beast was stalking towards him, growling deep within its barrel chest. Colin sensed someone behind him gently touching him on the shoulder. Startled, he whirled to see his Aunt Jennifer.

"Its leg's injured! We've got to get out of here. Run, Colin! Hurry!" she pointed towards the woods.

"Where do we go?" Colin asked breathlessly. His Aunt Jennifer was a slim girl, with long straight dark hair and gently lavender eyes.

"Just run! I'll follow you," she patted him on the back again, indicating the direction of the river.

Glancing at the beast stalking at them, Colin required no further prompting. He sped off into the mist that rolled in from the Hudson. Looking briefly over his shoulder, Colin saw Jennifer close at his heels. The creature was not far behind them, even with one wounded leg.

Colin ran until he thought his heart would burst with effort, his breathing ragged. The fog made it difficult to see. It was very dark, away from the ground lamps that illuminated the exterior of the house. They made no sound as they ran, since the grass was wet, as were the drifts of fallen leaves. Their brilliant colors were leeched by the night.

The shadowy trunks of trees rose up to bar their path, the branches reaching out to grasp them like the claws of some demonic sentinels. Still, the pair kept running, ignoring the minor scrapes from stray twigs and undergrowth. Each of them narrowly avoided tripping over roots several times. The thing pursued them inexorably.

Those glowing eyes cut through the mist and darkness. If not for its injured leg, it would've caught up to them already. It was much faster than an ordinary human. They couldn't talk to each other as they ran, because they were too winded. All they could do was flee. There was no time for rational thought.

Finally, the trees grew fewer and the path more open. Ahead of them they saw the river, with the boathouse and private dock. They stopped for a second to catch their breath.

"I can't run any further..." Jennifer huffed and puffed, exhausted. "Go to the boathouse. Bar the doors...hide. I'll make for one of the dinghies — try to row out into the river — maybe it can't swim..."

She was crying. Colin knew that she couldn't swim. She was risking her life for him.

"Good luck, Colin," she said, her voice breaking. "Love you, kid."

"You, too, Aunt Jen," Colin's eyes became moist, sobs building up inside, though he tried to fight them down.

"Go, then," she pointed to the boathouse. "Go now"

Colin nodded in response. Reluctantly, he went to the boathouse as she'd instructed. Looking over his shoulder, he watched his aunt walking onto the dock and fumbling to untie one of the dinghies from the post where it was moored.

The beast howled as it broke from the trees. Colin closed the boathouse door as quietly as he could then slid the bar into place. Unfortunately, there was a large window. How much good the bar would do, he wasn't certain.

Scanning the boathouse, Colin looked for a place to hide. In one corner, he spotted several wooden crates stacked up. There was a few all-weather tarps piled there, too. He unfolded one of the tarps and threw it partially over the crates so that he could hide under it. He knew that it was fairly obvious, but it was all he had to work with. Colin hoped the creature wasn't too bright.

Although he knew he ought to hide immediately, his curiosity drew him back to the window, to see if his aunt was okay. She'd managed to untie one of the dinghies and crouched down into it. Due to the rocking of the boat, the beast's swipe just missed her. Jennifer sat and began to row furiously away from the pier.

The creature refused to give up. It coiled and lunged at her. It missed her boat, yet came up out of the water and climbed into the dinghy. Jennifer hit it over the head with an oar, but the oar splintered futilely. When it reached out at her again, the little board became unbalanced. The thing fell back into the river.

To Colin's horror, Jennifer cartwheeled and fell overboard herself, with a big splash. He clasped his hands over his mouth to stifle his instinctive scream. Although Colin could swim, there was no way he could've reached her in time, or would have had the strength to pull her from the water, and that thing was out there, too. ..

CHAPTER 8

THE END OF THE BEGINNING
SEPTEMBER 12, 1982

His aunt never resurfaced, as he had feared she wouldn't. In the darkness and fog, Colin couldn't even see any bubbles. She was gone...just like his grandparents and his father's friend. Colin didn't know his mother or uncle's fates, or his father's whereabouts. She gave her life to save his. She could've remained hidden, back at the house. It was a deadly gamble and she had lost.

As Colin thought that, a wet, muscular arm, covered in dripping wet fur, appeared on the edge of the dock. It latched onto the wood of the pier with its razor sharp claws. Seconds later, the other hand gripped the dock. The thing pulled itself from the cold dark river. Water streamed off it, puddling on the dock as it regained its footing and stood. It resembled some monstrous denizen of the deep, its green eyes blazing neon in the night.

Looking around, it sniffed the night air. It was seeking for something — Colin! The beast knew that it had followed two people but only one was accounted for. It couldn't see him, yet it sensed his presence nearby. It sought to catch his scent.

There was no way he could outrun it back to the house. It would see him if he opened the boathouse doors. That was his only exit. He was still shaky with exhaustion and emotion. There was nobody at the house who could protect him anyway. None of the doors or windows there could hold it out any better than those of the boathouse. That monstrosity seemed immune to fatigue. Not even bullets were enough to stop it...

The thing stalked purposefully towards the boathouse. It had figured out where he had to be. Colin edged away from the window, his back against the wall. He bent down so that it couldn't see him through the window. Then he crept over to the crates and crawled under the tarp.

Colin sat facing the boxes, his knees drawn up to his chin. The situation was a nightmare. His chances of survival seemed slim. Colin's heart nearly stopped when the thing began to batter the doors, snarling in angry frustration. The doors groaned inward at the beast's savage blows. The bar held just barely.

Colin closed his eyes tightly, clenching his teeth until his jaws hurt. He covered his ears to shut out the sound of the wood being smashed in. Then, as suddenly as it began, the noise ceased. The silence was ominous, almost unbearable. He could scarcely breathe, his fear was so intense.

The silence was broken by the sound of glass shattering. It chose the easy way in, just as he was afraid it would. Colin was sure that he was doomed. It must hear him shaking beneath the tarp, or smell him. There was nowhere to run, and it was too fast for him to evade.

Colin heard the click of its claws against the wooden floor…the protesting whine when it placed its massive weight on each board. It stalked closer, taking its time as it sensed he could not escape. The creature savored the approaching kill. It breathed heavily, like the panting of some gigantic dog.

It sniffed the air as it neared where he was hiding. Colin felt certain it could smell him. How long before its claws raked him, or its fangs sank into his flesh, crunching his bones to get at the marrow? Then it stopped, sensing something. What was the damned thing waiting for?

In that instant it struck, its claws ripping the tarp away, eyes gleaming with unholy triumph. It bared its slavering fangs at Colin. He stared up at it, frozen in terror. Its gaze caught something which temporarily halted it. The pendant! It had seen the pentagram….

"Stop!" cried a familiar voice. It was Dr. Marsden, his dad's godfather. "I won't let you harm the boy!! It's gone too far this time! It has to end tonight! God, how I prayed I'd never have to do this…"

A shot rang out, its echoes bouncing back and forth in the boathouse. The beast yelped in obvious pain and surprise, but it didn't go down. Instead, it snarled in agonized, thwarted fury. There was another shot. The beast dodged it.

Then it ran at the already damaged doors, rending the wood like cardboard. An instant later, a splash told Colin that it had leapt into the river to escape the bullets.

"It's gone, Doc." The voice belonged to Robert Devon, Odyssey's former drummer, who had recently helped record his father's solo album. "You chased it off."

"I wasn't trying to chase it off, Mr. Devon," replied Dr. Marsden, his voice full of pent-up emotion and exhaustion. "I meant to kill it. I must not have hit a vital spot or it would be dead now. Damn fog and my lousy aim! When I was younger, I'm sure I could've hit it." The doctor was almost crying. Colin had never seen Marsden so emotional before. "I should've killed him...it," the doctor corrected himself, though neither Colin nor Devon knew what he meant. "God...I should've ..."

"Where's Ian, Doc? Or Jenny?" inquired Devon. Colin wondered where his father was, too. He would've told them about his aunt, but he was too stunned to speak.

"I...I don't know," Marsden answered haltingly, his voice cracking. "Ian was looking for her and Colin...I lost sight of him."

They found Colin a few seconds later. He was still too numb to talk. He couldn't even focus his thoughts enough to form coherent sentences. As they loaded him into the ambulance, everyone kept telling him that he would be alright, that he was safe and it was over now. Instinctively, he had known they were wrong. It was just a matter of time. It had not ended that night. It had only just begun...

"So that's what happened?" Cynthia asked, stunned by what she'd just heard. It sounded utterly impossible, but Colin had been completely lucid and sincere. She had been told that the assailant was never caught. There had been deaths. Still...a werewolf? Yet, what had it really been that night?

"They say I imagined it, or that it was a man in a mask or makeup. I know it was Halloween. Yeah, I was a kid then, but even then I could tell a...monster from a guy in a bloody mask! They didn't even look that good in the movies back then. It wasn't a mask! That thing was real. It's alive out there somewhere. Sooner or later, it'll be back for the rest of us — for me. It knows I escaped it. Dr. Marsden shot at it, but he won't admit it!"

"He wouldn't lie, Colin," Cynthia hated the naïve, almost whiny, sound of her own voice — the defensiveness in it. To be honest, she didn't know Dr. Marsden well enough to say if he would lie, but if he hadn't, then...werewolves were real. She wasn't quite ready for that yet.

"Yes, he would," Colin gritted his teeth stubbornly. "They all do. All he had to do was keep quiet about it, and he did. He doesn't want people saying he's crazy, but it's okay if they say I am."

"I'll ask him…" Cynthia fumbled for a response. Colin cut her off angrily.

"He won't tell you the truth. He hasn't in seven years."

"I'll make you a deal, Colin. It's hard for me to believe in… monsters, but I admit I wasn't there. I didn't see whatever you saw. For now, I'll withhold my judgment until I know more. Does that sound fair?" Cynthia offered. "I believe you saw something strange; I just don't know for certain it was a…werewolf. You admit yourself that there wasn't a full moon that night. You never saw it change to or from a man, though it wore human clothes. It's definitely a mystery. Do we have a deal?"

"I…I don't know," Colin hemmed and hawed, "Mmbe." He eyed her distrustfully.

"It's the best I can do, Colin. You must know how hard it is to accept. I'm not saying you're lying; I'm just saying that I don't know the answer."

"Okay," Colin grudgingly replied. "The deal's on. Just don't forget, he added stubbornly.

"I won't," Cynthia laughed wryly, shaking her head appreciatively. "You're quite the negotiator."

"I have to be," Colin gazed at her unblinkingly. For the first time in years, he wasn't afraid. He had found an ally.

CHAPTER 9

MUSIC OF THE NIGHT
SEPTEMBER 13, 1982

The next night, after dinner, Seth went to bed early and Jeremy to his own room. Since it was a school night, Colin went up to his room, too. The Jeffers were in the kitchen, cleaning up. Ian, Cynthia, and Lisa had adjourned to the study, and Ian allowed Mat to join them, much to the disapproval of Harlan and Aida. They considered Cynthia and Lisa closer to guests than employees, but Mat was definitely a servant. Aida liked him; Harlan resented that he was there at all.

Mat and Lisa sat on the green velvet sofa, while Cynthia was seated in a wing chair beside the fire in the hearth. Ian was at the piano, closer to the window. He was intent on the keys, playing a pretty, yet otherwise unfamiliar, melody, while occasionally jotting something down on a page of sheet music.

"What are you working on?" Cynthia inquired, taking a sip of wine.

"A new song," Ian answered, without looking up. "Well, to be more accurate, the reworking of an old one — a tune I left off my solo album because I wasn't satisfied with it."

"I didn't know you were still writing," Cynthia commented.

"I never really stopped," he replied. "I haven't performed live in seven years, but I still write, practice on the piano and guitar — even record in my studio down at the garages. I ...haven't released any of it, but I've done some rough-cut demos for those I've sold songs to. It keeps my hand in the business, even though I'm not up to touring anymore."

"He does quite well with it," Lisa observed. "He's in demand as a song writer, arranger, and studio musician."

"I had no idea," Cynthia was surprised.

"If you're interested, I can show you my studio sometime," Ian offered casually, with a self-deprecating smile.

"Is that like inviting me up to see your etchings?" Cynthia winked at him.

"It could be..." Ian grinned back, "if it's not breaking some doctor-patient rule."

"That's a bit dicey," Cynthia admitted, "but, technically, Colin is my patient, not you...unless you want to change that."

"No...that's okay," Ian chuckled. "Not that I probably couldn't use psychiatric help, but I would rather you focus on Colin. Besides, if I were your patient, wouldn't it be unethical to flirt with you?"

"Not for you," Cynthia giggled. "Unfortunately, it would be for me to reciprocate."

"Well, then becoming your patient is definitely out. I wouldn't want to force you to do anything ...improper," Ian cocked an eyebrow mischievously.

"Are you suggesting something?" Cynthia raised her own eyebrows.

"If you're open to it," Ian shrugged, with a smile.

"Mr. Holderness?" Lisa interrupted tentatively.

"Yes, Lisa?" Ian turned toward her.

"Irv wanted me to ask if you'd be willing to perform at their Oktoberfest picnic. It's three weeks from now," Lisa said, clearly hopeful. "Are you free?"

"Oh...I don't know, Lisa," Ian hesitated awkwardly. "I haven't played in front of an audience in a long time. Besides ..my monthly... treatment with Richard is on that weekend."

"Come on, Mr. Holderness," Mat chimed in. "I never did get a chance to see you with Odyssey. Isn't there some way you could do it?"

"I...I'll think about it," Ian responded uneasily."

"Why don't you do it?" Cynthia threw in her lot with the others. "It's just a picnic, not a world tour." She eyed him with exaggerated sweetness. Glancing at her, Ian knew that it was no use to fight it.

"Alright...I give in," Ian sighed in resignation. "I'll let Richard know. We do most of our...treatments at night, anyway. I suppose I could do it as long as I leave early enough."

"Or what? You'll turn into a pumpkin?" Cynthia laughed lightly.

"Something like that," Ian replied cryptically, his expression serious. He said no more, yet there was plenty behind his eyes. Only Cynthia seemed to notice. She let it pass. He had a right to privacy. It wasn't her place to badger him.

"You mentioned a treatment," Cynthia noted. "What's it for?"

"I ...got sick around the time Odyssey broke up. Richard's been treating me ever since. It's a rare...blood condition. I doubt you'd have heard of it...just another long Greek name. It would be meaningless to you, if you could even pronounce it. Richard wasn't familiar with it until he had to look it up to diagnose me," Ian sought to deflect the question. Cynthia could tell that was what he was doing, but the answer would have to satisfy her. He was her boss, after all. Yet, she wondered what he was hiding. Was it a drug addiction? It wouldn't be unusual if so. Whatever it was, hopefully it wasn't life threatening. Still, what sort of illness or addiction required monthly "treatments"?

September 15, 1982 Wednesday

The wind whistled and moaned around the window. Outside, the shutters clacked against the masonry of the walls. The ivy surrounding her windows created strange moving shadows on her walls in the colored glow of the ground lamps. The flames in her fireplace flickered low, since she was too tired to stir them with the poker, much less add another log.

There was a dank chill in the air, so Cynthia huddled beneath her comforter, luxuriating in its warmth. Her room was of generous size, nearly half as big as the apartment she'd rented in the city during her internship. She was grateful that it had its own bathroom, unusual in a Victorian house. It was cozy in an old-fashioned way, though simply furnished by the standard of the mansion's public rooms.

She had a big four-poster canopy bed. The lower portion of the walls were paneled, the wallpaper above that a pale mint green. An overstuffed wing chair sat beside the fireplace, with a round table next to it. Near the window was an antique vanity with an oval mirror. In one corner stood a full-length mirror made of the same wood. A tall chest of drawers flanked the window on the other side.

Facing the chest of drawers was a feminine secretary desk. To either side of the bed were twin nightstands; on one of them was an electric imitation of an oil lamp. Oriental rugs covered the polished parqueted floor. Cynthia put her clock radio on the nightstand nearest the door to the hallway. Its numbers glowed red in the darkness.

The wail of the wind kept her awake. Although a cliché, it did remind her of lost souls. Cynthia was unaccustomed to it sounding that way. Lack of sleep was going to tell on her in the morning. It frustrated her, but she couldn't help it. The bed was comfortable, yet all she could do was roll around, staring at the canopy.

Her mind just wouldn't stop working; the thoughts and images continually swirling through it. Cynthia kept thinking about all she'd seen and heard since she arrived. She was reluctant to believe that what Colin saw had been a werewolf. That seemed impossible, but she's promised not to automatically dismiss his testimony. He insisted what he'd seen was not a man in a costume. What else could it have been, though? Her rational mind fought the vow she had made.

There weren't many choices. Either Colin was wrong about it being a man in a costume or it had been something real — something extraordinary. Could it have been the creation of some isolated lab, like in a sci-fi movie? Was that any more believable than the supernatural?

The final option was possibly the most disturbing of all. What if the boy's fantasy was some reality that his conscious mind couldn't face? What if the killer was someone known to Colin and trusted by him? His mind might well have substituted a fearful image to block the awful truth. If so, of the potential candidates, only one stood out — Ian. He was unaccounted for in Colin's story and the most traumatic possibility.

For better or worse, though, it was all pure speculation on her part. She had no way to be sure it hadn't been a man in disguise. It had, after all, been Halloween. The assailant could've escaped simply by ditching the costume. That meant it could've been a stranger after all.

The poor kid had fixated on it since he was seven years old. The denial of others merely strengthened Colin's convictions. His self-esteem had become bound up with the creature being "real". That was a powerful motive for his subconscious to distort his memory.

The fact that nobody was found when the police dragged the river only proved that the assailant didn't die close enough to the estate to be discovered within the search parameters. Whoever it was could've died elsewhere, or simply escaped altogether.

Cynthia had only just met Ian. It was unfair to accuse him of something so heinous on such flimsy evidence. His charm and good looks were obvious, but so were his guilt and temper. Was it grief combined with survivor's guilt, or was it more? He admitted to some sort of illness, yet was extremely vague about what it was.

Those closest to the victim were the prime suspects. Danny... and television, had taught her that. It often seemed to be a cruel, unfair accusation, but just as frequently it turned out to be true. Yet, it was still way too soon to form conclusions.

Although a psychologist, not a detective, she might need to be both to help Colin. Simply denying what he believed he saw had not helped the boy. Cynthia had to take a different tactic. She couldn't convict Ian on the grounds of tenuous speculations. Neither could she afford to absolve him because she found him attractive. The jury was out, but the trial hadn't been canceled. There had been a "monster". The question remained; who...or what was it? It was up to her to find out.

September 16, 1982 Thursday

Colin was in a bad mood when he came home from school. The local boys had been harassing him again, particularly Andy Foster, who was a year older, and bigger. It wasn't just that Colin was an outsider, a foreigner, or even that he was Ian's son. Foster had heard that Cynthia was hired and made fun of Colin for needing a "head-shrinker". The bullying was becoming more physical, too.

Cynthia wasn't sure of the best advice. She knew that bullies rarely stopped merely because one tried to ignore them. Most perceived that as fear, a sign of weakness they could exploit; conversely, she didn't want to advocate violence, either. It set a bad precedent for him. Unless taught to fight, he could well get hurt. On the other hand, if he injured any of the other children, Colin might get in trouble at school and the other parents could complain or file suit. Ian's money would be a tempting lure, were there even a minor scrape.

While retreating from the world did not seem like a good permanent solution, it did appear the best option they had at the moment. So, it had been decided to withdraw Colin from the local school in order to tutor him at the estate. If it could be worked out with the government, Lisa suggested that Moira might be willing to do it, since she still had her teaching certificate. Ian planned to ask her over the weekend.

Colin didn't want to go back to school in the morning, yet acted differently about being tutored. He knew it was either stay in school or be tutored at home. Even boarding school wasn't a real solution, since the same sort of bullying was likely there. If he was away at school, it would be harder for Ian to watch over him. Ian was anxious to make up for past neglect. Sending Colin away didn't exactly do that.

Quickly discerning that Colin did not want to talk about the situation at school, Cynthia changed the subject. "I'm curious, Colin. Do you have any family pictures I could see? It might help me to know you better." It was a half-truth. The photos probably would give her a feel for the boy's past, but Cynthia had an ulterior motive. She wanted to see if the girl she'd seen in her car was Colin's aunt, who'd died by drowning. Could they be the same?

"Sure, if you want," Colin shrugged. "I've got some in my bedroom. I'll show 'em to you if you're interested." He appeared surprised that she would be.

"Thanks," Cynthia smiled, following Colin as he headed for his room. The hall was dimly lit by a combination of wall sconces and table lamps. He opened the door and left it that way. Cynthia went in behind him. It was a typically messy boy's room, except for the antique furniture. Clothes were tossed everywhere, often several layers deep. She nearly tripped over a pair of sneakers, with dirty socks balled up inside them.

The room hadn't been personalized much since Colin returned a few weeks before. He had brought a couple of posters for The Cure, and Souixe and the Banshees, which partially explained his dyed hair. He was evidently into the "Goth" scene. Cynthia had heard of it but didn't know much about it.

On top of his chest of drawers was a faux leather box full of cassettes, along with a boom box. That was all he had, except a rather ragged stuffed animal left over from seven years before. Cynthia couldn't even tell anymore what type of animal it was supposed to have been.

Colin paid no attention to her as he rummaged through his desk drawers, searching for the pictures he'd promised. He mumbled to himself, annoyed that he couldn't find them. "Where the bloody hell are they?" he cursed softly, under his breath. At last he whistled triumphantly and straightened up. "I found 'em!" Colin turned around with a small stack of photos in his hands.

He laid them out on his writing desk. Cynthia saw several of Colin as a much younger boy, with his father and some with a beautiful auburn-haired woman who must be his mother. Few included Seth, even peripherally. A few had other band members she recognized from the back sleeves of Danny's Odyssey albums.

She saw a couple of a gray haired man in his late fifties or early sixties. He wore a white suit, with a vest and a blue ascot. In other pictures, the same man stood beside a slight, middle- aged woman with dark hair and violet eyes. Cynthia guessed that they must be Colin's grandparents.

Colin pointed to a photo of a young brunette with violet eyes, like the older woman, beside him, when he was about four or five. "That's me," he indicated the boy in the picture. "And that's my Aunt Jennifer…"

Cynthia's eyes flared for a moment. She paled. It was the girl from the car! She recognized the girl, despite the fact that she'd been deathly pale and dripping wet when Cynthia last saw her. It was just as she'd suspected. The apparition was indeed connected to the estate. She existed outside of Cynthia's imagination, but the girl had been dead for seven years. Shocked, she put her hand to her mouth to stifle a reactive gasp.

"What is it?" Colin asked, baffled. "You look startled. Why?"

"Noth...it's nothing," Cynthia stammered.

"Come on! Don't lie to me. What is it you saw?" Colin insisted angrily. "You want me to trust you, but you won't trust me. It's not fair!"

"Al...aright," Cynthia sighed, slumping into the chair next to the room's fireplace. "I was...just surprised when I saw your aunt's picture. I realized...that I'd met her somewhere before — maybe in college. Do you know if she went to school over here?" Though not the truth, it was the best she could do, under the circumstances. Telling him the truth might gain his confidence, but if he told anyone else she would surely lose her job.

"I think for about a year, but I don't remember where she went," Colin answered.

"I just didn't expect to have met her before," Cynthia fibbed. It made her feel guilty. So much for her promise to him.

"I miss her," Colin said in a subdued voice. "She wasn't like the others. She paid attention to me. She never acted like it was a chore. Everybody else just...put up with me...or else ignored me. That meant a lot."

"She sounds like a great person. I wish I'd gotten the chance to know her," Cynthia commented neutrally.

"She was," Colin reflected quietly, his eyes far away. Cynthia felt sorry for him. She could easily understand why he missed his aunt. It must've been lonely for him here. She wished she had known Jennifer...when she was alive...

What should she do now? How could she deny that Colin had seen a werewolf, when she was beginning to believe that she'd actually seen a ghost? It made Cynthia feel dizzy, her world-view threatened. Ghosts were real! She couldn't believe it. She didn't want to. It left her with no bearing on reality. If ghosts existed, what else might? It meant the dire warning might be valid after all...

CHAPTER 10

OLD NEWS
THURSDAY, SEPTEMBER 16, 1982

Again, she couldn't sleep! It was becoming a habit — a bad one. Cynthia headed down to the library to find something to read. She needed to get her mind off things. It was late. Everyone else had probably already gone to bed. The lighting in the foyer was dimmed at this hour. She descended to the foyer.

The library was the largest room in the house. Its ceiling soared fifteen feet overhead. It was coffered with an inset bronze medallion. There was a massive carved fireplace, done in the Renaissance style. To either side were curtained French doors that led to the terrace. A pair of wing chairs faced the fire.

There were two sofas in the middle of the room, with a low coffee table between them. On the west wall was the door to the screening room, which had originally been the estate's office. At the other end of the room, three tall bookshelves stretched out like giant fingers. Cynthia guessed that there must be thousands of volumes. It was nearly as big as some public libraries.

Glancing at the hearth, Cynthia noticed that she wasn't alone. Ian sat in one of the chairs beside the fire, holding a drink in one hand as he gazed into the flames. He said nothing as she entered the room.

"Trouble sleeping, Doctor?" Ian asked in a conversational tone, without looking up.

"A little," she admitted. "I'd thought I'd come down to find something to read."

"You definitely came to the right place," Ian observed in a wry tone, indicating the shelves.

"What about you?" Cynthia turned the tables on him. "I see you're still up, too."

"You got me," he shrugged with a grin. "I'm a night owl...always have been. When the sun comes up, I know it's time for bed."

"I guess rock stars can work that schedule," Cynthia chuckled. "Not all of us are so lucky."

"Ouch!" Ian winced theatrically. "I guess I deserved that."

"Do you miss it? Touring and all that, I mean." Cynthia asked, though she knew it was none of her business.

"Sometimes," Ian answered sadly. "It wasn't all fun and games, but it was like nothing you can imagine…the sounds, the lights, the audience…oh, and the concerts were great, too," he added with a laugh. She smiled back.

"Why'd you quit?" Cynthia pressed further into risky territory. "I understand taking a break when everything happened, but it's been seven years. From last night, I can tell you haven't lost your ability and that you still love the music."

"I do miss it," Ian acknowledged, "at times, but it's part of my past now. I'm not a kid anymore. I'm pushing thirty-eight. Rock is a young man's game," he continued.

She could tell he was rationalizing, but she didn't contradict him.

"Besides," he continued, "I've been out of it too long. A year in rock is like a lifetime anywhere else. Since I retired, disco and punk have both come and gone. They're shifting from vinyl to CDs. I'm a dinosaur now."

"You don't even look close to extinct to me," Cynthia laughed lightly. "Not even partially fossilized yet. Aren't there plenty of veterans still on the charts? McCartney, The Stones, Pink Floyd… Bob Seeger?"

"You know your rock," he chuckled. Ian seemed a bit embarrassed. "But thanks. It's flattering of you to say." He decided to change the subject. "How are you getting along with Colin?"

"Okay, I think. He's a smart boy. He's understandably upset about the way things are at school. I've made an agreement to try to take seriously what he said happened. It angers him that people automatically dismiss his word. I admit being skeptical, but I told him that since I wasn't there, I wouldn't draw conclusions about what he did or didn't see. I noted that he didn't see whatever it was change shape, and he admitted it wasn't a full moon that night. But no one likes to be treated like they're lying, crazy, or stupid — as he put it," Cynthia summarized briefly. "He's none of those things."

"I can understand your point, Miss Akers, but is it really a good idea to encourage him?" Ian raised one eyebrow questionably. "Should we let him continue to believe in… werewolves?

"I'm trying to convince him how unlikely it is that such a thing could exist, but I don't want to antagonize him by calling it impossible. He's had seven years of people telling him that, and what good did it do? It depressed him and made him hostile. None of us know what he actually saw that night. It was probably someone in makeup or a mask as a disguise, but we don't know it for sure. I don't know what other answer there could be. I just need for him to trust me. I know how it feels to be dismissed and ridiculed," Cynthia explained, as well as she could. "It's not pleasant or helpful."

"Perhaps you're right," Ian sighed. "All the drugs and denial did no good." He gazed back into the fire, with a sad, wistful expression. "All I can ask of you is to do your utmost for Colin. If his mother and I were better parents, maybe what occurred seven years ago would never have taken place, or have affected him as it did. I should've been more security-conscious. If we'd been more attentive to him — less self-absorbed — he might have recovered better. I want to rectify that as much as I can, but it won't change the past."

"I'll do everything in my power," Cynthia promised earnestly. "This opportunity means a great deal to me, Mr. Holderness."

"Then we have an understanding, Doctor. I want you to do whatever it takes to help him." Ian sank back into his chair, putting down the now-empty glass he held. "I shouldn't have forced him to go to the local school. They know he's my kid. I shouldn't have subjected him to that."

"If you feel so unwelcome here, why do you stay?" Cynthia tilted her head slightly and eyed him curiously

"I…I'm used to it here," Ian inhaled deeply. "I really have nowhere else to go anymore. Despite some bad memories, this is my home. It…suits me. I refuse to be run off by a few yokels," there was a stubborn edge to his voice.

"It is a…spectacular place," Cynthia noted honestly, not wanting to antagonize him.

"Oh, I'm not kidding myself," Ian shook his head in self-deprecation. "I know the impression this place makes. If there was ever a haunted castle, this is it. I suspect Nicholson built it to create that effect. It was the heyday of gothic fiction. It's one reason I bought it. Seth and I used to love the old horror movies, even though we had to sneak in to see them. The Hammer stuff anyway. We were in our teens before they showed the Universal ones on TV over here. In England, they had their own certification letter, like your "R" or "X". Only adults were supposed to be able to see them. My stepfather used to bring us across the pond on business, and we'd visit Richard while we were here. That was when we got to watch them on TV."

"Do you miss England?" Cynthia asked in a conversational tone, hoping to draw him out, since he seemed willing to talk. "I know Colin does."

"In a way," Ian responded. "Mostly out of nostalgia for when I was younger. God, how I hated it at the time...everything seemed so dingy, narrow-minded, and dull. I could say it was too overcast, rainy, and foggy, but it wasn't always — and this isn't exactly sunny California. The bureaucracy and taxes there could be outrageous, but you did get something back, too. So, it's a tradeoff, I guess. I haven't lived there in so long; I doubt I'd recognize anything except the Queen and the national monuments. Even before I moved here, I toured and recorded so much in other places that I only saw merry old England for a few weeks at a time since I was, what? Twenty-three? But mostly there's nobody left there for me now, except maybe Rob — our drummer. But it wouldn't be even close to the same. It would just remind me all the more that you can't go home again because, in my case, it doesn't exist."

"I'd love to see it someday, if I can ever afford to travel," Cynthia mused dreamily, her expression far away. "I've never been out of the country, except once in my teens. We visited the Canadian side of Niagara Falls on vacation, but with my student loans to pay off, it'll be a while, if ever."

"Perhaps I'll show it to you one day," Ian hinted with a wink. "It might be fun to play tour guide. Colin would love it. I might enjoy seeing it through someone else's eyes; maybe next summer."

"I can't wait," Cynthia chuckled. "They say travel broadens the mind."

"Then we'll have to be certain to do it. I wouldn't want to deprive you of any...broadening," Ian was definitely flirting this time. It amused her. It was the first time a celebrity, even a retired one, had ever flirted with her before.

Cynthia returned to her room with the book she'd chosen. The moment she entered her room, she saw a folder laying a top her bed, the sort students used to take notes. It had to have been Colin who'd left it for her. She wondered what it contained. What did he want her to read?

Cynthia picked up the folder and flicked it open. Inside she found a series of photocopied newspaper articles taped onto notebook paper. Most were from the local newspaper, The Corchester Gazette. It was a small afternoon paper, scarcely more than a newsletter, but it was the only source of local information.

The articles began in November, 1974, and ran until the following autumn. Colin had gone to a lot of effort digging up and copying them off, she presumed from the town library. He'd put them all in chronological order. Aside from the pieces about what occurred at the estate, the articles derived mainly from 1974.

The earliest was dated a few days after Thanksgiving. George Bollan, a local dairy farmer, called the police when several of his cows were slaughtered. Whoever did it had tried to break into the farmhouse after Bollan shot at them with his rifle. The police drove the assailant off, but lost the trail in the woods. They never saw the assailant clearly.

Officially, the police labeled it the work of a vagrant. Yet, both Bollan and his wife insisted that what they saw wasn't human or any known animal, though it walked on two feet. Bollan claimed he'd shot it, but the bullets hadn't phased it. People just laughed at him. Two nights later, a boy named Tommy Zimmerman disappeared. He had been riding his bike toward his home near the edge of town not long after sunset. He never made it. His battered bicycle and a bloody sneaker were all that turned up. Nothing further was ever found. Fear and frustration gripped the town.

Between Christmas and New Year's, a pair of homeless men was discovered dead, near the abandoned train depot that once served the estate. Though half-frozen due to the cold, their bodies were savagely mutilated, like Bollan's cows the month before. They were said to have died of exposure and later savaged by wild dogs. Yet, no one ever saw them, though canine-like tracks were sighted. Tabloids reported that some hairs found were neither human nor from any known animal.

The next night, a young couple out on a date was attacked by…something. The girl was brutally murdered; the boy a bloody, incoherent mess. He had a few lacerations, but most of the blood belonged to the girl. The boy insisted they were attacked by a creature that looked like a beast, yet walked like a man. Although there was some weird tracks and damage to the car, the boy was blamed. He "managed" to hang himself in his cell.

Then there was a gap until March, 1975. There was a farm near the estate which belonged to an immigrant family from Romania, though the locals called them gypsies. A call came into the police from the family patriarch, but the sheriff's men arrived too late. The whole family, the patriarch, his three sons, and daughter-in-law were found in or near the house. It was ransacked and they were all virtually torn apart. They'd shot at whoever did it, but to no avail. The case was never solved. The sheriff's department was baffled.

Finally, there were the stories regarding what happened at the estate on Halloween that year. They reported little that Colin or Seth hadn't already told her, but the articles did confirm what she'd heard. The official articles in the Gazette and New York Times merely repeated the same details, but the tabloids gave a grizzlier picture, and noted canine tracks like those at the other scenes. They even called it the "werewolf killer".

The tabloids unabashedly suggested drug deals gone wrong, or some sort of twisted occult goings on. Some pointed to a local serial murderer, as memories of Charles Manson and the Zodiac killer were still fresh then.

Blame both direct and indirect was laid on Ian's doorstep, for his lack of proper security, presumed drug activity, and interest in the occult. It all made nice lurid headlines the press found irresistible.

Cynthia was impressed by the compilation. Something sinister did seem to have been going on at the time. Colin had included a list of full moons. Except for the final incident, all the events took place during the full moons or the nights just before or after. Yet, nothing occurred between April and October 1975. Why not?

The mystery haunted her as she finally drifted off to sleep. It was not a restful night. She had a lot to mull over. She better understood why Colin believed as he did. Cynthia prayed Colin was wrong about it still being out there. That was enough to scare anyone.

CHAPTER 11

AN AFTERNOON SWIM
SEPTEMBER 17, 1982

Cynthia met Colin at the head of the stairs. He studied her expression carefully.

"Did you read it?" he asked breathlessly.

"Yes," Cynthia replied. "It was...very interesting." She tried to sound encouraging, given all the effort he had put into it.

"What do you think?" Colin barely waited for her answer. "I didn't make it up."

"I'm proud of the work you put into your...dossier. It's very impressive. Unfortunately, the most incriminating stuff is from the tabloids, but they're not the most trustworthy sources of information. But I'm not insisting they made it all up. It is intriguing about all those full moons, though what happened here wasn't during a full moon. We don't know where...it was for most of 1975...or since then. Yet, I'll admit it's enough to show something very odd was going on then," Cynthia concluded diplomatically.

"But you still don't believe me," Colin was crestfallen, his head drooping, his posture visibly slumping. She saw the sting of betrayal in his eyes.

"Don't jump to conclusions," Cynthia admonished him gently. "Did I say that? I don't know what the answer is. I'm just not quite sure it was a werewolf, or that werewolves actually exist, but something very strange and deadly was here. You're not the only one to describe it in similar terms. There were tracks. Whatever it was, it existed. You didn't imagine it. The problem is we don't know what it was. It appeared to be connected to the full moon, yet not dependent on it. It's up to us to figure out what it was."

"Then you do believe it's real?" Colin sounded suddenly hopeful, his face brightened.

"I told you so, didn't I?" Cynthia replied.

"I ...guess that'll have to be enough for now,Colin seemed disappointed again. "But just you wait. I'll prove it to you yet. I promise I will."

"I'll bet you will, at that." She patted him on the back before continuing down the stairs. He watched her go with renewed determination, standing a little straighter. It wouldn't be easy, but he would do it. Colin vowed that he would.

"Mr. Holderness?" Cynthia knocked on the door to the study.

"Yes, Doctor?" Ian glanced up from the book he was reading.

"Since the weather's nice today, I agreed to take Colin to the pool-house. Would you like to join us? If you're not too busy, that is."

"How busy could I be? I'm retired," Ian chuckled in self-deprecation. "I was just reading; I can do that anytime. Just let me get my suit and I'll go with you. We could have Mrs. Jeffers pack us a lunch."

"Sounds great," Cynthia smiled broadly. "I'll let Colin know you're coming with us."

"I'll drop by the kitchen on my way to the room, to tell Mrs. Jeffers to make the lunch for us." Ian stood and headed towards the kitchen. Cynthia waved and ascended the stairs to Colin's room. She had to get her own suit as well. The late morning sun beamed through the windows.

"You're sure it's heated?" Cynthia shivered, rubbing her arms for warmth even though she wore a coat. "It's a beautiful day, but it's awfully chilly."

"It feels fine to me," Ian grinned, his eyes twinkling. He was only wearing a short- sleeve pull-over shirt and an old pair of jeans.

"How can you stand it like this? If it was overcast, it could snow..." She eyed him enviously. "It can't be above 40 degrees."

"I love the autumn — at least the weather," Ian shrugged. "The fall colors are nice, too." He indicated the red, gold, orange, and brown leaves on the trees and carpeting the ground.

Colin giggled at them. It was the first time Cynthia had seen him laugh. It was a nice picture. She hoped to see it more often. It was pleasant to see Ian at ease, too. For a moment, the gloom at the estate seemed to lift. They crunched through the dry leaves. There was hardly a cloud in the brilliant azure sky. The few that were there were wispy and high up.

After a short stroll through the woods, the pool-house came into view. It was a gray- white building in the classical style, resembling a Greco-Roman temple, with its portico and tiled roof. A modest stairway led up to the entrance.

Vents hidden in the coffered ceiling pumped in warm air. There was an interior colonnade in warm golden-colored marble. A large skylight directly over the pool let in the sunlight. A mosaic of Neptune and his dolphin nereids was visible through the clear water, which was also lit from below.

Paintings similar to those of Pompeii lined the walls. A few classical white marble statues stood guard between the columns. Water gushed from the mouth of a bronze fish ridden by a mermaid.

"It's gorgeous," Cynthia observed, surveying the interior. "It's like something out of a palace or royal villa."

"It was one of the most expensive things to restore, but it's been worth it. I can be a real sanctuary from the house…warm in winter, cool in summer," Ian explained. "It was a pain installing air conditioning, as it wasn't extended up there. I'd planned to but never did."

Colin wasn't paying attention to them. He'd gone into the changing room to remove his clothes. He couldn't wait to get into the pool. He would come here more often, except that it felt creepy when he was alone, but the whole estate was that way….

"It's almost as good as going to the beach," Ian observed. "And you wouldn't be going to the beach at this time of year, unless you were a lot further south."

"You don't leave the estate much anymore, do you?" Cynthia inquired, trying to sound casual rather than nosey.

"No, not often," Ian acknowledged. "I have what I need here. I have no reason to leave frequently. I traveled enough for a lifetime with Odyssey, though I mainly saw hotels and not much else."

"I guess there wasn't much time to sight-see," Cynthia commented with a nod.

"Not while I was on tour anyhow," Ian agreed. As they spoke, Colin emerged from the changing room in his bathing suit. He jumped into the pool, with a loud splash. Cynthia raised her hands futilely, to fend off the spray from the splash.

"I suppose that's my signal to change," Cynthia giggled, blushing. "Now that I'm already soaked…"

"Don't look at me," Ian responded with mock-defensiveness. "I didn't do it," he shrugged.

"You're his father…" she gently chided him.

"I never said I was good at it," he laughed. She cast him a stern look before laughing herself.

"When I was growing up, I would've loved to have a pool at home. I always had to use a public one or the one at school. I was on the swim team back in high school," Cynthia recalled.

"You'll have to show me if you still have it." Ian gave her a mock skeptical look.

"I said I was on the team. I never said we won anything," she winked at him wryly. "Swimming wasn't considered all that high a priority at my school and girls' sports even less." She smiled over her shoulder as she got up, and went to change into her bathing suit.

Ian already wore his suit. So, he merely pulled the t-shirt over his head and took off his jeans. He had worn sandals rather than shoes and socks; so, he didn't have to remove either. He'd already slipped into the pool's heated water before she returned to the pool.

Cynthia chose a simple cyan-blue one-piece suit to match her turquoise eyes. Although she owned bikinis, they seemed too provocative for the occasion. Colin was, after all, her patient and Ian her employer. It was what amounted to a family picnic, not a tropical resort. Even as it was, she felt self-conscious. Not only was Holderness her patient's father, but he was a former celebrity who could've had any woman he desired.

Cynthia wasn't normally that shy. Her figure was pretty good, though to her own eye it could use some improvement. Ian appeared to like what he saw. Instead of the bun or pony tail that she often wore, she let her hair hang loosely around her shoulders. For her part, Cynthia appraised Ian. While not bulky like a body-builder, he was more muscular and defined than she'd expected, resembling a gymnast perhaps.

"You'd have patients knocking down your door if they saw you now, Doctor," Ian said appreciatively.

"A sexist way to look at it," she admonished him, and then

laughed. "But thanks for the compliment."

"You deserve it," he chuckled, "even if it was sexist of me. We dinosaurs have a lot of evolving to do."

"As long as you're ascending the evolutionary ladder," Cynthia laughed, jumping into the water. "Brrr! I thought you said it was heated..."

"It is," Ian grinned. "The thermometer of the heater is set at seventy-nine degrees. The water is heated to seventy-five degrees, a whole four degrees difference."

"It's okay...I'm adjusting," Cynthia fibbed, shuddering slightly as she wiped the water and the hair out of her eyes. Behind them, Colin continued to splash about contentedly, oblivious to the adults.

"This is nice," Ian closed his eyes for a moment, leaning back against the edge if the pool. "I ought to do it more often. It's ...hard for me not to always dwell on the past or worry about the future. I'd forgotten how to just live in the moment."

"I know what you mean," Cynthia said, inhaling then exhaling slowly, luxuriating once she became used to the temperature of the water. "Most of my life, I focused so much on the future....the next test, when the grades were coming out, whether or not my student loans were going through, that I rarely paid much attention to day-to-day stuff."

"It must've taken a lot of discipline," Ian commented. "I remember my mother encouraging my music, but my stepdad thought it was frivolous — a waste of time. He insisted I find a 'real' job. So, I decided to go into medicine, mostly because of Richard I suppose. He was always good to me. I admired him. He was my real father's best friend. They first came to England during the war. My dad died a few months after D-Day. So I went to med school. I had to get near-perfect grades to qualify. It wasn't easy. I wasn't bad at it, but it wasn't my first love."

"I didn't have time for my music anymore. I couldn't even retreat to it like I used to. After a couple of years, I couldn't take it anymore. It was like being an addict and having your drug of choice cut off. So, I finally quit. Richard was really hurt and disappointed, but he forgave me like always. Roderick, my stepfather, was less happy about it. He threatened to throw me out. I did leave home then. It was hand-to-mouth for a while then...Rob...Robert Devon still called me 'Doc' because of that."

"When was that?" Cynthia asked with genuine interest. "How long ago?"

"I quit med school in '65," Ian replied. "After a few months, I managed to get some studio work....I founded a band called the Hawksmen. My real dad's last name was Hawkwood. We practiced a lot—finally got to play a few clubs in London. To us that felt like the big time, coming from a fairly small town and all. But we never got close to being signed by a record company. We didn't make much money. It probably cost us more to get back and forth than they paid us. We did get some free drinks—and a few birds..." he smiled mischievously.

"Be careful." Cynthia wagged her finger at him, "you're at risk of devolving."

"What can I say?" Ian shrugged. "I've been hiding out through most of the women's movement."

"Ignorance of the law is no excuse," she giggled easily. "You must've driven your wife crazy."

"Oh, I did," Ian admitted. "But not with my neanderthal behavior. She said I ignored her too much—didn't take her on tour with me, barely talked to her when I was home. Kate said it was like living with a bloody ghost. In fact, she said a ghost would've been better company most of the time. She's probably right. I was pretty self-absorbed. I guess I still am. I ...tend to live in my head a lot, but I'm really great at self-pity. I've got that down to a science."

"It couldn't have been entirely your fault," Cynthia tried to be sympathetic.

"It wasn't," Ian admitted, remembering. "Kate's dad, Henry Haine, doted on her—gave her whatever she wanted whenever she wanted it...until she decided she wanted me. He didn't approve of that at all; a scruffy, lazy hippie? I ...always suspected she got pregnant on purpose; at least back then I did. My friends said to blow her off. Her father was furious. Roderick freaked out. Seth got a kick out of the whole thing. My mom was...disappointed.

It wasn't exactly a shotgun wedding, but I did feel …herded into it. She found out that she was pregnant in late February. We got married in mid-April. Colin was born on September 4th that year. We considered pretending he was premature, but by then most of my friends and family already knew. So, we didn't bother. Kate got me in the end, but she decided it wasn't worth the effort. I'll admit that my resentment of the situation didn't help. It wasn't the way to start a marriage. We both gave up after a while."

"That's too bad." Cynthia didn't know what else to say.

"It's okay," Ian sighed. "It was over a long time before we divorced. If we'd both been less childish and selfish we might've stood a chance. Kate was and still is gorgeous. She's got a sharp tongue, but so do I when I want to. Neither of us was particularly responsible back then. While we weren't kids—I was twenty-three and she was nineteen—we weren't terribly mature either. What about you? Why hasn't any lucky guy snagged you yet?" he winked at her.

"I'm not something to be snagged," Cynthia stated disapprovingly. "I dated in high school, but I was obsessed with my grades so I could try to get a scholarship, which I did. I had a boyfriend in my junior and part of my senior years, Peter Berk. We split up because we wanted different things. He wanted to go to college out of state, and for me to follow him like part of his luggage. I planned to attend college in the city. So, we drifted apart after graduation," she reminisced. "In college, I dated Larry Sandridge, Darrel Parsons, and Cory Muldrew. None of those 'relationships' lasted, for various reasons. Obviously, I'm not married now and never have been. During my internship, I had a crush on Blake Donaldson, a surgical intern a year ahead of me. We dated a few times, but he was too caught up in becoming a surgeon to get serious. I was no better. We're still friends, but we don't see each other much."

"Well, I guess you just haven't found the right person yet," Ian observed.

"Sorry I gave you such a bio," she rolled her eyes in mild embarrassment. "I'm sure it was a lot more than you wanted to know. I …think about everything too much. I should've just made a joke and left it at that."

"You didn't say too much," Ian smiled reassuringly. "I gave you more of a biography. I didn't mean to imply you were some sort of spinster. You're what, twenty-nine or thirty? You've got plenty of time."

"You should know a girl never tells her age…and none of us ever hit thirty," she giggled lightly. "I'm in no hurry to find romance. If I'm meant to, I will."

"You never know when or where it will find you," Ian raised an eyebrow, flirting.

"No, I suppose you don't," she glanced back at him with a subtle grin. He was so good-looking it would be easy to get carried away…

"I've wondered about the tension between you and your stepbrother, if you don't mind me asking. I realize it's none of my business, but I couldn't help but notice," Cynthia said tentatively.

"I'm sure you couldn't help but notice," Ian sighed wearily. "I see no reason not to tell you. It's no secret. Seth was always a partier, despite my stepfather's efforts. He's had a drinking problem since we were teenagers. Roderick would blame me and my 'evil' influence. Seth used to laugh that it was the other way around. He can still be like an overgrown teenager at times. He likes to shock people. Anyway, nine years ago, he snuck out to see one of my concerts in New York. Roderick didn't want him to, because Seth had to work in the morning. Roderick was afraid Seth would get drunk at the after-party and miss work. He'd done it before. Roderick didn't feel it right that they just leech off me. It was a matter of pride, and he thought Seth should feel the same, but Seth was fascinated by music and acting, and the whole backstage thing. He has his pride, but it was less tied to his work than for Roderick. He wanted to enjoy himself. Roderick could never understand that. They fought about it all the time."

"Seth got smashed, just as Roderick feared. I offered to send him home in our limo. He refused….insisted he was fine. He acted insulted that I didn't think he was up to driving himself. At the same time, he hated Roderick's lectures. So, he begged me to make sure he and his car got home by morning. I knew he'd never make it to work that day. I should've ignored him and put him in the limo myself, but I admit that I was preoccupied, so I didn't."

"A pickup truck hit him on the way home. His reaction time was too slow to avoid it. He says his brakes didn't work. Who knows? Maybe they didn't. It took the Jaws of Life to get him out of the car. He hasn't been able to walk in since. He sees it as my fault. Perhaps it is."

"I'll tell you what I'd tell Colin," Cynthia began gently. "No matter how hard you try, there'll always be things we could've done but didn't or did do when we shouldn't have. We're not omniscient. It's natural to blame ourselves when things go wrong, but we can't let the guilt overwhelm us. It may sound like a platitude, but it's still true."

"Thanks for your concern," Ian sighed once more. "I appreciate the sentiment. I really do, but I'm stuck with my brother. He's my responsibility. We were raised together. We used to be inseparable. I owe him a hell of a lot, even if not for the accident. He does a lot for me —running this bloody place and handling my business affairs. He's good at it, too. Maybe this place is cursed...or we are. I don't know which. I realize it's terrible for Seth in that goddamned chair. I'm sorry about that, but I can't turn back the clock for him—for any of us..."

"Hey!" Colin called out from the end of the pool. "Are you two gonna talk all day? I can hardly hear myself splash. You can talk anytime..."

"You know...I think he's right!" Ian laughed then, and dove with a great splash. Cynthia sighed, and then dove in herself.

CHAPTER 12

SOMEONE IS WATCHING YOU

SEPTEMBER 17, 1982

"I'm going, Richard. That's all there is to it," Ian gulped the glass of brandy that he held. "I told them I would, and I won't break my promise."

"It's not that I don't want you to enjoy yourself," Marsden stated, his concern evident. "I'm just worried about you, Ian. You know how close you're cutting it. If you miscalculate even slightly, it could be disastrous."

"I'm aware of it," snapped Ian defensively. "How could I forget? But I had no valid excuse. Colin's anxious to go, since we missed the Renaissance Faire a couple of weeks ago. I can't keep begging off all the time..."

"Are you sure that's all it is?" Richard fingered his bearded chin thoughtfully.

"What if it's not?" Ian folded his arms defiantly, and looked away. "Does it matter? Don't I deserve some fun, too?"

"Of course you do," Richard sighed "I'm not saying that. I can see the way you look at her. I'm happy for you. You've been alone too long. Just be very careful. The situation's complicated."

"I'll be careful," Ian frowned. "I won't take advantage of her. Nothing may come of it anyway. There's no guarantee she's even interested in me. She's been pleasant, and I've enjoyed talking with her. It doesn't mean more than that. I know there can't be more than that with anyone."

"I never said that, Ian," Marsden retorted. "You're twisting my words. I don't want you to be alone forever. I'm just saying to take it slow."

"You might not have said it, Richard, but it's what you were thinking. I'm enjoying this little interlude, but I know that's all it can possibly be. There is no cure. We both know it. Without one, there can be no normal life for me—not ever. Everyone thinks this estate is my sanctuary. It's not. It's my prison. I won't forget that. I couldn't if I wanted to, and Lord, do I want to..."

September 18, 1982

The alarm went off and the radio came on. Cynthia groaned resentfully, rubbing her eyes and yawning. Morning always came so damn early! She opened one eye to glance at the clock. It was seven already...she had an hour to get ready for breakfast. Delicious as Mrs. Jeffery's food was, Cynthia wished she could stay in bed longer. She's never been a morning person, and doubted that would change.

She rolled over briefly, intending to take a couple of more minutes. When she turned over again she saw that it was 7:18! How could almost twenty minutes slip by without realizing it? Those last few minutes always felt the most luxurious, but they were the riskiest, too.

Sighing in annoyance, Cynthia thrust aside the comforter and sat up reluctantly. She yawned and stretched again. Throwing her legs over the side of the bed, she donned her slippers and staggered into the bathroom.

The light came on slowly, flickering eerily, with a hissing static noise. The bulb was dim, nearly yellow. The sconce looked Victorian, although it was electric. The wiring was probably ancient. Still, it gave her the creeps.

The bathroom had no windows, so the flickering bulb was the only source of light. The room was lavish, compared to what she was used to. It had expensive Italian tile on the walls, and polished gilt frame above a sink of veined gray marble.

The tub was a white Victorian with clawed feet. The knobs and handles on both the sink and the tub were made of brass and ivory. The only concessions to modernity were the blue plastic shower curtain and matching cloth covers of the toilet and rug beside the tub.

The lights continued to flicker, almost as if creating a Morse Code, but Cynthia was too sleepy to try to translate it. She went to the sink, took a swig of mouth wash, gargled and spit it out. Then she brushed her teeth, savoring the minty flavor after the muddy taste that had developed overnight.

There were dark circles beneath her eyes. It would require a lot of makeup to cover them up. ""Vanity, thy name is Cynthia," she laughed wryly at herself.

Having finished doing her teeth, she turned towards the tub and twisted the knobs to start the water. Bending over, she tested it but found it too cold. The tub was a long way from the water heater down in the basement. Straightening up again, her gaze fell upon the mirror.

Cynthia gasped, and jumped at what she saw there. A hooded

figure stared back at her from beyond the glass, the cowl pulled down so far that it hid most of the wearer's face. The hood was of crimson silk. Only the tip of his nose and sliver of his dimpled chin was visible, save the hint of a brown or dark-blond mustache. His eyes glowed in the shadow beneath the cowl, like red-orange flames. Almost as soon as she saw it, she blinked and the face was gone. She must've imagined it, but why that particular image and why now? Cynthia was aware the house had been built by an occultist. Although it was only a few days since she'd heard the story, she hadn't focused on it since then. The lighting did make her nervous, and she felt vulnerable even in the bathroom of this strange house. So, it might be enough to cause the hallucination. She hoped it wasn't a sign that she was losing her mind.

Shaking her head at the thought, Cynthia checked the water once more. It was warm enough this time. Cynthia removed her nightgown, and doffed her slippers. She laid the night gown atop the closed toilet seat, and stepped into the tub, feeling mildly self-conscious. There was nobody there to see her. Though the bathroom door wasn't locked, the bedroom door was. Yet, she sensed scrutiny, making her uneasy.

Rubbing her arms for warmth, she pulled the shower curtain around the tub. Cynthia let the warm water pour over her, turning slowly to revel in it. She closed her eyes. It felt glorious. For a while, Cynthia shoved her fears to the back of her mind. Time slowed down. Clocks ceased to matter to her.

Cynthia took the shampoo bottle from its niche, and poured some of it into her hands. Then she snapped the bottle closed and put it back up, and then worked it up into a rich lather. The flowery smell was pleasant and soothing. She wished she could hold onto the moment forever, but deep down Cynthia was aware that she didn't have forever. She had started late, and so needed to hurry.

As soon as she finished rinsing off the soap and shampoo, she turned off the water with a reluctant sigh. The cool made her shiver briefly, raising goose bumps after immersion in the warm water. Dragging aside the shower curtain, Cynthia grasped one of the towels. She blinked until she wiped the water and residual shampoo from her eyes.

Stepping out of the tub, she began to dry herself off. Once she felt sufficiently dry, Cynthia wrapped the large towel around herself, then took another and wound it around her head like a turban. She picked up her night gown from where she'd left it, and donned her slippers again.

Cynthia headed back to the bedroom, when her eye caught sight of the mirror. It was covered in steam, obscuring the reflection of the room. What she saw there made her jaw drop. A message was inscribed there, as if by an invisible finger. It was impossible! How did it get there?

It read: "He's watching you. He knows why you're here. He will try to stop you. Be careful! If you fail, doom will descend on the Blood Moon." Again with the blood moon! What was it? Why was it so important? What sort of "doom" was she in danger of? Who did the warning come from and to whom was it referring?

Despite wishing she could pretend that she hadn't seen the message, its tone was unmistakable. It was almost the same wording as that apparition she'd seen on the drive to the estate. Could the face that appeared in the mirror have been real after all? If so, he—whoever 'he' was—must be the one threatening the amorphous 'doom' Cynthia was meant to avert, but who was 'he' and how could she stop him?

It was insane! Here she was seriously contemplating 'spirit messages'. Cynthia examined the mirror more closely, opening it. She ran her fingers carefully along the back, seeking any sign that it might open up to reveal wiring. She found nothing. It seemed to be nothing more than an antique mirror. Of course, she was no expert in 'spyware'. By the time she'd closed the mirror, most of the steam had evaporated and, with it, the message. Had it ever really been there?

Briefly, Cynthia checked the wall across the room, to be sure there was no place the image could've been projected from. If anything was there, she couldn't find it. Switching off the bathroom light with a frustrated swipe of her hand, Cynthia returned to the bedroom.

Before she began to dry her hair and get dressed, she strode over to the bedroom door and checked it; to be sure it was still locked, as she'd left it. It was. Unfortunately, Ian, Seth, and the Jeffers all had access to the keys. Her employer was wealthy enough to, though why he would, Cynthia couldn't guess.

If that's what it was, did it work two ways? Could she be watched through it like a monitor, as well as having pictures projected onto it? Was it for security or just some sick practical joke? If the latter, it pointed more toward Seth, since it fit his warped sense of humor and he handled the money. Had he done it, no one else might know about it.

The grin certainly resembled Blackthorne more than his brother. Sadly, suspicion was all that she had. There was not a shred of proof that there was a technological explanation for what she's seen, much less who was behind it.

Without more to go on, she was just wasting her time. Could Seth Blackthorne have rigged her car, too? Could he have made the seat wet? Even I so, why bother? It made no sense to her. It was almost easier to believe in ghosts—almost. Disgusted with the whole thing, Cynthia decided to put it on the shelf for the time being. Until she knew more, there was nothing she could do about it anyway.

She sat down before the vanity, and unwound the towel she wore so that she could brush and blow-dry her hair. Cynthia plugged in the hair dryer, and used the flow of warm air and the sound in an effort to shove the speculations to a corner of her mind. It wasn't easy. They resisted going...

After her hair was dried and brushed, Cynthia picked out what she planned to wear and got dressed, periodically glancing at her watch or the bedside clock with growing impatience and urgency. She applied her makeup hurriedly, trying not to muss the process, but years of being rushed had trained her well. She grabbed a scarf, intending to use it to tie her hair back then changed her mind, deciding to leave it loose instead.

The morning sunlight streamed in through her window, which faced east. The new day had begun. It was time to set aside the fears of the night. Checking her make-up one last time in the vanity mirror, Cynthia was satisfied. Turning, she unlocked the door and headed for the stairs. Breakfast and Ian were waiting for her in the solarium.

CHAPTER 13

REMINISCING
SEPTEMBER 18, 1982

"Are you ready, Doctor?" Ian flashed a blinding white smile, his eyes glinting like silver in the morning sunlight.

"I'm ready Mr. Holderness," Cynthia answered as she finished her coffee. "But you can call me 'Cynthia'. 'Doctor' sounds so formal. Besides, I'm not on duty today."

"Cynthia," Ian enunciated it slowly, in his lilting British accent. "I like it. It's a pretty name. It suits you."

"Thanks." She blushed. "I didn't always like it. Some of the girls in school used to make fun of it..."Cyn-the-uh'..." she imitated the whiney, nasal sing-song tone her adolescent tormentors once used.

"Then they were ruddy idiots," he laughed warmly. "Kids can be cruel. I should've remembered that for Colin's sake. Blokes used to push me around because I was quite shy..."

"You were shy?" Cynthia asked skeptically, with a raised eyebrow.

"Hard to believe now, eh? I was into music and reading and movies as a kid, not football—you'd call it soccer—like Seth does. He was the popular one back then...the athlete...the partier...the teacher's pet..." Ian recalled wistfully. "That's one reason it's so hard seeing him in that damn chair."

"Well, I can't say I know how you feel," Cynthia commented thoughtfully. "But I can sort of understand. My brother, Danny, used to pick on me when I was a girl. He loved to tease me, but we'd do anything for each other. He chose to join the Marines, so that the college fund my parents set up could be used for me. He didn't know what he wanted to do then. He knew I did. My parents weren't rich. They couldn't afford to send us both to college. Because he was the boy, they assumed he would be the one to go. He gave me my shot. I'll never forget that."

"I missed him while he was in the service, but I was busy in college, then at Columbia. I'd managed to get a scholarship, too, which helped a lot, but even with that and the college fund, I owe a lot on student loans from when I was going for my Master's. Danny floundered a bit after he got out of the Corps. I worried about him. So did my parents. It was hard for him to readjust to civilian life. He just made detective a few months ago. I'm so proud of him."

He went to the police academy, but got laid off during the

financial crisis in '75. They called him back two years later.

"It sounds like the two of you are close," Ian said, a faraway look in his eyes. "I miss that. Seth used to look out for me when we were younger. He was just a couple months older, but more athletic and outgoing, but we both liked motorcycles. Our parents hated them. Mom, as always, spoiled me. It scared her, but she let me ride, although my step-dad wasn't very happy about that; not at all."

"I used to let Seth sneak rides on my bike. He would go out to parties at night against our dad's orders. I'd try to make excuses and cover up for him, though it usually didn't do much good. Roderick tended to blame me for being a bad influence on Seth. Seth was proud of it being the other way around."

It was clear Ian's relationship with his step-brother had soured over the years, but it had once been quite close. They'd both lost a parent when they were too young to remember them. More recently, they had lost their remaining parents and half-sister. Seth's bitterness over his accident, combined with Ian's guilt, had proven corrosive. Cynthia couldn't think of anything to say. Whatever she might come up with was bound to seem like a feeble platitude or unsolicited analysis.

"What about your sister?" Cynthia couldn't resist the question, though she realized that it was potentially insensitive. "It's alright if you don't want to talk about it. I just wondered. Colin mentioned her to me—showed me her picture, along with some of your parents. Neither you nor Seth ever speak of her. I just wondered what she was like."

"Jen?" Ian's voice cracked slightly. "No...I don't mind. I ...don't like thinking about what happened, but that doesn't mean I want to forget her...I could never do that. I wouldn't want to. She deserves to be remembered."

"Did you know she saved Colin?" Cynthia inquired tentatively. "He was in shock when he found your band mate. Wha....whoever it was...was still there. Your sister got Colin to run and hide in the boat-house while she got into one of the boats to distract...the attacker."

"No...I...I didn't know; not for sure. Colin wouldn't, doesn't...

discuss it with me. He didn't talk for weeks after that night. Kate took him away with her before he did. We didn't have much contact after that, but I'm not surprised. That was Jen, alright. She looked fragile, but she was brave. It must've taken everything she could do to get into that boat. She couldn't swim. She was terrified of the water. She loved Colin, though,as if he was her little brother rather than her nephew. She'd risk it all for him in a minute...I guess she did."

"I wish I could've been there, too," he agreed. "I...I'm glad you're here for Colin now."

"So am I." Cynthia smiled, with a nod. "He's a great kid."

"You'd know better than I would," Ian sighed sadly. "I barely know him...not that I can blame anyone but myself."

"Did you want custody back, then?" Cynthia felt the need to ask.

"To be honest, no," Ian admitted, embarrassed. "I didn't feel I could take care of him properly. I've been too wrapped up in my guilt and grief for too long. This isn't the best place for him, but I couldn't...can't leave it. I knew Kate loved Colin, however she felt about me. She'd take him far away from here. He'd be safe...have the chance to get better. I've told you some of my reasons for staying here. Richard is another. He's treating me—I can't trust another doctor to handle it as he has. The sanitarium and his family keep him here."

"I couldn't ask him to pull up stakes for me. He's given up enough for my sake, as it is. If it wasn't for Kate needing some time, I would've left things as they were. But she deserves another chance. I know Colin's got bad memories of this place, and few good ones of me to balance them out. Believe me; I've considered it from every angle. I couldn't send him to boarding school because he'd face the same bullying there with no one to support him. It would be me shunting him off again. So, unfortunately for him, it was here or nothing."

"You want him, don't you?" Cynthia persisted. She felt that she needed to know.

"Of course I do!" Ian sounded offended at the question. "I don't deserve him. It's my fault the tragedy occurred, and my fault he has to return here due to my…limitations. I want what I can't have—a second chance. It may be too late for that now, but I owe it to him to do whatever I can for him." He looked away for a moment, his face set in hard lines.

"I'm sorry for implying you didn't, but I had to be sure, if I'm going to help him," Cynthia said apologetically, feeling guilty at having pressed him.

"That's alright," Ian replied with resignation. "I realize you need to know where things stand here. It's just not pleasant to talk about it."

"I shouldn't have said it like an accusation," Cynthia blushed.

"That's okay…I've accused myself often enough," Ian acknowledged. "We should go now. The ride's about forty-five minutes. I'd like to have some time to talk to Irv and Moira. After that, we could shop or go to a movie or visit one of the parks in Newburgh—maybe stop for lunch…" Ian changed the subject, and she didn't try to change it back. It was best not to upset him further if she didn't have to. Things would go easier if they got along.

"I'm ready," Cynthia grabbed her coat as she stood. Ian pulled out her chair for her then returned it to its former position. She donned her coat, and followed him into the foyer. Ian opened the main doors, and gestured for her to go first. Then they began to stroll down the drive together.

It was a cool morning, with a light breeze rustling the leaves in the canopy above them. A few that had already fallen skittered across the cobblestones, and a dappling of sunlight and shadow fell across them. It was a beautiful early autumn morning. Cynthia inhaled deeply.

At the garages, they met Mat. He and several men in coveralls were setting up the new monitors in what he originally been the stables and more recently storage. Mat had been cleaning it out for days. Today, he'd brought in a desk and some office chairs, file drawers, a water cooler, a coffee-maker and a microwave.

The other men were taking down wiring, and plugging in the new monitors. Elsewhere, more techs were installing the new cameras around the estate. These were color instead of the few older black and white ones.

The security company was also adding more motion detector lights away from the house, which already had them. They were forced to put in new fuses and breakers to handle all the equipment, as the stables had not had electric before—except some jury-rigged lights.

"Say hi tuh Leese for me, will yuh?" Mat grinned broadly. "She's at the Dragon tuhday. Wish I could be, too, but we're almost finished here. They'll be bringin' the dogs out in a few days. The golf carts'll be here later this morning. In a few minutes we'll be testin' the cameras and monitors..."

"That's good. It's got to be safe, now that Colin's here—and Dr. Akers and maybe soon, Moira. I should've done this a long time ago," Ian's tone was serious, his face unreadable.

"I will not allow anything like what happened here seven years ago to occur again."

"Sure, boss," Mat was taken aback by Ian's intensity. Cynthia watched and listened, but said nothing. It wasn't an unreasonable attitude. It was just oddly delayed. There had been some security added in the mid-70s, although it was being stepped up notably now. Was there more to it? Since she had no way to know, it was useless to speculate.

"Before we go, do you want to take a look at my studio?" Ian's mood brightened. "I promised you I'd show it to you."

"I'd love to," Cynthia responded enthusiastically.

"Follow me up the stairs," Ian directed her to a stairway from the garages to the second floor. "Mat's rooms are up here, and my studio, where the grooms used to live above the stables."

"You mean over what's going to become the security guardhouse?" Cynthia asked.

"Yes," Ian replied. "The current garage used to house the carriages."

They continued up the stairs, to a corridor that was dimly-lit by overhead sconces. There was a series of doors to what had been rooms for the coachmen and stable hands and later the chauffeur. "We combined a couple of these to give Mat a decent-sized room with its own bathroom, since servants a hundred years ago didn't receive such luxurious accommodations," Ian winked humor in his expression.

They came to a door and Ian took out his key-ring. He chose the correct key, and unlocked the door. "I probably don't need to keep it locked. I trust Mat, but until recently there wasn't much security down here. I keep a lot of my favorite instruments here and some of the master tapes. There are a few people who might want to steal one or the other."

"They'd probably be worth a small fortune," Cynthia commented. "Maybe not so small."

Within the room, she saw that it was divided in two by a partition with a large window in it. On one side of it was a large mixing-board that looked relatively new. In the other room there were a piano and several electronic key boards, as well as multiple electric and acoustic guitars. There was even a bass guitar, and a selection of tambourines, maracas as well as a drum set.

Wires were everywhere, and also two stand mics and a few overhead. In the mixing room were shelves of albums, cassettes, reel-to-reels, and even a few eight- tracks. The only things missing were compact discs. Doubtless, he'd soon add some of them, too.

"Do you play all of these instruments?" Cynthia asked, fascinated.

"Most of them," Ian answered matter-of-factly, "except for the drums. I started doing bass around the time Odyssey was falling apart. Rick, our bassist, got along better with our lead-singer, Dave. I didn't want to have to rely on him to record my own stuff, and I was too impatient to do a cattle call for bassists. Of course, I learned piano before I was allowed to learn guitar, but Paul was better at the electronic keyboards than I was, especially the moog and the melotron. I still like the sound of the melotron better than most modern synthesizers, because it uses real tapes of vocals or strings instead of simulations, but they're rare beasts these days, and temperamental to play and maintain. Whenever I need a drummer, I call Rob and he hops across the pond to help me out. I keep a set of drums for him."

Robert Devon—Odyssey's drummer?" Cynthia wondered aloud.

"Yeah," Ian answered "We've kept in touch over the years. I was always close to him and Paul. With Paul...gone, it's only Rob and me left now. Dave and Rick don't speak to me, though they did revive a new version of Odyssey last year. With Rick, it's more disinterest than enmity, but Dave still resents me, and he had an affair with Kate back in the day. I fought to retain the name and logo for a while, since both were my idea back in '68. When everything happened here...I just didn't care anymore. So, I sold them my portion of the rights. They're welcome to them."

"Did you do any of your albums here?" Cynthia continued to wander about, examining everything.

"We'd finished 'Sojourner' and toured for it before I bought the estate. Richard had purchased what's now his sanatorium a few years before, in '69 or '70. Seth noticed Falcon's Aerie on a visit to Richard in '71, if I recall. Later, we found out the owner, Marcus Howarth, wanted to sell it, yet had never found a buyer. He was Jared Nicholson's nephew, son of his younger sister, Alexandra. We began negotiations to buy the place in the fall of '72 and the sale was finalized the next spring. So, I did some of my bits from 'Legend' here, and most of 'Eclipse' was done here in '74. My entire solo album, 'Nocturne', was.

"Danny was a fan of Odyssey in high school, but he missed a lot of your albums while he was in the Marines. I think he had the first three. When he got out, I bought him the rest for Christmas and his—our—birthday, December 23rd. That was in 1976," Cynthia remembered.

"I'm flattered that you bothered," Ian said in self-deprecation.

"I owed him. He bought the Cougar in his senior year of high school. It was a couple of years old by then. He let me have it when he joined the Marines. I doubt I could've afforded a car of my own for years after that if not for him," Cynthia reminisced, with a faraway look in her eyes.

"Since it got you here, I'm grateful to him," Ian smiled

"'Legend' went platinum, didn't it?" Cynthia asked, searching her memory.

"Eventually," Ian responded. "It was our top-selling album.

Sadly, it tore us apart, too. Dave was used to being the star of the show. Sometimes he started acting like we were just his backup band. He got sick in late '71, so I began to write more of our songs and sing lead sometimes, where I'd only done backups before. By the time of 'Legend', it was about half and half. It pissed him off that the biggest single was one I sang and wrote. He started to withdraw after that. On 'Eclipse', we recorded almost everything separately. When I got…sick, during the Eclipse tour he was quick to blame me for the dates we missed. He wanted to replace Paul, too, because Paul had…his problems then. I refused to go along with it. Rob sided with me and Rick with Dave. That was pretty much the end, though the legal…entanglements took months to undo."

"That's too bad. It was a great album, but I guess there's a lot of money and egos involved," Cynthia observed.

"You have no idea," Ian shook his head, with a wry smile. "Whether mine or Dave's was worse, I still don't know. Maybe it was a tie…" he chuckled easily.

CHAPTER 14

A MORNING RIDE
SEPTEMBER 18, 1982

Once they'd finished up in the studio, Cynthia and Ian went down to the garages, where his motorcycle was parked. It was a customized 1981 Harley Softail. Ian got him. Cynthia got on behind him as he'd instructed. "It's been a long time since I've done this. Danny had a bike in high school before he got the Mercury. He used to take me on it once in a while, when he thought his friends wouldn't see. They'd have ragged on him for letting me ride with him," she laughed softly.

"They must've been jealous you weren't with them," Ian mused with a wry grin. Then he gunned the engine, and they rode off through the open gates onto the estate's service road.

The wind rushed past them, whipping through their hair. Cynthia brushed her hair away from her face, laughing. She felt like a teenager on a date. She'd been so focused, it was hard to let loose in those days. Ian seemed to enjoy himself, too; the cloud that often hovered over him was temporarily forgotten.

The engine's roar combined with the breeze prevented them from conversing, but neither seemed to mind. The sun was warm, yet the wind cooled them. It didn't take long to reach Route 9, which ran along the east bank of the Hudson. The traffic was fairly light, even for a Saturday morning.

The river sparkled in the sun. The toll bridge over the Hudson from Beacon to Newburgh was roughly fifteen miles north of Corchester. On the way, they passed through Peekskill, Garrison, Cold Spring, and Beacon, before they got to the bridge. The towns were quaint and scenic, though traffic was slightly heavier while going through them.

Cynthia held tightly onto Ian. There was the same sort of thrill as she got on a carnival ride, just a hint of fear-yet a delicious fear. She could feel the hard, lean muscles through the rust colored t-shirt he wore beneath his suede vest. The beating of his heart was clear and strong. He seemed to revel in her presence.

With rare exceptions, Ian admitted to having made himself a virtual hermit at the estate over the last seven years. For a man who toured the world previously, that was quite a change, but was the estate his haven or his prison? And if it was a prison, why had he sentenced himself to it?

Once they arrived in Newburgh, Cynthia felt on more familiar ground than she had amidst the woods, farms, and small towns of the valley. Newburgh was tiny compared to the Big Apple, yet its density, architecture, and ethnic mix was more like the city than any of the other towns they'd passed through. Here and there were hints of the Hudson Valley's historic charm, but it was recognizably a city. Newer, shinier buildings mingled with urban decay but, as a city girl, Cynthia was used to that.

The Silver Dragon was a modest concrete and brick building at one end of a small strip mall. At the corner of the parking lot, a large oak stood, providing shade even as its roots began to break up the nearby pavement and sidewalk. The parking lot was empty.

The main window bore a painting of a silver dragon copied from the cover of a paper- back fantasy novel, above it the name of the store in Old English script. On the glass door a sign was pasted bearing the store's hours. It was not quite ten o'clock by Cynthia's watch and the shop did not open until 10:30 AM, explaining the lack of customers.

One of the cars was Lisa's red '65 mustang, with its white rag top. Another was a late 70s bronze colored Buick sedan, whose model Cynthia failed to recognize. She didn't know cars like Danny did. The final vehicle was battered dark-blue dodge van with an airbrushed fantasy painting on the side panel.

"This is it." Ian stopped, turned off the engine. "It's not much to look at, but Irv's a real artist. He did the paintings on the van and the store window. He's great at working metal, too. He even makes decorative daggers and swords they sell at the shop at the nearby Renaissance Faire at Tuxedo Park. It just ended last weekend."

"You never mentioned what you're picking up..."Cynthia wondered idly.

"Nothing much," he deflected her question. "I mainly came to talk to Moira, and to let you meet them both. They're not usually here on the same day."

Why had he avoided so simple a question? He was hiding something, but what? She decided to let it pass. What did it matter?

He had a right to his privacy. Still, it struck her as odd.

Ian opened the door, and Cynthia heard a cowbell clang as she entered. Ian held the door for her, following close behind. The door banged shut. Lisa stood beside the checkout counter, talking to an attractive woman with dark blond hair at the register. Lisa smiled and waved. Cynthia and Ian both waved back.

Lisa wore jeans and a printed t-shirt, instead of the skirts and blouses she sported for work, her long brunette hair loose about her shoulders. Cynthia smoothed the windblown tangles from her own hair. Removing her suede jacket and laying it aside, she went over to greet Lisa.

She guessed the blond woman was Moira Sorenson. Her hair was not as long as Cynthia's. It was a deep-honey color, pulled back into a loose ponytail at the nape of her neck. Sunglasses rested atop her head. Her large violet eyes were framed by long lashes. She wore a colorful peasant blouse over designer jeans.

"Dr. Akers, this is Moira," Lisa introduced her.

"So pleased to meet you," Moira smiled warmly.

"Call me 'Cynthia'," she suggested.

"Cynthia, then," Moira agreed.

"Is Irv in?" Ian interjected.

"He's in the back," Moira responded, pointing to the beaded curtain behind her.

"There were just some items I wanted to pick up while I'm here. I'll go back in a moment. I came mostly to talk to you, Moira," Ian said tentatively.

"Lisa told me," Moira nodded. "If you can set it up with the school board, I'm willing to tutor him. I just need the curriculum. What grade is he in?"

"The eighth," Ian replied. "Lisa can fill you in, then. She's been on the phone to the school board. We should have the curriculum by next week. Then we'll get whatever books he doesn't already have."

"That'll be fine. I'm free during the week anyway. When do you want me there in the morning?" Moira appeared genuinely enthusiastic over the thought of teaching again. Lisa had explained how Moira was forced to retire, when the parents of her students discovered she was a Wiccan. Although they couldn't technically fire her because of it, the tense atmosphere made teaching impossible for her.

"Nine o'clock should be fine," Ian stated, rubbing his chin in thought. "Or 9:30. We eat breakfast at 8:00 and have lunch at noon. You're welcome to have lunch with us, or even breakfast if you want to come that early. Should it be five, or six hours a day?"

"It's usually five, plus one for lunch," Moira noted. "Maybe 9:00 to noon and then 1:00 to 3:00, after lunch.

"It's settled, then," Ian reached out and shook hands. "I'll let Lisa handle the financial end. Just let her know what you need and it's yours."

"Be careful, Mr. Holderness," Moira chuckled. "I don't come cheap."

"I'm sure you're worth it," Ian laughed. "Now that we've discussed the matter, I'll leave you and Dr. Akers to get acquainted. I'll go back to see if my order's ready," he grinned and waved perfunctorily as he circled the counter. He passed through the curtains and disappeared into the backroom. The beads jangled before becoming still once more.

Cynthia felt a bit awkward, since she'd just met Mrs. Sorenson and had only met Lisa less than a week before. She didn't really know what to say. If they were going to work together, it was best to get to know each other, but she wasn't sure where to start. While not terribly shy, Cynthia was not especially outgoing either.

"So...Lisa tells me you've made a good start with Colin. What's he like?" Moira broke the ice for her.

"He's bright," Cynthia answered, trying to think of how best to describe her patient.

"But he's defensive. He's been neglected a lot. He feels people dismiss whatever he says because of his age and the things he claims he saw. It's been hard for him."

"Nobody likes to be told they're lying or imagining things," Moira nodded sympathetically. "What does he say happened?"

"I shouldn't say until I've spoken to him. He's my patient, regardless of his age..." Cynthia hesitated. "He witnessed what occurred at the estate seven years ago. He found his grandparents and his father's friend dead, and was chased by the ...killer. He saw his aunt drown trying to lead the killer away, but it didn't work. Only Dr. Marsden's arrival saved Colin."

"That's awful," Moira commented. "I can understand why he'd be troubled."

"I told Moira about your dreams," Lisa interjected.

"Has it helped you with Colin?" Moira inquired, studying Cynthia's face closely.

"A little," Cynthia replied, her mind racing for the safest answer. "At first, he was skeptical that I might've just made it all up to gain his confidence, but once I convinced him I hadn't, things got better. He just wants someone to trust, who'll take him seriously. I promised to do my best."

"We all want to be taken seriously," Moira observed thoughtfully.

"What's your opinion of the supernatural?" Cynthia asked warily.

"I try to tread the line between rationality and openness to the unknown. I don't think science has all the answers and may not be equipped to answer some of the 'big' questions. Some scientists tend to deny what they can't prove," Moira explained as carefully as she could. "Did you have anything in particular in mind?"

"No, not really," Cynthia fibbed. "I guess I was thinking of things like psychic powers...monsters...ghosts...that sort of thing."

"Well, monsters I'm not sure about," Moira admitted with a smile. "Big Foot and the Lochness Monster could be real, but I haven't studied them enough to say. I do believe psychic abilities are real, though there are plenty of fakers out there. I can see auras, for example."

"Really?" How interesting," Cynthia tried to sound neutral. "What about ghosts?"

"There are loads of theories," Moira said, carefully considering the question. "Science presumes they're all hoaxes or mistaken natural phenomena. Traditional believers are convinced they are the spirits of the deceased. Some fundamentalist Christians say they're demons masquerading as the spirits of the dead. Certain investigators theorize that ghosts are psychic impressions endlessly replayed on the psychic 'ether', sort of like a tape loop. Others hypothesize they might be 'slips' in time, or between parallel universes. A few hypothesize that they could be thought forms conjured up by our own minds, especially if belief is strong enough. Those are the ideas I've read. I don't know which, if any, is true; possibly more than one. Any particular reason you asked?" Moira raised an eyebrow, her curiosity aroused.

"Uh...no," Cynthia stammered embarrassed. "I was just... curious." Lisa and Moira shared a knowing glance, but didn't press Cynthia further. She'd come forward on her own when she was ready. If that was never, so be it.

"So, what do you think of Ian? I mean, Mr. Holderness?" Moira changed the subject.

"He's quite nice," Cynthia over simplified.

"Gorgeous, isn't he?" Moira giggled conspiratorially. "As a happily married woman, I'm not supposed to notice, but I do. I love that British accent, too—so sexy."

"He is...attractive," Cynthia blushed.

"It's alright. We won't tell him you said so," Lisa nudged Cynthia with a sly wink and a smile.

"Am I that obvious?" Cynthia sighed.

"Just to us," Moira laughed good-naturedly.

"You'd have to be deaf and blind not to be attracted to him. Don't worry. He's pretty oblivious. He won't notice unless you thunked him on the head with it...maybe even not then. He's a very nice guy... but moody and very preoccupied. Don't give up on him, though. He needs somebody as much as Colin does. He's become a virtual recluse. Things will be better for Colin if his father stops carrying that cloud around with him wherever he goes. You might be the one who can lift it. I hope so."

"I'd like to think you're right," Cynthia fidgeted. "But it's a tall order. Colin is my patient. I really shouldn't involve myself too closely with his father. It's frowned upon. I really need this job. I don't want to mess it up."

"I wasn't suggesting you seduce him," Moira chuckled. "Though that could be fun, but I do think the best way to help the son is to help the father. The kid needs a parent, not a self-absorbed martyr."

"I …suppose it wouldn't hurt to be nice to him," Cynthia suppressed a giggle, seeing the humor in the situation.

"There are a lot of women who'd die for the chance to make that sort of sacrifice," she fought back another laugh.

"You have what I asked for?" Ian asked in a half whisper, as if he feared being over- heard.

"Yeah," Irv replied with a broad smile. "I just finished 'em yesterday. This is under the table, you understand, Mr. Holderness? Gotta be careful. The law frowns on bikers and witches. They'd ask me what yuh wanted 'em for. None o' my business really, but why silver bullets? Why'd yuh need Moira tuh bless 'em for yuh, again?"

Irving Sorenson was a jovial-looking man of medium height. He was in his forties. Stocky and a bit thick in the waist, his long brown hair was thinning on top and pulled back at his neck by a leather cord. There was gray at his temples and in his full wiry beard and upturned mustache. He had friendly blue eyes, from which laugh lines radiated, and a pug nose broken at least once. He wore an off-white tunic shirt under a brown leather vest. His faded denims were shoved into laced moccasins to mid-calf. He wore a spiked wristlet on his right arm and rings on every finger, save his thumbs.

"Yes," Ian answered. "I'm grateful for your help, Irv. You two have always been good about not asking too many questions. I have my reasons." Ian glanced about furtively, visibly nervous.

"Moira said silver's traditionally fer demons, an' o' course, werewolves," Irv laughed. "Least in the movies."

"The movies aren't always wrong," Ian sighed. "They're just a precaution. Hopefully they'll never be used…"

"Whatever you say, Mr. Holderness. The customer is always right," Irv handed the bag to Ian.

"One more thing," Ian snatched the bag possessively. "Can you make a necklace for me—a pendant? Cost is no object, you're the artist. Make it a pentacle. I don't care what other designs you include. It has to be the purest silver you can get, and I want Moira to use her strongest protective spells on it. I need it as soon as possible…"

"Fer a special lady, eh?" Irv winked knowingly. "Is it the pretty doctor? She seen the one I made for Lisa?"

"Uh….yes….yes she did," Ian lied.

CHAPTER 15

BROWNIES
SEPTEMBER 18, 1982

Cynthia and Ian waved goodbye as they rode from the shop. They spoke little for a while, both preoccupied with their own thoughts. After a few minutes, Ian offered to take her to lunch. Cynthia took a rain check, as she wasn't hungry yet. They considered going to a movie and bought a paper to check the listings, but they couldn't find anything that they both wanted to see.

In the end, they rode around Newburgh; window-shopping at a local mall, and then strolling awhile at a park facing the river, just south of the bridge. Ian seemed to enjoy her company; he remained largely silent regarding his self-imposed exile over the last seven years, as if they had never occurred. Was it just reticence or something more?

Cynthia was charmed by the man she was getting to know, yet troubled by his omissions, periodic silences, and far-away glances. As pleasant and warm as Ian appeared, the cloud that hung over him gradually reasserted itself as the day wore on. As evening approached, she saw what Moira meant. The tragedy haunting Ian refused to release him. As long as he was still at its mercy, so could Colin be.

By 4:30, the day had grown overcast. The breeze picked up. It was cool with a hint of moisture suggesting that it might rain. They decided to head for home. It had been a lovely day, and Cynthia would treasure it. They hopped onto the Harley and rode across the bridge towards Beacon.

Luckily, there was no real rush hour, since it was the weekend, though traffic was a bit heavier when they passed through the towns along the way. They went through Beacon, Cold Springs, Peekskill, and Garrison.

As they left Garrison behind, Ian reminded Cynthia that it was the Jeffers' night off. Aida and Harlan had gone to visit her sister, Zelda, in Poughkeepsie. Lisa and Mat were going out to a movie. Aida had left a cold supper for Colin, Seth, and Jeremy. She hadn't left anything for Ian or Cynthia, assuming they'd planned to eat out.

South of Garrison, there was only Corchester, unless they rode beyond it. Cynthia suggested Brownies, the local bar and grill. There wasn't much else, except a couple of chain fast-food places along the highway south of town. Despite the extra travel, Ian said that he would prefer one of them, but that would mean getting home after dark; with rain threatening, Cynthia was anxious to get back to the estate. Reluctantly, Ian acquiesced and they pulled into the parking lot at Brownies.

"I'm not sure this was a good idea," Ian gave a weary sigh. His eyes darted about uneasily. "I'm not the most popular man in town."

"Then we'll eat quickly," Cynthia offered. "We're here now. What can happen in a few minutes?" Stupid question, she thought.

"If you say so," Ian shrugged in resignation, with a skeptical roll of his eyes. He turned up his collar, having put on his jacket as the sky had darkened. He kept his head down, and brought the sunglasses down from the top of his head to hide his eyes. The moves were as futile as they were instinctual.

All eyes were on them as soon as they entered, though a few tried to pretend they weren't looking, but the expressions of some of the patrons were distinctly hostile.

They chose a booth relatively close to the door, so that they could leave quickly. The waitress looked directly at them, but made no move to greet them. It annoyed Cynthia, yet didn't surprise Ian. He gave her an 'I told you so' look. She gave him an apologetic half-shrug.

Cynthia sensed the atmosphere and almost immediately and regretted her decision, but she hated to admit it even herself. She was not a scared little girl, afraid of a few hooded glances. They had as much right as anyone else to be there. No small-town hicks were going to chase her off with her tail between her legs.

With a disgusted expression, the middle-aged waitress came over to the booth, note pad and pen in hand. She appeared about forty-five, with wavy, reddish-brown hair and makeup that was a little too harsh. Her uniform, while clean, was not crisp. Her name tag read 'Hetty'. She eyed Ian with veiled curiosity.

The bartender, a balding man in his fifties, pointedly ignored Cynthia and Ian, concentrating on wiping out a glass mug. The patrons at the bar pretended not to glance over their shoulders. Another pair stood beside one of the bar's three pool tables, each

illuminated by low-hanging lamps. Each held a cue. They had temporarily stopped game to glare at Ian and Cynthia with ill-concealed anger and contempt.

Both men looked to be in their mid- to late-thirties. One stood over six feet tall. The other was a couple of inches shorter. He was a thin, wiry man with sharp features and lank, greasy brown hair that was long in the back and short on the sides.

They both had heavy stubble, yet were otherwise clean-shaven. The taller man's gut drooped over the belt of his rumpled jeans. They each wore flannel shirts and had dirty, scuffed work boots. Behind them Asia's "The Heat of the Moment" played on the jukebox, having followed a song by the Cars.

Cynthia and Ian ordered hamburgers, without fries, as it would take too long to eat them. Ian asked for a beer, whereas she went with a Diet Coke. The waitress scribbled down their orders then headed straight for the kitchen, making no attempt at chitchat. The two men at the pool table continued their game, yet never ceased to watch Ian and Cynthia. The jukebox clicked and a new song began; Rainbows' "Stone Cold".

Cynthia and Ian couldn't help but feel the unwanted scrutiny. Ian impatiently thrummed his fingers on the table, clearly ill at ease. He couldn't wait to get out of there. Cynthia felt increasingly guilty for insisting that they stop here. The tension in the air continued to grow thicker.

After what seemed like forever, the waitress finally brought their orders. Anxious to leave, Ian stuffed a twenty into the waitress's hand and told her to keep the change. He explained in a whisper that he was out of fives and tens, and in no mood to count singles. Cynthia understood, though he'd paid almost twice what they owed.

Ian wolfed down his burger, despite its thickness. Ketchup, mustard, and juice from the meat dripped onto his plate, staining a couple of his fingers, but he scarcely noticed. Cynthia ate quickly herself, conscious of Ian's desire to leave, and not feeling very welcome either. The jukebox fell silent, now out of songs.

Brownies definitely would not be a regular stop for her. Ian finished before she did, wiping his mouth and hands with the napkin. She forced herself to chew carefully, regardless of their haste. She refused to choke to suit these cretins.

"Look a' that," smirked the shorter man. "The great big Rock Star's gracin' us with his presence. Ain't that nice o' him?"

"Real nice, Eddie," grinned the bigger one, nastily. "We oughtta greet 'im-show 'im how honored we are..." he laughed. "Jus' like his brat at school. 'Cause o' him, Andy got suspended. We gotta thank 'im right and proper..."

"Who gets the girl first, Carl?" Eddie snickered lasciviously. "Can I buddy-can I?"

"Not yet, Eddie. We gotta deal with our buddy here first..." Carl grimaced.

"Damn Brit faggot thinks he's better'n us. Daffy, here's, gotta pay fer what his brat caused..." Carl reached out, and grabbed Cynthia's arm tightly before she could react, dragging her from the booth. Frowning, she inhaled sharply.

"Get your hands off me!" Cynthia shouted angrily, glowering at Carl.

"Shut the fuck up!" Carl snapped, raising his other hand as if to strike her.

"Don't even think of it!" Ian snarled, half-rising from the booth, one hand stretched out towards Cynthia and Carl. Yet before Ian could free himself from the booth, Eddie's boot shot out, tripping the Englishman. It sent Ian sprawling onto the floor with a harsh thud. Cynthia cursed under her breath, and glared furiously at Carl and Eddie.

"Leave him alone!" she cried, her anger and worry out-weighing her fear.

They were just a pair of over-aged bullies. For now, they had the upper hand. Eddie kicked Ian several times in the gut. Holderness grunted in pain involuntarily, seething at the situation.

Carl squeezed Cynthia's forearm until it hurt. She spat at him and aimed her free hand to slap him across the face. Gritting his teeth, he caught her hand before she could hit him. "None o' that, bitch!" He let her hand go for a second to wipe the spit from his cheek. Then he back- handed her in the face, leaving a visible welt.

She reached out to scratch at him, but never got the chance.

Livid, and refusing to give him the satisfaction of tears, Cynthia glared at Carl. Knowing that her time was short, she kicked him in the shin and elbowed him in the gut with her free arm. She'd aimed for the groin, but the unexpected pain in his shin caused Carl to shift positions. So, she struck his ample stomach instead. Carl hissed, infuriated. "You fuckin' bitch! You're gonna pay fer that!" He moved to punch her.

Eddie watched in fascination, distracted from Ian. Hearing movement, he glanced down, intending to kick Holderness again. His boot passed through empty space. Ian caught it mid-kick. He'd turned over while Eddie wasn't paying attention. In an instant, it was Eddie who lay on the floor, staring up at Ian. Holderness had risen to his feet almost too fast to see. Carl failed to notice, focusing on Cynthia.

Carl's fist connected with Cynthia's face, sending her reeling. He held onto her arm to prevent her from escaping him. Blood dripped from the side of her mouth, where she'd accidentally bitten her lip, but Carl was not through with her. He lifted his balled fist to hit her again.

The blow never landed. It met Ian's left palm instead, as if crashing into a brick wall. Foster looked stunned for the moment, and totally baffled. It was the first time he realized that Ian was even on his feet again.

Carl wasn't used to resistance. He'd pegged Ian as a coward who required bodyguards and lawyers for protection. He assumed that Holderness would be easily cowed. Ian's earlier nervousness radiated "victim" to Carl. He was skilled at finding potential victims.

"Back off, Foster or I'll crush your hand," Ian spat. He tightened his hold on Carl's fist, visibly causing Foster pain, controlling himself, with difficulty. Ian let Carl's hand go. Foster unintentionally let Cynthia loose when confronted by Ian. She stumbled back as she broke free. Holderness moved quickly to help steady her.

Shaking off his initial shock, Foster charged at Ian, taking advantage of his temporary distraction. Carl pulled a knife from his pocket and flicked out the blade. It glinted in the neon lights of the bar. In his blind fury, Foster sought to stab Ian in the back, even though Ian was unarmed. He assumed no one would dare to testify against him and was too angry to care. "Get the fuck up, Eddie!" he yelled helplessly. "Help me get 'im! This fucker's gonna die!"

Eddie, back on his feet by then, took out his own knife, grinning viciously. "Get 'im, Carl! Stick 'im good!" Hastings circled around, looking for an opening. He always did as Carl told him to.

Cynthia noticed that Ian's eyes looked as though they were lit from within. They had a strange greenish cast she'd never seen in them before. In fact, it was unlike anything she had ever seen before in anybody. Scanning the room, Cynthia found no green bulbs to create such a reflection, if that's what it was. Ian's features looked coarser, too; heavier—even sinister. It was an unnerving effect. Could she have imagined it?

She could almost swear his teeth looked longer...sharper. His hand, where it held hers, was like a steel vise, his nails unwittingly biting into her flesh, the pressure of his grip crushing. Ian was too preoccupied to realize it. "Ian! Watch out!" Cynthia shouted in warning.

He whirled to face the pair without fear or hesitation, though both were armed whereas he wasn't. Carl darted out, slashing Ian on the forearm. He ignored the wound as though he didn't feel it. Cynthia watched in sickened fascination.

While grateful for the rescue, she resented the need for one. She ought to have been able to extricate herself without Ian's help. She really should've taken those self-defense lessons Danny offered to give her. She'd just been so busy back then...

Before Carl could lunge at him again, Ian's arm shot out as if it was spring-loaded. He grasped Foster by the throat, tightening his fingers to constrict Carl's windpipe. Ian lifted the taller man off the floor...All 350 plus pounds of him, one-handed. He revealed no signs of strain, or even much effort. Carl choked and flailed, his air cut off, visibly afraid for the first time. He dropped the knife from his numb fingers.

Eddie gasped at the sight, in surprise and terror. Then he bent down and ran at Ian, his knife extended to slash or stab; whichever opportunity presented itself. He had to save his friend. Carl wasn't much. He often bullied Eddie, but he was the only friend Hastings had. With Ian focused solely on Carl, Eddie prayed he would get his chance, though fear ate at his gut like battery acid.

Ian appeared to ignore Eddie. Cynthia failed to see Hastings coming, her eyes on Ian and Carl. At the last possible instant, Ian swung his free arm, swatting Hastings away. Eddie was helplessly flung backwards, knocking over a chair as he tumbled to the floor.

Hastings' knife skittered away from his grip, across the floor. Neither Eddie nor Cynthia saw where it ended up. Hastings lay where he fell, slightly dazed, eying Ian in abject terror. The merest "tap" by Holderness had sent him halfway across the room...How the hell had he done that? What was he? Was he even human? Maybe the stories about him were true after all.....

Carl's eyes bulged as he gasped unable to breath, "How does it feel to be helpless, Foster? Do you like it? I see where your son gets his manners from..." Ian glowered at Foster, unblinking, his temper building...straining to be set free. "Should I finish this here and now, Foster?"

"Ian..." Cynthia whispered. "He's not worth it. You've proved your point..."

"Have I?" he snapped irritably, not looking at her. "Let's ask Carl, here. Have I made my point?"

Foster was nearly unconscious, not able to respond. Ian shivered slightly with the emotions running through him—surging adrenaline. He wanted to hurt Carl. He would enjoy doing it. Part of him knew that was wrong, that he was becoming the bully now.

He struggled internally for an endless moment. He felt little direct sorrow for Carl. He probably deserved worse than he was getting, after years of terrorizing others.

But this was not the way to handle it. Ian was perilously close to crossing a line from which there was no return.

"Aach!" Ian growled, and then dropped Foster. Eddie rushed to his friend's side, helping him sit up. Foster massaged his throat, coughing as he began to breathe again. He was unable to speak, yet stared with mingled fear, rage, and embarrassment. "Remember, Foster!" Ian sneered. "If you ever-EVER-hurt me or mine again, you won't get off so easily" Then he turned on his heel and stalked from the bar. Cynthia, glancing about nervously, followed after him.

"We gotta go get 'im Carl—make 'im pay...maybe call the cops..." Eddie stuttered, his words tumbling out in an unthinking rush.

"Shut up, Eddie," Carl croaked, his voice hoarse and raspy. "We ain't callin' nobody. Yuh hear that?" he yelled as loud as he was able. "Nothin' happened here tuhnight! Got that?"

"But, Carl...." Eddie broke in, confused.

"But nothin', Eddie," Foster almost whispered. "He's got money.... lawyers. He ain't gonna get off that way. His time's comin'. He's gonna pay real good. So's his bitch, but they ain't gonna survive the lesson..."

Eddie grinned knowingly. "Right, Carl. I'm with you. Jus' let me know when it's goin' down."

"Don't worry, Eddie," Foster frowned deeply. "I will...believe me, I will."

CHAPTER 16

A CHILL IN THE AIR
SEPTEMBER 18, 1982

Although not usually dark at this hour, the clouds obscured the late afternoon sun. The wind whistled about the house. As they reached the gate, it began to rain. They did not speak as they rode, each lost in their own thoughts. Knowing Mat wouldn't be home, Ian had brought the remote with him. He took it out and pressed the button. The gates swung inward.

They rode through the gates, the only sound coming from the Harley's engine and the ever faster beat of the rain. Since Cynthia had arrived, Mat had oiled the hinges of the gates and they moved almost silently, save a modest clank when they closed.

Ian parked his bike in the garage and they both got off. Along with the van that Mat used were Ian's cars, a red Jaguar XKE and green '69 Camaro SS396 convertible, with hidden headlights. A pair of electric golf carts had been delivered that morning for the security guards. They were charging.

Ian remained silent. Cynthia could sense the roiling of competing emotions going through him. "You okay?" Cynthia reached out to Ian tentatively, doubting that he would say anything unless she did first—perhaps not even then.

"I..." he began haltingly. "I don't know. I'm sorry I ruined the day."

"You didn't," Cynthia objected. "I had a wonderful time. What happened wasn't your fault. They started it. I should've taken your word, and chosen someplace else for lunch. You saved my stupid neck back there."

"Maybe..." Ian remained conflicted. "I couldn't let them hurt you. If I'd moved quicker, Foster would never have hit you once, let alone twice."

"I gave him some pretty good reasons," Cynthia chuckled ruefully. "If I'd taken the self-defense lessons Danny offered me, I wouldn't have needed to be rescued, but you have nothing to apologize for. I'm grateful to you."

"If I hadn't been so clumsy, you wouldn't have those bruises," Ian persisted, gently brushing her face with his fingers.

"How could you help it?" She laid her hand on his arm, gazing into his intense eyes. The silver mingled with the stormy gray green, still visibly troubled. "That creep took advantage because he knew he had no hope any other way."

"I wasn't fast enough." Ian gazed at her longingly, his voice sad. "He hurt you."

"These?" Cynthia indicated the welts. "They're nothing. Badges of honor...."

"You're brave," he half-smiled appreciatively. "And very generous, but I don't deserve your generosity. I went too far. Those two could sue me, even have me arrested."

"They're bullies. They might be afraid to broadcast what you did to them, beyond those who saw it. You trashed them without raising a sweat. They'll probably pray nobody finds out," Cynthia said encouragingly.

"That was foolish of me." Ian turned away. "I should've stopped them in a less...showy fashion. Now, I've made everyone there fear me—perhaps even you."

"You did what you had to do," Cynthia continued to try to soothe him.

"You don't understand." He walked a few steps away, wrapped up in his feelings. "I could've killed them—Foster especially. I wanted to. It would've been so easy. I would've enjoyed it, too. I could barely restrain myself.... "

Cynthia sensed how close he'd come to killing Foster. It disturbed her, but she owed Ian. She was also attracted to him. It wasn't hard to understand why he'd gotten so angry. It was the intensity of that anger that frightened her, combined with his unusual strength. He might easily hurt or kill someone without intending to. The consequences, if he did, were worrisome. His problem controlling his temper made that a serious risk.

Where had he gotten that strength? Carl, being dead weight, would equate to well over his three hundred-plus pounds. Ian hadn't appeared to be using just some martial arts technique. Yet, if not, what was it?

Ian might well be capable of what Colin said the beast had done. He was the only person she knew who could. His temper offered a possible explanation for why he might've lost control seven years before—if he had. Cynthia didn't want to believe it, but the potential was unmistakable.

"You must think I'm a psychopath after tonight," Ian sighed, shaking his head in frustration. "Maybe I am."

"I don't think that," Cynthia smiled. "You could use a little... anger management," she laughed.

"Ouch! I guess I deserved that." Ian rolled his eyes in self-deprecation. "I really did enjoy today. I'd forgotten what it felt like to just go out and have fun," he sounded wistful.

Impulsively, Ian reached out and drew Cynthia closer, bending to kiss her. Instinctively, Cynthia flinched in surprise at his touch and the tightness of his grip. Immediately, she regretted her reaction, but it was already too late. Feeling her tense, Ian pulled away from Cynthia, embarrassed. He stepped back and turned from her, with a stricken look that he quickly sought to hide.

"I'm sorry...I shouldn't have done that," Ian stammered.

"No...you don't have to apologize," Cynthia blushed, embarrassed at her own reaction, though it wasn't intentional. "I was just surprised, that's all. I wasn't expecting it..." She could've kicked herself at that moment. Cynthia had secretly hoped that he might kiss her, though she hadn't expected it. What an idiot she was! Why had she done that?

"It's understandable, after what you saw, that you'd react like that," Ian's tone was dull, lifeless, his eyes averted. He seemed tired. He muttered to himself, though Cynthia couldn't hear what he was saying. Giving her a brief perfunctory wave, he strode away, heading towards the house. Ian ignored the rain and made no effort to fend it off.

Cynthia watched him go, with mingled bafflement and disgust with herself. Ian had withdrawn into his shell so deeply that it would be very difficult to pull him out of it again. "Great job," Cynthia sighed to herself. There was nothing she could do now, but damage-control...if she could repair things.

September 19, 1982
The next day, Ian was polite, yet distant, towards Cynthia

whenever they met. He avoided direct eye-contact. He tended to leave the room if she walked in, and said as little to her as he could. He was clearly embarrassed by what had occurred between them. If she hadn't flinched at the wrong moment, things might've been so different...

Maybe it was for the best, she tried to tell herself. It really wasn't appropriate for them to become personally involved. It might affect her treatment of Colin. She would've tried not to let it, but it would've been difficult for it not to. Cynthia did her best not to dwell on it. Yet, that made it all the harder to forget...

September 20, 1982

"Would you like to inspect the perimeter, Mr. Holderness?" asked the man in the security uniform. His name tag read 'Peterson'. The uniform consisted of a crisp, long-sleeved white shirt with arm patches, and dark-green trousers that had gold piping. He wore laced, shiny black shoes. He had a medium build and was shorter than Ian. He appeared to be in his mid-thirties. His posture suggested he'd once been in the military.

The symbol on his cap matched the patches on his sleeves, a five-pointed star in silver thread, within a circle atop a shield. Mirrored sunglasses covered his eyes. He moved with energy and confidence. "After I show you the perimeter, we'll go to the monitor room and I can introduce you to some of the guards," Peterson offered.

"That sounds fine Mr. Peterson," Ian answered in a distracted voice. Fighting a yawn, he got into the golf cart beside Peterson. The guard noticed Ian's mood.

"Officer Peterson," the man corrected him, with a mild touch of annoyance in his tone.

"Alright, 'Officer', then," Ian raised an eyebrow. He fought the urge to smile. Although he found the man's attitude a bit too gung-ho for his taste, he had little doubt Peterson knew what he was doing. Seth and Lisa had checked out the company in detail, before signing the contract with them. Ian trusted their judgment.

"Our first stop will be the new kennels. I want to show you the dogs, and introduce your scent to them. Later, we'll do it for each of those in the household, so they get used to who is supposed to be here," Peterson explained as the cart rolled along just inside the wall of the estate. Ahead, he saw a couple more guards holding a pair of Doberman hounds on leashes.

Officer Peterson stopped the cart, and both he and Ian got out. Together, they approached the two guards holding the dogs; although the leashes were taut, and the dogs attentive, they made no sound. Peterson strolled over and petted them. They sniffed him and licked his hand.

All that changed when Ian drew near. The dogs turned their gaze on him and began to growl, snarl, snap, and bark. They strained violently at the leash, desperate to lunge at Ian. They bared their teeth, growling viciously at him. Ian stepped back warily, with a sharp intake of breath.

"Down!" Peterson commanded them. They reluctantly calmed themselves a little, but the dogs continued to snap and whine. "I said down!" Peterson repeated in frustration. "I don't understand it! They've never acted like this before." He seemed confused.

Ian turned around and walked back to sit in the cart. "That's alright, Officer Peterson…we can go on with our little tour. The dogs don't have to like me. They'll get used to me in time." But his expression suggested otherwise, his eyes unreadable. "By the way, you'll be storing guns and ammunition on site, won't you?"

"Uh…yes, sir," Peterson answered, still focusing on the dogs. "We have to. This place is too remote to do it any other way."

"I'm not complaining," Ian said calmly. "Just asking. We hired you as armed security. It's just that I have young son. I…need to be careful."

"I understand, Mr. Holderness, We'll be careful," Peterson responded in a professional, though stiff, manner. "He won't get hurt. We watch our weapons and ammo closely."

"Good," Ian observed cryptically. "That's very good…I'll be sure Colin doesn't bother you." Ian had learned what he needed to do.

September 21, 1982 Tuesday

"Were you able to read the folder I gave you yesterday?" Cynthia asked as soon as they were alone after lunch. "Colin is anxious to know what you think. So am I."

"I read it," Moira replied. "It was very intriguing. He obviously did a lot of work digging up and collecting those articles. I hope he puts as much effort into his school work."

"I know what you mean," Cynthia agreed. "I told you what he said happened here seven years ago and the....official version. I know it's incredible, but could Colin be right? At least, could it have been something more than a man in a costume? What do you know about werewolves? Danny used to watch the movies, but I wasn't allowed to because of my nightmares."

"One of these days, we're going to have to talk about them, but for now I'll focus on your question," Moira answered. "As for werewolves, I've seen the movies, read a few novels, and some books on the folklore. It's pretty hard to believe that a person could physically transform from human to animal shape, and then back again. It's easier to accept that someone might think that they were an animal and act accordingly. Similarly, a crook might disguise him or herself but, at the moment, we don't know that it was a shape-shifter. Colin only saw the beast-like form. That makes a man in disguise likelier. It was, after all, Halloween, the one night such a disguise wouldn't seem out of place. By removing it, the man could more easily escape. Still, it could have been something... extraordinary."

"It wasn't a full moon that night," Cynthia noted. "Aren't werewolves only supposed to change when the moon is full? Yet, the incidents Colin documents did all occur during full moons!"

"It's odd about the moon. In folklore, the full moon was important for the working of magic and it still is for wiccans like Irv, Lisa and me, but it was rare as a catalyst for Lycanthropy, even though one method of transforming involved a ritual. When a period of years was invoked, it was often during a lunar cycle. It was cited by the Roman writer, Petronius, and in medieval times, by Gervase of Tilbury. I've read some hints that a connection had sometimes been made by the mid-nineteenth century. So, for now, it's too soon to say if the association with the full moon is enough to prove or disprove the case. The movies are where the full moon became a necessity."

"There's some mystery here," Cynthia sighed with a shrug. "But I can't figure out a plausible explanation. If it wasn't a man in a costume, what could it have been? Even if we accept that idea for what happened here, how do we explain those other incidents? What really bothers me, and I probably shouldn't say it, is the possibility that Colin created the image of the monster to hide the killer's identity, because he couldn't face it. I know it's a terrible thing to even consider. Yet, if that were true, Mr. Holderness is the one it would've been most traumatic to have seen that night. He was here then, and may be the only one I'm aware of, who could've done what Colin says the beast did."

"Why do you say that?" Moira asked in surprise.

"He's not just moody, Moira," Cynthia responded. "He has a violent temper he only barely controls. He's also very strong. When we stopped to eat at a bar and grill, two of the locals started to harass us. They grabbed and hit me, and tripped then kicked Ian..."

"So that's where the bruises came from...I wondered," Moira broke in.

"Yes." Cynthia blushed. "I might've upset them a bit," she over-simplified. "My point is that Ian got to his feet so fast I could hardly see it. He easily stopped the fist of the one who hit me. He didn't flinch for a second. He only used one hand. Later, Ian grabbed the man by the throat one-handedly and lifted him off the floor. The man had to weigh at least three hundred pounds. He was taller than Ian. He was able to throw both men for several yards, using only one arm. I don't want it to be true. Ian acts guilty, but maybe it's just survivor's guilt. I don't know what to think."

"I can see some of the points you made," Moira acknowledged. "But I doubt it was Mr. Holderness. I don't want to add to the confusion, but there's something you ought to know, Please don't tell Mr. Holderness I told you. It could get Irv and me in trouble. His order last weekend was for silver bullets...a lot of them. I blessed them for him. He told Irv that he knew he couldn't get a Catholic priest to do it. It's not the first time, either. He ordered some back in 1975, before we opened our shop. He ordered several pentacles back then, too. Colin has one of them, from what you told me. It sounds like he believes more in werewolves than he's admitted."

"Then you think he knows about it and has been trying to protect everyone?" Cynthia asked hopefully.

'Maybe," Moira replied. "He told Irv he hopes that the bullets will never have to be used, but he wanted them as a contingency. That could be why. He seems to be going by the movies. The question is whether he's right to do so."

"Ian did tell me that he and his stepbrother were fans of those films." Cynthia recalled. "I know he feels responsible for not having enough security back then."

"Perhaps," Moira mused. "He feels he should've recognized the signs sooner and prepared appropriately. He did try, yet he was too slow to act. Possibly, he thought he had until the full moon..."

"That makes sense," Cynthia agreed, almost relieved. "I get the impression he's used to blaming himself for whatever goes wrong."

"Then he might think he's protecting his son by denying what Colin saw...taking it all on himself," Moira suggested.

"From what I've seen, he would do that," Cynthia nodded with a weary smile. "On a ...related topic, have you ever heard of something called the 'Blood Moon'?"

"Sure," Moira responded readily. "It's also called the 'Hunter's Moon'. It's next month—the night after Halloween, I think..."

CHAPTER 17

CONFLICTING MESSAGES
SEPTEMBER 21, 1982

"Really?" You're certain?" Cynthia was surprised by Moira's answer.

"Yes," Moira answered. "It's the night of what Catholics call All Hallows' Eve. At least, that's when the true full moon is. It'll appear full for a few days about then. The next full moon this weekend is the Harvest Moon. We hold our rituals on those nights. That's why I keep track of them. Why do you ask?"

"I...I just heard it someplace and was....curious what it was," Cynthia fibbed "I thought you might know the answer."

"It's only every few years we get a full moon or one that's nearly full at Halloween—All Hallows' Eve. It derives from the Celtic festival of Samhain—essentially their new year. It was the end of summer and the onset of winter. It's said that the boundary between our world and that of the other world was thinnest on that night. The other world was that of the dead—of the Fairy folk, or Shining Ones. It was believed that there were overlaps between the two worlds then. Fairy folk and the dead could enter our world, while mortals might become trapped in the other one. That's where we got all the ghosts and goblins and ...witches from at Halloween. The Christians felt obliged to adapt it, calling it the Eve of all Hallows, as All Saints Day is on November 1st. The next day became All Soul's Day. Some call October 30th, Devil's Night or Mischief Night. Other cultures also had days of the dead at about the same time. In Egypt, for example, there was a festival for the Lioness goddess, Sekhmet, the warrior daughter of the sun god, Re. Myth said that she nearly destroyed mankind when it rebelled against her father."

"That's....interesting," Cynthia tried not to gulp audibly. It was an ominous thought.

September 22, 1982 Wednesday

Ian was in the library when Cynthia entered. He stood to leave, wordlessly. It was what he'd done for the last several days. This had to stop, Cynthia decided. It had gone on for too long. Ian's avoidance of her was hurtful and embarrassing, regardless of what lay behind it.

"Ian…Mr. Holderness…can we talk? If…if you have time, that is," Cynthia forced herself not to hesitate, though it was an awkward but necessary, moment.

"Yes, Cyn…Miss Akers?" Ian carefully corrected himself. The change stabbed at her. "What do you want to talk about?"

"Us," she answered simply. "You're my employer. I understand that. We don't have to have anything more than a professional relationship, but the way it is now, we avoid each other. I thought we were becoming friends. Yet, lately, we can't even be in the same room together."

"We're in the same room now," Ian raised an eyebrow, his tone ironic.

"You know what I mean," Cynthia persisted. "Please don't make a joke of it. I know you can ignore me—fire me if you want. I'm sorry if I offended you, but if there's any way of ending this chill between us, I'd like to do it."

"I'm not sure I should've brought you here. It's nothing you've done really. I'm pleased that you and Colin get along well, but I'm not certain he can ever get better here. I've already told you boarding school was not a solution. I believe I was wrong to move towards a more…personal relationship between us. It was unfair to you. I'm unpopular in this town, as I've told you before. The other night reminded me of that fact. By appearing to get too close to you, I'm putting you at risk. I won't always be there when that problem arises. Even when I was there, you were hurt. That's a risk I'm not prepared to take. I was being selfish before, by seeming to make our…relationship more than professional. Since you're here and you've established a rapport with Colin, I hope you'll stay."

"Of course I'll stay, if you want me to," Cynthia responded, though what he'd said stabbed deeper than his previous sarcasm. "I…I won't trouble you again."

"Perhaps that's for the best," Ian commented, looking away. "I believe you've been good for Colin, Miss Akers. Yet, for a moment, I forgot myself. For that, I apologize. I never intended to make you… uncomfortable here. If I've seemed to avoid you, it's only because I was afraid of my own weakness. My life is…what it is. I cannot let myself think it could be different. It can't. I've resigned myself to that fact—but I don't want you ever to think I'm upset with you. The mistake was all mine."

"Was it such a mistake?" Cynthia wondered aloud. "What secret forces you into this...prison you've sentenced yourself to?"

"A secret that is mine to keep, Miss Akers. The prison you cite is well-deserved. That is all you need to know." Ian turned and left the room. As before, all she could do was watch him go, as baffled as ever.

"You seem....pensive, my dear," Seth interrupted Cynthia's thoughts as she left the library. "Is anything wrong? I saw Ian leave a moment ago. He didn't look happy. Was he in one of his moods again?"

"I ...don't really know, Mr. Blackthorne. He appeared ...serious, but I don't know him well enough to say more."

"I wouldn't worry too much about it," Seth smiled. "Ian's mood shifts are unpredictable, but they rarely last long. What set him off this time?"

"An incident a few nights ago at Brownies," Cynthia replied distractedly. "Some local bullies harassed us when we stopped to eat there. Your brother dealt with them, but it angered him. He was also worried that he might've put me in danger by being seen with him."

"He could be right in that," Seth mused. "The townsfolk are ridiculously hostile. I'll never understand why Ian puts up with it. He doubtless only made thing worse, though there was probably no choice. I know how Ian hates to...put on a show, unless he has to."

"You knew he was that strong?" Cynthia couldn't resist asking.

"Ah...you noticed," Seth seemed amused.

"I ...noticed," Cynthia understated it. "It was hard not to."

"You shouldn't give up on my dear brother. If he's giving you the cold shoulder now, it doesn't mean he won't be his usual charming self tomorrow—the next day at the latest. If he wasn't a man, I'd swear it was....his time of the month."

"Maybe that is all it is," Cynthia nodded. "I know it bothered him that I saw what he had to do—because he got so angry. I tried to convince him it wasn't a problem, but he didn't believe me."

"He is a sensitive soul," Seth chuckled. "I suppose it's what makes him such a good musician, but it doesn't make him easier to live with."

"No," Cynthia acknowledged. "I guess not."

September 23, 1982 Thursday

Class was over for the day. Mrs. Sorenson had headed for home. Like Dr. Akers, she was sympathetic, but he could tell she didn't fully believe he'd seen an honest-to-god werewolf. At least they didn't deny it. That helped some. Colin knew it was hard to accept. It wasn't easy for him either. Yet, he knew what he'd seen.

Colin was bored. There ought to be so much to do here. There was the pool-house, tennis courts, the greenhouse, the boathouse and docks…but the latter had bad memories for him. The greenhouse hadn't been kept up since his grandmother died. There was no one to play tennis with, even if he knew how. He wasn't supposed to use the pool-house unattended…besides, it was…eerie when he was alone. The woods creeped him out. The library maybe?

He wished there was something to watch on TV, but the choices weren't spectacular on a weekday afternoon. There might be more if they had cable. Yet, rich as his father was, he'd never had the estate hooked up to cable, in part because of how isolated the place was. It would cost a small fortune for the cable company to extend its lines to Falcon's Aerie. Perhaps he could ask his father to install a satellite dish.

Colin had spent all day with books, so the library held no appeal for him. Besides that, his uncle was frequently to be found there. Something bothered Colin about his uncle. That chair made him uneasy. His uncle's constant sarcasm put Colin off. Seth was always watching everyone, with that sly, self-satisfied grin of his. He seemed to imply more than he actually said. Everybody else ignored it, or failed to notice. Colin noticed. It scared him.

He decided to go exploring in the north wing. It was normally kept locked, but he'd learned where his father put the keys, a drawer in the secretary desk in the study. Hopefully nobody would be there when he snuck in to get the keys.

The study was empty, thankfully. Colin had feared his father, uncle, or one of the servants might be there. The drawer was not locked. Colin opened it and took the key ring, stuffing it into his pocket. Then he crept out of the study as quietly as he could, hoping nobody noticed he'd been there. No one did.

His excitement grew as he hurried up the main stairs. First he went to his bedroom to get a flashlight. Then he made his way down the hallway to the door to the north wing. Glancing both ways to be sure no one saw him, Colin inserted the key in the lock and turned it until he heard the expected click. Removing the key, he returned the ring to his pocket and pushed the door open.

Beyond the door, it was like entering another world. There was no electricity in this part of the house, so it was almost pitch dark in the corridor, until Colin flicked on his flashlight. There were no windows along the hall to relieve the darkness.

The air was stifling without circulation, and it smelled musty. Dust was everywhere; a grey-white patina was on the doors, furniture, even the carpet. Here and there were tables along the corridor between the doors. Cobwebs draped the objects on the tables and between the legs. The few lamps he saw were Victorian oil globe-types—the real thing, not the electric imitations used elsewhere in the house.

While the whole mansion was like a museum, the north wing made Colin feel like he'd stepped into the nineteenth century. It was fascinating, yet eerie, too—depressing. He found it hard to imagine life going on here. No one had dwelled in the north wing for sixty-five years, not since the death of the man who built the house.

Colin slowly made his way down the hall, testing the doors as he went. Most were locked. Finally he found one that wasn't, and he went in. The air inside was so thick and still that it was difficult to breathe. The spider-webs were even more prevalent than in the hall, like gauzy veils over almost everything. The dust on the Oriental carpet was so thick it was hard to discern the patterns and colors.

This room might well not have been touched for even longer than sixty-five years.

Heavy damask curtains and begrimed windows virtually blotted out the sunlight, save for a few slivers. Suddenly, Colin felt a waft of frigid air. Whirling around, he saw nothing. A wave of unease swept over him. What caused the chill? The air otherwise was stifling. There was no place for the cold air to have come from—if it was a natural breeze.

Aiming his flashlight around the room, its beam fell upon a long, rectangular mirror along one of the walls. In the middle of the glass he saw a pinpoint of light. A quick search of the room revealed no source for it, since the mirror faced away from the windows. So whatever it was, it wasn't a reflection.

To Colin's surprise, the light increased in size and brightness. It had a greenish cast to it, expanding outward gradually; it became swirling, ropey spirals of light interlacing as they spun. The room's reflection grew hazy and somehow indistinct. Although part of him was scared, Colin could not move. He was riveted in place, eyes locked on the mirror.

After a while, the light coalesced into the semblance of a human figure. Initially just an outline, in time a more detailed image formed. It was a tall man, with dark blond hair parted in the middle, and heavy mutton-chop sideburns that merged with his upturned mustache. His clean-shaven chin was dimpled, his cheekbones wide. Thick eyebrows glowered over brilliant azure eyes that gleamed like stars.

He wore a high stand collar and dark frock coat above a brocaded waistcoat, with a purple silk ascot and bejeweled tie pin. His black shoes were polished like mirrors. Over it all, he had a dark brown Inverness caped coat. On his hands, he wore gray gloves in which he held a shiny, black cane. Its ivory and gold handle was in the shape of a lion's head, with sapphire eyes that matched those of its bearer.

The hair on the back of Colin's neck stood on end. The chill intensified. The boy recognized the man's garb and hairstyle as Victorian, from the era when the house was built. Even beyond the fact that he was an apparition in a mirror, the man's stare made Colin queasy. Who was he and what did he want?

The boy's apprehensions grew when the figure stepped out of the mirror into the room, seemingly as solid as though he were alive. The man's grin broadened; a sardonic twinkle in his eyes. He continued to gaze at Colin wordlessly without blinking. It was an eerie, hypnotic affect. He seemed to be lit from below, though there was nothing to produce the effect.

Words began to form in Colin's mind; at least he thought they were in his head, not spoken aloud. "Who are you?" Colin gasped, his fear growing. "What do you want from me?" The man did not visibly reply, but the answer come to him in his mind.

"You....you're the guy my uncle said died in the fire," Colin stammered. "A hundred and one years ago!"

The figure nodded in assent, his lips curling into a virtual leer.

"I still don't understand," Colin said, bewildered. "What do you want? Why did you appear to me here—now?"

The man frowned, glaring balefully at the boy. "Why do you say I'm the blood of your enemy? Who's that? What am I supposed to do?" Colin demanded.

Once he understood what was being asked of him, Colin grew pale, his eyes wide, icy terror clutching his heart. "No! I won't do that! I won't help you hurt anyone! You can't make me!"

The man grimaced angrily, reaching out with his free hand in a claw-like motion. He began to close the fingers like the petals of a flower. In that instant, Colin could not breathe, the air cut off by invisible fingers tightening around his throat. His fear surged through every vein like liquid fire.

"Please...please don't make me do that..." he croaked out barely. "I ...don't want to hurt..."

The man's fingers tightened further, and Colin fell to his knees, no longer able to stand. What could he do? There was no one here to help him. Nobody knew where he was. "Al...alright...whatever you say....I'll do it....I won't tell anyone..." The man smiled triumphantly. His plans would succeed; through the heir of his old foe he would live again—and all those who once opposed him would die.

CHAPTER 18

THE PENTACLE
FRIDAY SEPTEMBER 24, 1982

Dinner was over. Seth headed to his rooms, accompanied by Jeremy. Harlan and Aida cleared away the dishes, glasses, and cutlery. Lisa went down to the garage to visit Mat. Colin, too, seemed in an unusual hurry to go to his rooms. The boy had said barely a word during the meal, and seemed to play with his food rather than eat it. In explanation, he mumbled that he wasn't hungry. Since it wasn't unusual for him to be sullen, no one pressed him about it.

Ian and Cynthia found themselves alone at the table. For a while, they both stared at their plates, avoiding each other's gaze. The silence between them was awkward. Ian fidgeted with the silverware until Aida collected it to clean. Once everything had been cleared away, Cynthia sighed and got up to leave.

She'd had enough of the chilly atmosphere between her and Ian. He could remain or go, but she wasn't about to sit indefinitely, not talking and trying not to look at each other. He didn't have to converse with her. Cynthia, for her part, did not feel the need not to be spoken to.

Ian glanced up, catching Cynthia's eyes with his own for the first time in several days. "Please, don't leave yet, Cynthia," he requested quietly. His expression was sad, yet resolute.

"I'm Cynthia now, am I?" she glared haughtily at him. "I thought we'd reverted to 'Doctor' or 'Miss Akers'."

"I deserved that, Cynthia...I'm sorry," Ian sounded genuinely contrite. "I shouldn't have hurt your feelings the other day. Though I said then that it was my fault not yours, it must still have seemed that I was blaming you..."

"Weren't you?" Cynthia threw it back at him. "Isn't this about my reaction in the garages? I'm not sure whether you were hurt or embarrassed or angry. Maybe it was all of those, but you didn't tell me. You just walked away and tuned me out."

"You're right," he admitted sadly, "I did. That was ...unfair of me. I could say that I've grown...unused to dealing with people these last few years. It would be true, but it's no excuse. I'm torn, Cynthia. This isn't easy for me. It's been very lonely for the last seven years. In one way, I hate that, and am desperate for it to end but, on the other hand, there are very real forces restricting my life. Those forces put others around me at risk, you included. That troubles me a great deal, but I should never have let it appear that the onus was on you."

"I can understand you being lonely, Ian. I can also understand your grief, and even guilt over what happened seven years ago. I know that you've said this is your home; that you've got nowhere else to go. Yet, because of that, you willingly put up with outright hostility, even violence, from the locals. You tell me you have an illness that Dr. Marsden is treating, but you won't tell me what that condition is or what sort of treatment you're receiving, or why its timing is so important. I realize you don't have to explain yourself to me. Still, you're so mysterious about it all, how am I supposed to respond?" Cynthia sat down again.

"I wish I could explain it to you," Ian replied wearily, looking away. "I'm not sure how. It's very complicated."

"Then why did you want to speak to me now, if you've got nothing to say to me?" Cynthia retorted, genuinely baffled.

"Because I...I didn't like the way our last conversation ended. I blame myself for it, but I don't enjoy this...chill between us either. I thought I was doing it for your own good, but you're right. I was embarrassed by what you saw me do—my loss of control. Your reaction, however natural, convinced me that I'd made even you afraid of me. Maybe it did, despite what you said. If so, you had every right to be uneasy, but I ought to have taken you at your word that you were just startled. We're all such a mass of conflicting emotions that we don't always have complete control over. I should know that better than most." Ian looked tired.

"What disease is so rare or terrible that you can't describe it or explain what Dr. Marsden is doing about it?" Cynthia continued to press him.

"I've told you as much as I can about it," he responded defensively.

"No," Cynthia refused to back down. "You told me as much as you're willing to. I don't know if you're embarrassed by it, or if there's some other motive, but the choice to reveal the truth or hide it is yours."

"Then I guess there's not much more to say," Ian observed sadly.

"But before you go, there's something I want you to have. I asked Irv to make it while we were at his shop last weekend. He just finished it yesterday, and Moira brought it with her this morning. Despite our apparent impasse, I still want you to have it." He reached into the pocket of the coat he wore, and took out a small velvet-covered jewelry box. Wordlessly, he handed it to her.

"Is this some sort of peace offering?" she inquired skeptically.

"No, Cynthia. You have a right to be upset with me, but I hope you'll accept this…gift anyway. I ordered it before…before everything happened. I still want you to have it, regardless of how you feel about me," Ian's voice was plaintive. Warily, she took the box, examining it in curiosity.

"What is it?" she asked, still uncertain of his motives.

"Open it and see," was all he would say. Cynthia lifted the top of the box and gazed at that lay inside. It was a pendant in the shape of a pentagram, with the single point directed upward. The star and circle were of polished silver. Small diamonds were set in the outer circle. They glinted in the light of the chandelier. Behind the star, within each point and between them, was Celtic knot-work-interlaced patterns in red gold to set off the silver. At the center was opalescent moonstone. Its iridescence mesmerized her. The chain upon which it hung was likewise of gold.

"It's gorgeous!" she gasped in surprise, never having expected anything so exquisite or costly. She'd never owned anything like it before.

"Irv did a great job, especially given that I rushed him on it," Ian agreed, pleased that she seemed to like it. "I told him to make it as beautiful as he could. He took that to heart."

"Yes—he really did," Cynthia half-whispered in awe. I'll have to compliment him when I see him next…Thank you, Ian. I mean that. You didn't have to get me a gift. We barely know each other."

"Maybe not," he replied sheepishly. "But I'd like to. I've made a bloody mess of it so far. You deserve it just for putting up with me. I'm not the easiest person to be around."

"I've noticed," she giggled good-naturedly. Ian removed it from the box and draped it about her neck. Cynthia pulled her hair to one side so that he could snap the clasp at the back of her neck. Then she let it fall, adjusting it so that it was comfortable.

"It looks good on you," Ian smiled in appreciation.

"It's lovely," Cynthia sighed with pleasure, briefly forgetting her earlier anger.

"Yes—you are," Ian quipped, eyes twinkling.

"Silly," Cynthia rolled her eyes, "I mean the necklace."

"I know what you meant," Ian replied, "And what I meant." He bent and kissed her forehead. He was such a jumble of contradictions, she thought; infuriating one minute and courtly the next. How could she relate to someone so unpredictable? It was certainly a challenge, but she'd always sought out challenges before. Why change now?

"Wear it for me always," Ian requested with a gentle smile.

"I'd be happy to hear it anytime," she answered, holding it so that it caught the light.

"No...I mean all the time..." Ian hesitated awkwardly.

"If you really want me to, but why?" Cynthia asked in confusion. Then the realization dawned. She recalled her recent conversation with Moira. "She was right! You...you believe in it. This...is for my protection isn't it? Like the one Colin got from your stepfather?"

"Why...why do you say that?" Ian stammered weakly, growing pale beneath his tan.

"Colin told me how he received his pentacle from his grandfather that night—that it was the one originally intended for your mother, but that one had been intended for him, too. He was told it would protect him, and he believes it did. That's why Lisa and Moira wear theirs—as protective talismans. Moira said she blessed them. Is this one blessed, too?" Cynthia put him on the spot.

"Yes," Ian gulped nervously. "I had her use her strongest protective spells on it."

"What is it to protect me from, Ian? Colin said your stepfather had one, too, yet chose not to wear it, because he didn't believe. That...creature is real somehow, isn't it? I promised Moira I wouldn't mention it, but she told me Irv not only made the pentacles, but he also made silver bullets for you—both then and now—a lot of them," Cynthia pressed him harder.

"She shouldn't have told you that," Ian frowned. "They promised not to tell anyone."

"Well, perhaps she didn't consider me just….anyone, since you had Irv make this for me," Cynthia interjected. "It's true what Colin saw, isn't it? He didn't imagine or misinterpret it. That thing exists."

"At this point I suppose I can't deny it, can I?" Ian shook his head, slumping into his chair, a pained expression on his face.

"You must've figured out what it was somehow," Cynthia observed, "and tried to arm yourself against it."

"Not fast enough." Ian appeared sick with guilt. "Not nearly fast enough. I…I knew the signs from the movies, but my rational mind resisted the evidence. I couldn't believe it was really happening. It seemed too incredible to be true, but it was."

"Colin collected articles of things that happened in 1974 and 75 that might be related," Cynthia noted as much to herself as to Ian. "He was right about it all, then."

"It seemed so impossible," Ian almost groaned. "But the clues kept piling up, and eventually I couldn't deny them anymore. Until that final night, it only appeared during the full moon or nights before or after when it looks full. The Bollans described what sounded like a werewolf. Bullets seemed to have little effect on it. It tore its prey apart like an animal, but one as big as a ruddy bear. Its tracks always disappeared. Sometimes there were human footprints nearby. The police couldn't make the connection, but I could. I realized nobody else would believe the truth. I barely did. It was up to me to deal with it, then. I knew enough that it matched the movies, but not the folklore. I still don't know why. Initially, I guessed about the significance of silver and the pentagrams. I never got to test the pentagrams. I hope Colin's right about them. Richard agreed to help me, though he was skeptical. I told him to keep a pistol, loaded with silver bullets, on him at all times and he did, thank God. I was too slow in giving my family the pentagrams.

The moon wasn't full yet. I thought there was still time. I was wrong. It only fled the house because Richard hit it in the leg…and then grazed it again down at the boathouse. Roderick didn't believe, so his bullets weren't silver. You know the result."

"You think it's still out there, don't you?" Cynthia took the next logical step.

"I don't think...I know it is. I wasn't killed that night. I don't know if it can die, but if it can be slain, I intend to do it. You can't imagine how much I hate that damn thing—it's shattered my life—killed most of my family, and who knows how many others? It has to be destroyed. I'll do it even if it kills me." The light of obsession burned in Ian's eyes. He scarcely saw her for a moment, his gaze far away on something only he could see. His determination, though understandable, frightened her.

"Is that where you're going this weekend? Hunting the beast?" Cynthia inquired perceptively. "You said what you had to do had to be done at night. If it is a movie-style werewolf, that's the only time it would appear. All he incidents seven to eight years ago took place at night, too."

"Nothing gets past you," Ian shook his head with a wry smile, breaking the tension. "But you...you could say that's what I'm doing. If nothing else, it's up to me to make sure that thing doesn't break free again. Maybe now you understand better why I can't leave—why I'm tied here, but it's not a duty I can pass on to anyone else. That might sound melodramatic to you, but it's true.

"I'll take your word for it," Cynthia shuddered involuntarily. "Just be careful. I know how inadequate that is, but I don't know what else to say under the circumstances. You've dealt with this... problem for years. It's all new to me. I trust your judgment, but remember, Colin needs a living father."

"I'll try not to," Ian gave her a sad smile, brushing her face with his hand. "But the day may come when I won't have a choice..." She reached up and brought his head to hers. He put his arms about her and kissed her, long and deeply. It was too late to pretend anymore.

CHAPTER 19

CONTRARY APPEARANCES
SATURDAY OCTOBER 2, 1982

Richard stepped away from the beast, the syringe still in his hands. The creature struggled weakly, despite the drug that had just been administered and the silver-plated manacles that chained it to the wall. Experience had taught Marsden that regular steel chains worked no better than normal bullets.

The drug would calm the beast, easing the pain of the convulsions and a second to put it to sleep. The serum contained colloidal silver combined with wolfsbane, or the sedative wouldn't work either.

Once the beast settled into its uneasy slumber, Richard left the cell and closed the massive steel door, locking it in case the drug wore off early. In the outer room, he switched on the monitor and hit the button for the tape to begin. He no longer bothered to record the transformation; he'd seen it so many times before. These days, he just used it as a safeguard in case he fell asleep. That happened more often these days.

With that done, he went over to the sofa, briefly stopping to pour himself some coffee. Then he slumped onto the cushions, picking up a book he'd begun earlier. He was running out of books. He would have to bring down some more. It was going to be another long night...with two more to follow...

October 3, 1982 Sunday

Ian was already at the table in the solarium when Cynthia came down for breakfast. No one else was there yet. It was just past 7:30. She was startled at his appearance, yet resolved to say nothing. He did not even look up when she came into the room. Once he did notice her, he seemed embarrassed and did his best not to meet her worried gaze.

Ian was uncharacteristically disheveled; his hair remained uncombed, almost matted, and looked longer than when she's seen him the previous afternoon, but that was impossible in just one night. His mustache and goatee were equally ragged and untrimmed. Stubble covered his cheeks.

Ian looked haggard, his skin pale beneath his tan, dark circles around bloodshot eyes. His expression mixed weariness and pain.

He wore old, ragged jeans and a flannel shirt long past its prime. He was barefoot. All of that was unusual for him. He didn't say anything to her when she sat down.

In front of him on the table was a dish of raw red meat, and several glasses full of water without ice. The place was awash in juice from the meat and some of it dribbled down Ian's chin. He ignored it, making no effort to wipe it away. Instead, he ate the meat, which looked raw, with his hands.

He stuffed it into his mouth, chewing and swallowing quickly as though starved. Then he would periodically stop to drink the water, guzzling almost a whole glass at a time. He appeared dehydrated. His nails were long and sharp...

After he'd gone through several glasses of water and three or four good-sized steaks, Ian took a napkin and roughly wiped it across his face and then his hands. Without a word, he left the plate and empty glasses and left the room, pretending Cynthia wasn't there.

The sight appalled her. What was wrong with him? What could affect him like that in just one night? Where had he gone in search of the beast? Sometimes people were advised to eat protein after giving blood, but Cynthia saw no sign that Ian had done that; no bandages anyway. And why the extreme thirst for warm water? It made no sense to her.

A moment later, Mrs. Jeffers came out to clear away the plate and glasses. She wore a disapproving frown as she did so. She asked Cynthia if it would be alright if she put the plate and glasses into the sink before taking her order for breakfast. The housekeeper appeared almost as embarrassed as Ian. She wanted the ...evidence out of the way as soon as possible, before anyone else showed up.

Upon finishing her own breakfast, Cynthia approached the housekeeper. "Mrs. Jeffers? Can I ask you something?"

"What is it, Doctor?" Aida responded.

"Does Mr. Holderness...eat like that often? He doesn't look well," Cynthia said haltingly.

"Best not to ask, Doctor. We're...not supposed to talk about it. I ...I know it's...not right, but thankfully he's only like this a few days out of the month. He'll be fine next week. I shouldn't say any more. I've already said too much. Harlan always scolds me for being a terrible gossip…"

"I won't tell anybody what you said. Thanks for answering my question. I was just…surprised and worried," Cynthia tried to reassure the housekeeper.

"You've got a good heart, Doctor," Aida smiled genuinely. "I've seen you with him and the boy, but he's a strange one—so moody and unpredictable. I'd be careful if I was you."

"I will," Cynthia lied. It was too late to be careful…Much too late. She loved him.

An hour and a half later, Ian came downstairs once more. He'd shaved, trimmed his beard and mustache, combed his hair and dressed more in his usual manner. He wore a black t-shirt under a dark brown leather jacket, with a high collar and wide lapels. He'd also donned black denims and square-toed Dr. Martin's boots of a type favored by bikers. Though he hid his eyes behind mirrored sunglasses, Cynthia was willing to bet they were still bloodshot.

"I'm ready," he stated laconically. "We can go at any time. I need to be able to leave on my own, so I'm taking my bike. Would you mind driving Colin in your car? If you'd rather not, I'm sure Mat and Lisa will be happy to do it." He did not mention a word about what she'd seen at breakfast, as if it had never happened. Two could play at that game, Cynthia decided. Men and their secrets! Then again, she had some of her own…

"I'll take him. I don't mind, but it's too bad you have to leave early," she aimed a mild barb at him.

"Yeah, I know," he deflected without a blush. "I'm taking my chances as it is, but I know how much Colin and everyone else has been looking forward to this. I didn't want to disappoint him…or anyone else. This is…the best I can do."

"I'm sure it is," Cynthia replied, cocking an eyebrow. Every time she thought she knew him…

"I'll meet you two at the garages." He straightened the cuffs of his jacket and adjusted his collar then headed out the main doors. His expression was stiff and unreadable as he passed by her. She did her best to do the same.

Observing the exchange, Seth grinned wryly, enjoying it. "I see you've finally met my dear brother's alter ego this morning. He's trying to pretend you didn't see it now, like he does with everyone. It's quite a spectacle, don't you think?"

"I'm certain he has his reasons. It's none of my business really," Cynthia responded defensively. Yet, now she felt it was.

"If you say so, my dear," Seth smirked. "But if so, he's never revealed what those reasons were and if they're any good or not. It makes one wonder which is the real Ian. Is it the dapper bloke who just left, or the inarticulate disgrace you saw this morning? Which is real and which is the façade?"

"I wouldn't know, Mr. Blackthorne. I only met him three weeks ago. You've known him all your life. You tell me," Cynthia snapped, as annoyed at Seth's gleeful venom as she was frustrated by Ian's reticence and mood shifts; and it had been such a good week...

"That's true, Doctor." Seth eyed her coldly. "I'd keep that in mind if I were you. Ian can be quite the charmer when he chooses, but it's only one of his faces. You never know which one he'll show you next. It might well be a sight you don't care for. There's a reason he and Kate split up. It wasn't all due to her."

"No doubt," Cynthia acknowledged guardedly. "He told me so himself."

"Just friendly warning, my dear; Ian can be...mercurial." Seth's eyes twinkled with sardonic glee.

"I'll keep my wits about me," she shot back at him, a little more harshly than she planned. If only that were true, she thought.

"You know, Doctor? I do believe you will," he chuckled, and then wheeled himself back to his own room. Cynthia glared at him as he went. Seth was annoying, but was he right?

"Why didn't he come with us?" Colin asked, avoiding direct mention of his father. "Wouldn't it have been easier?"

"He's got an appointment with Dr. Marsden tonight." Cynthia knew it was a half-truth, but it was the best she could think of without lying. "He didn't want to force us to leave early just because he did.”

“If you say so. He never wants to do anything with me. He never wanted me to come back here,” Colin said sullenly.

“You didn’t want to come back either,” Cynthia noted. “He knows that.”

“Yeah, but I didn’t have any choice. I wanted him to want me here, but he doesn’t. I’m just baggage—a problem he’s gotta worry about. If Mom hadn’t pawned me off on him, I wouldn’t be here,” Colin frowned, folding his arms across his chest. It reminded her of Ian.

“You’re wrong,” Cynthia insisted. “He does want you here. He doesn’t think he deserves for you to be with him. He blames himself for what happened seven years ago, and neglecting you before that. He’s still grieving. They were his family, too, Colin...his friend. He just doesn’t know how to talk to you about it.”

“Then why didn’t he ever tell me himself?” Colin almost whined. “I was here for three weeks before you came. I’m invisible, unless he’s yelling at me. He doesn’t even do that often. I only see him at breakfast, lunch, and dinner. We don’t talk then. Matthew and Miss Ramirez talk more to me than he ever does. So does Uncle Seth.”

“He’s...preoccupied, Colin. It’s not easy for him either,” Cynthia defended Ian weakly, uncertain what other excuses she could make. “He hasn’t been well for years.”

“So...what’s wrong with him then? He doesn’t tour anymore. If he’s so sick, what is it?” Colin asked pointedly. He stared out the window without turning to glance at her. His tone was weary, disappointed....skeptical—Colin needed to know that his father wasn’t intentionally ignoring him. Yet, if she told him the truth, Ian would be angry at her for breaking a confidence; while Colin would doubtless be upset that his father had known the truth but denied it for so long. Although tempted to tell the boy what his father was doing, Cynthia didn’t feel she had the right to make that decision on her own.

“I...I don’t know, Colin. He didn’t tell me what the name of his... condition is. It’s not my place to press him about it, but I’m sure he didn’t make it up,” Cynthia hesitated.

“Whatever.” Colin rolled his eyes, and sighed.

CHAPTER 20

OKTOBERFEST
SUNDAY OCT 3, 1982

Ian's bike was already in the parking lot at the park in Newburgh when Cynthia arrived there. The park faced the Hudson, beside the Beacon-Newburgh Bridge. There were dozens of cars, vans, pick-ups, and motorcycles. It was a glorious autumn morning. The air was crisp, with few clouds in the sky. The sunlight had that peculiar golden quality that only occurred in the fall.

The motorcycles easily outnumbered the cars. Ian's Harley fit right in. Cynthia hadn't spoken to him at the garages, so she was mildly surprised to see that he'd brought one of his guitars, since he had been so resistant to perform when originally asked. In the distance, she saw speakers and mics being set up on a makeshift stage.

Elsewhere there were people putting out food in pans covered with tin foil and Saran Wrap beside coolers full of ice for the beer and sodas. Others sat or lay atop blankets, or relaxed in folding chairs. A few played with Frisbees or tossed footballs. Most were in shorts and t-shirts and tank tops, despite how cool it was, or else jeans and pull-over polo shirts. Not many wore jackets or sweaters. Everybody seemed to be enjoying themselves.

Above the stage was a large homemade banner that read "The silver Dragon Oktoberfest Celebration" In quasi-Old English script. Irv had doubtless made it. A few smaller ones hung on the covered hutches. Cynthia parked, and she and Colin got out.

"Try to have a good time," she pleaded with him. "Don't let... what we discussed ruin the day for you." Or her either, she thought.

"I'll try." Colin rolled his eyes again. "At least there's gonna be music and tons of food, even if they're probably mostly gonna play a lot of mouldy-goldies."

Cynthia rolled her eyes in response and she laughed. "I guess that makes disco and punk oldies."

"They're bloody pre-historic!" Colin groaned. Cynthia laughed, but it made her feel old. She's be hitting the big 3-0 in a couple of months, but being around a fourteen-year-old on a daily basis reminded her how vast a generation gap can be.

Lisa and Mat were already with Irv and Moira. They waved as Cynthia and Colin walked towards them. She wondered idly where

Ian was, since she didn't see him there. He had to be around somewhere. The others were in one of several roofed hutches, each with its own barbeque grill.

"Hello!" Moira called out, the others following suit.

"Hi!" Cynthia smiled broadly and waved back. Colin gave a half-grin and waved perfunctorily, as if bored, though he'd seemed anxious to come until the last day or so. Cynthia theorized that Colin feared that he would look immature if he seemed to be visibly excited. Appearances were important to Colin. Being taken seriously was critical to his self-esteem.

'Where's Ian—Mr. Holderness?" Cynthia quickly corrected herself.

"He's with the band we hired," Moira replied. "Showin' em the list'a songs he'll do. He brought some sheet music, in case they don't know all the songs," Irv added. "He's agreed to a couple'a cover tunes, too."

"I can't wait," Cynthia commented.

"Me, too!" Lisa chimed in enthusiastically.

"It should be cool," Mat nodded. "I never heard Odyssey live. So, this is the closest I'll probably ever get."

"Yeah," Cynthia agreed. "From what he's said, a reunion isn't very likely. He's still close to the former drummer, but there's a pretty deep rift between him and David Westbury. I gather the bassist sides more with him than...Mr. Holderness,"

"It's a shame," Mat sighed. "They did some great albums. The new stuff, since they got back together without Mr. Holderness, just ain't the same. They songs're all shorter...more commercial...it sounds too much like all the other crap these days..."

"It's doing well on the charts," Lisa disagreed. "I like some of the old songs, but every song doesn't have to be half an album side or like it's the soundtrack for Star Wars or Lord of the Rings. Sometimes those songs are depressing and put me to sleep."

"You n' me both," Colin interjected. "That '70s stuff is mostly for potheads," he snorted derisively. "Or leftover acid freaks."

"What's wrong with potheads?" Mat gave them a mischievous grin. "Not that I know of any..." he added with a knowing laugh.

"I like the musicianship, melodies and instrumentation" Moira tossed in her own appraisal. "I love the fantasy, sci-fi and horror imagery—it's evocative;poetic. Not everything needs to be dance music."

"Some o' the drum, keyboard n' guitar riffs got a nice metal crunch to 'em," Irv gave a hearty laugh.

"Everybody's got their own taste," Cynthia tried to strike a compromise.

"Different music suits different moods. They did some nice harmonies, too..." Moira added. "You can't please everybody all the time."

"I guess," Colin acknowledged grudgingly. "Some of the songs on Legend, Eclipse, and Nocturne were...kinda cool, I suppose...sorta like Goth—nice'n'dark," he smiled crookedly, rubbing his hands together in an exaggerated comic villain style. It was as close as he could come to an outright compliment. Cynthia knew Colin was a Goth fan, but no teenager could admit their parents were cool. It went against the code.

"Nocturne's right out of Edgar Allen Poe," Lisa observed. "Real Halloween rock."

"I always thought it was kind of romantic," Cynthia blushed slightly. "It shows you how messed up I am..."

"It is romantic in a Jane Eyre-Wuthering Heights sort of way," Moira rose to Cynthia's defense.

"Livin' in Castle Dracula, is it any wonder?" Mat chuckled. "He did record it at the estate."

As morning wore on into the afternoon, the band that called themselves "Dark Water" was introduced and began to perform. They played at several local clubs and bars that catered to bikers as the Silver Dragon did. It was there that Irv heard the group and offered to hire them for the picnic. Later, they were thrilled when Ian agreed to perform.

Since the banners were already completed when Ian agreed to go on, only the band and decided it would be a surprise for those attending. Ian was just as grateful. He didn't want the press to get wind of it beforehand. He feared that they might be hypercritical of him after so long. On the other hand, he worried that nobody would even care.

Irv went up to the stage to make the announcement. "I'm happy tuh introduce an old acquaintance of mine and Moira's who's agreed tuh make a special guest appearance here as a favor tuh us. He hasn't appeared in concert…fer awhile, so we feel very privileged that he accepted our invitation. We'd like yuh tuh welcome our friend, Ian Anthony Holderness, best known from his work with the band, Odyssey…"

Even though she couldn't see Ian behind the stage, Cynthia could imagine his sigh and the roll of his eyes at Irv's introduction; not that there was any way to do it that he would totally approve of. Ian was torn between the desire to perform again, and the worry that he was just setting himself up for indifference or even outright ridicule…

The keyboardist began quietly, slowly building notes, and then the drummer and the bassist joined in. It was the opening of "The frost that burns, the flame that chills", one of Odyssey's bigger hits off the "Legend" album from 1972. The audience began to cheer.

Ian stepped on stage, guitar in hand. He'd already initiated the lead guitar parts, its piercing screech dominating the melody before going into the familiar power chords. His fingers worked the frets on the guitar's neck. He strode forward to the mic to do the vocals. It was the first hit that Ian sang lead on.

His voice was clear and strong; confident. It was as though the last decade had never been. Ian still sounded as he had then. Cynthia didn't notice any uncertainty in his performance. She'd seen him play piano and sing before, yet never on stage in front of a band. Both were good. Yet, he seemed born for the stage. The crowd went wild. All that was missing was the dry ice fog and colored lights.

For a moment, however brief, Ian was a star again; not a self-loathing, guilt-ridden recluse. He reveled in it, temporarily forgetting why he'd been forced to give it up. It didn't matter that there were fewer than a hundred people at the picnic rather than thousands in a stadium or amphitheater. He remembered what it used to feel like—how much he'd loved it. All the long lonely years faded away.

Ian had only promised to do a few songs, but in the end he did roughly two hours on stage. He sang most of the songs for which he'd originally done the vocals, along with a couple of cover songs that came out recently.

Two he played acoustically. Since he had not brought an acoustic guitar, one of the band members gave him one to use. He did two encores due to audience response. One of them he chose because Cynthia had mentioned liking it, Foreigner's "Waiting for a Girl Like You".

Everything seemed fine for most of the afternoon. Ian laughed and kidded, seemingly enjoy himself. It was the charmer that Cynthia first became attracted to. There was no sign of the haunted man she'd seen that morning. It was partially an act for everyone else's sake, but she sensed it wasn't all a put-on.

As evening neared, the clouds began to gather and the cool, damp breeze grew stronger. Ian became increasingly withdrawn and fidgety, his eyes constantly darting about nervously between the western horizon and his expensive Swiss watch. It was still daylight savings time. However, the sunset was fast approaching...despite the clouds now obscuring it.

These were not, light fluffy clouds turning orange and pink as the sun slid towards the horizon. They were ominous and oppressive, dark and heavy with the potential for rain. The band began to pack up their speakers and instruments. The crowd slowly dispersed. Mat and Lisa agreed to stay to help Irv and Moira clean up. Cynthia offered, too, but Irv and Moira said it wasn't necessary.

Ian fingered his key-ring, packing away his guitar and eying his motorcycle. It was clear he was anxious to leave. Finally he walked over to say his goodbyes to everyone. He waited until last to go to Colin and Cynthia, feeling guilty.

"I gotta go," Ian said tersely. "I've already stayed here too long. It's almost dusk."

"I understand," Cynthia responded.

"Well, I don't," grumbled Colin. "Why're you in such a hurry?"

"I've got an appointment at the sanitarium, Colin," Ian explained haltingly.

"And you're friends with the guy who runs it," Colin frowned. "Is he gonna cancel on you if you're a minute or two late?"

"I'm sorry, son…I don't have any choice. The appointment's been set up for some time. I can't change it now. Richard's expecting me," Ian squirmed.

"Yeah, yeah," Colin shook his head in impatient frustration. "Just like always. I'm the lowest on your list every time. Go on, Dad—go do whatever you need to. I'll get by ok." He turned and walked away without looking back.

Ian closed his eyes, his face falling into hard lines as if his head hurt. He inhaled sharply, his hands briefly clenching. "I've got to go," he reiterated. "See that he gets home alright, will you? I wish I had the time to explain things to him—that there was a way to make him understand, but there isn't. What the bloody hell can I say?"

"I …I don't know," Cynthia replied helplessly. "Unless we tell him the truth…"

"I …we can't!" Ian hissed. "He'd never understand. I've denied what he saw for so long. He'll never forgive me…Cynthia, I need to go. I…I'll talk with him about it as soon as I can."

"I know," Cynthia nodded. "I'll do what I can. He's upset right now. It's not a good time to talk to him anyway. I know you've got to go. Just…please be careful, Ian. You can't talk to him if you're not there to do it."

Ian smiled wanly. Then suddenly his eyes widened in shock, though he tried to hide it. He had seen something startling, though she couldn't tell what it was. He paled visibly, fear entering his eyes. "I…I'll see you later," Ian said hesitantly, his voice a bit shaky. Turning, he hurried to his bike. He never looked back. He mounted his Harley and gunned the engine, waving back at her perfunctorily without turning around. It was as though something dreadful was pursuing him. Maybe it was; but if so, what could it be? What had Ian seen that upset him so?

Cynthia was baffled by what had just occurred. They'd been so close for the last week, nearly inseparable. She grudgingly admitted that she had slighted the time she owed to Colin in order to be with his father. Creeping back to her own room each morning or watching him go to his room had become a habit, but he still constantly surprised her. No matter how many layers of the onion that she peeled away, would she ever really know him?

CHAPTER 21

INTERRUPTED JOURNEYS
OCTOBER 3, 1982

Carl Foster glared intently through his truck's windshield. The old dodge was parked half hidden, several dozen yards away from the entrance to the estate. It was the only way to drive in or out of the place. If Holderness left, Foster would see him and follow.

In the days that he'd been watching the gates, he had gotten to know every vehicle, from Holderness' motorcycle, the doctor's Mercury, the secretary's mustang, Dr. Marsden's Mercedes....the servants' beat up ford wagon, the handyman's van...

It would be harder to see if Holderness left with the old doctor. At least the car's windows weren't tinted, Carl thought to himself as he sat there, fingers impatiently thumbing the wheel. That bastard was going to pay for what he'd done, Foster vowed.

Carl would've acted sooner if he could have, but with the dogs and security guards, he couldn't get onto the estate without being detected. That's why he came here every day after work, and now on the weekend...waiting. He'd begun to clock out early, though his boss was not happy about it. Though it was boring and uncomfortable sitting here for so many hours, Carl usually stayed until well after dark before heading home, exhausted.

But his perseverance would pay off. Carl felt sure of it. Holderness' time was coming. Foster was going to make sure of it. Holderness should return any moment now...

Ian rode down Route 9, the wind whipping through his black hair. There was comparatively little traffic, as it was a Sunday night. The breeze grew colder and he felt droplets strike him with ever-increasing frequency. Risking getting a ticket, Ian revved the engine and sped up. He had to hurry. There wasn't much time left.

Far too soon, the moon would rise. Ian had to reach the house by then. Richard said he'd be there tonight. Ian had timed it all out carefully and, barring the unforeseen, ought to make it, but the best laid plans had a way of being over turned by fate. Ian knew that only too well. He had been foolish to stay at the picnic so long. He hadn't wanted to leave, letting his reluctance retard his steps. Now, he might well pay for it.

A truck lurched onto the road behind him, its headlights flicking on. Preoccupied as he was, Ian didn't see it. The sound of the truck was drowned out by that of his motorcycle. It raced to match his speed. Ian noticed its rattling before he heard the engine. When he looked into his mirror, all he could see was a dark shape beyond blinding headlights. It wasn't even recognizable as a truck.

At first, Ian didn't think much of it, assuming the driver simply wanted to pass him. Nothing else occurred to him. Carl was grateful that the road was otherwise empty. He wanted no witnesses for what he had planned. Carl moved the truck alongside Ian's Harley.

Ian waved it away as it edged closer to him, still suspecting nothing; but it kept coming, gradually pushing him toward the side of the road. Then it bumped Ian, attempting to knock him off the pavement. The Harley careened onto the gravel and grass beside the road. The gravel spewed like shrapnel behind the bike's wheels, screeching to a halt.

The rain streamed down, plastering Ian's hair to his skull. Water dripped into his eyes. Above him, thunder rumbled like toppled bowling pins. Lightning flashed dramatically. Ian grimaced angrily. What was the fucker trying to do? Had it been an accident? Or was it intentional? It was a virtual miracle that he hadn't crashed. Almost anyone else in the same circumstances would have.

If Ian had any doubt about the driver's intentions, they were soon dispelled. The driver clearly wanted to run him down. Once he determined that, everything clicked for Ian. It no longer mattered who the driver was or why they were doing it. They were not going to get away with it.

Whoever it was had made a bad mistake....a very bad one. This was not the night to piss him off. Ian always had to fight down the anger that boiled inside him, the rage of the beast within, but the closer it got to a full moon the harder it became to control. The nights of the cycle itself were the worst of all—like tonight. The fool was going to get what he had coming—in spades. Ian revved his bike and roared at the truck...

Ian gritted his teeth as the wind rushed past, the sound of the engine rumbling in his ears. The truck's headlights blinded him. If the driver wanted to play chicken, Ian would give him a proverbial run for his money. Their tires splashed through puddles on the road, the rain still coming down in sheets.

They rushed directly at each other, neither willing to turn aside. Ian knew the bike wouldn't fare well if it hit the truck head-on. In his rage, he no longer cared. Practical considerations meant nothing to him at the moment. Carl was equally committed, his injured pride urging him on.

Only at the last possible instant did Ian swerve to avoid the oncoming grill of the truck. "Fuckin' coward!" Carl snickered triumphantly. "Showed him!" His adrenaline pumped. "Put 'im on the run..." he guffawed gleefully. Foster quickly lost sight of the bike's taillight in his rear-view mirror.

On the road behind him, Ian turned the Harley around, switching off the headlights. He watched the truck's taillights recede, although Foster had slowed down. Carl had no reason to keep speeding. Ian had fled to escape him. Without the bike's headlights, he could not see the motorcycle coming until it was too late. Foster heard the Harley before he saw it.

Ian rode up from behind until he was alongside the bed of the truck, keeping pace with it. He reached out with one hand and grasped the edge of the truck's bed. Quickly, despite the rain beating down, he gripped it with the other hand as well. The bike slid away beneath him as he swung his legs to release it. The Harley slowed, wobbled, and finally toppled onto the road behind them. He regretted damaging it, but it could always be fixed, or he could buy another one.

Carl still didn't comprehend what Ian was doing. Holderness clung to the truck, slowly pulling himself upward. Water ran down Ian's face. His clothes were thoroughly soaked. Then Ian managed to swing one leg up and over the side. Within another moment, he was in the bed of the truck. He crept carefully to the back window of the cab....

Foster sensed something, yet did not know what it was. He saw the bike fall away and thought Ian had crashed with it. Then he heard a thump and a vibration, as if something heavy had landed in the bed of the truck, but what? He couldn't see anything in his rearview mirror.

By the time he could, Carl couldn't do a thing about it, except curse lividly. "Damn! How the fuck did he get there?" A fist burst through the back window of the truck cab. Glass showered the interior. Foster cursed again, only for it to be cut off as Ian's wet arm encircled Carl's throat.

"I gave you one chance!" his voice guttural and slightly garbled, as though his mouth was full. "You don't get any more." Ian's eyes blazed like emerald fire, his hot breath rank, almost bestial...

To Carl's confused horror, Ian's fingernails began to grow longer and sharper, his features heavier and courser. Dark hair sprouted on his arm and hand. More of it climbed his face. His ears became pointed, his teeth like the fangs of a wild dog...or a wolf. Ian's words slurred into a deep rumbling growl.

Foster tried to scream, but his air was cut off. The creature that had been Ian briefly raised its shaggy head, baring its ivory fangs, and buried them in Carl's shoulder with a twisting, chewing motion. Foster was in agony, blood spurting from the wound, staining his torn shirt.

Beyond rational thought, he lost his grip on the wheel. The Dodge clattered toward the side of the road, going faster because Carl accidentally hit the accelerator when he tried to reach the brakes. He was in a panic, never having expected anything like this. Holderness was some kind of monster...

The trees at the edge of the road appeared in the truck's headlights. The Dodge hurtled towards them, shaking and rocking as it went.

After Ian left, Cynthia began to grow restless. She saw the dark clouds gathering. They looked ominous. The wind was rising, getting colder. Much of the crowd was departing. Irv, Moira, Lisa, and Mat had already begun to clean up.

Colin was becoming impatient and fidgety, now that the food and music were over with. Cynthia sensed that he was upset that his father had insisted upon leaving early with such inadequate excuses. When it came to stubbornness, he was as bad as his father.

Cynthia decided that it was time to head back to the estate. "Colin? We'd better get going. The sky doesn't look good. I'd rather not get caught by a storm if we don't have to."

"If you say so," Colin mumbled, fingering his pendant. He glanced at his own watch. "But we can't get home in time. It's already too late."

"Too late for what?" Cynthia asked, feeling a chill. It wasn't from the breeze.

"The moon's gonna be full tonight. We waited too long. Dad was right. It'll be up before we get home," Colin said quietly. His eyes reflected his nervousness, but he sought to hide it.

"We should be ok," Cynthia said, more definitively than she felt. "There have been lots of full moons in the last seven years. Nothing has happened since then. Why should tonight be different?"

"I...I don't know," Colin admitted warily. "It just feels different." He knew more than he was saying. Cynthia decided to drop the subject, knowing the boy was not going to tell her anything more. Still, she prayed that Colin's instincts were wrong. If they weren't, the results could well be deadly.

Cynthia approached Moira to offer her good-byes. "Moira, Colin and I are heading out. I want to try to get home before the storm hits."

"Good idea," Moira replied, turning towards her. "It looks nasty. That's why we're trying to hurry with the clean-up here. If you don't think Mr. Holderness will mind, Lisa and Mat were going to spend the night at her old apartment over the garage. They'll drive to the estate in the morning."

"I doubt he'll mind," Cynthia responded. She and Colin then went to her car and got in. She slid into the driver's seat and clicked on her seat belt. Colin did the same.

Cynthia pulled out of the parking space for the drive home. It had begun to rain, ending any chances of beating the storm. Peering through the windshield, she could barely see the road. It reminded her of the night she first driven to Falcon's Aerie. Could it really have been only two weeks? It didn't seem possible. It felt so much longer to her.

She was tired, but she had to watch the road carefully, given the way the darkness and rain obscured it. Cynthia dared not let her attention slip. During most of the drive, she and Colin did not speak, each lost in their own thoughts. They'd said what they had to say already. Perhaps he was tired, too. He could be as moody as Ian.

They had just passed through Garrison, with Corchester only a few miles further south. The estate, which lay north of the town, was closer still. In no time, they reached the estate's service road.

Cynthia perked up when she felt the temperature in the car drop suddenly. Since it was cool outside, she didn't have the air conditioning on or the vents open. There was no rational reason for it. She'd experienced the same sort of unearthly chill before. Who... or what was it this time?

"Why is it so cold?" Colin broke in, briefly startling her. She noted that he'd gone very pale, fear in his eyes. Did he recognize the sign?

Instinctively, Cynthia glanced up at the rear-view mirror. The pale, dark-haired girl sat there, as she'd half expected. It was Jennifer Blackthorne again! Colin immediately noticed where Cynthia was looking. His eyes went wide.

"Aunt Jen!" he called out, stunned. So, he saw her, too... Cynthia wasn't sure whether to be relieved or not. Though a shared experience, could it still be an hallucination? If so, why? She had not told Colin that she'd seen his aunt's apparition.

"Turn back now...or it will be too late." Then she was gone. The backseat was empty. The car grew warmer, but a chill still gripped Cynthia's heart. What danger did the warning refer to?

"What did she mean?" Colin voiced her own question. It was then that Colin's earlier warnings returned to her—what night it was. Tonight was the full moon—the harvest moon. Had the boy been right after all?

At that moment, Cynthia saw a huge, dark figure in the road ahead. It was too late to stop. Cynthia slammed on the brakes, sending the car screeching to a halt.

CHAPTER 22

THE WOLF MAN COMETH
OCTOBER 3, 1982

She wasn't sure that the car would stop. Before it did, there was an audible thump in front of them. There was a series of splashes from the puddles they passed through. The car shuddered for a few seconds.

Looking out carefully through the windshield, Cynthia saw nothing, but she was certain that they'd hit something. What if it was a person and they were hurt? Cynthia wanted to check her bumper, too. How badly was it dented? Yet, she was leery of getting out of the car on this isolated road at night in a storm. Normally, the biggest danger would be getting soaked. Now she wasn't so sure.

"What did we hit?" Colin shattered her reverie.

"I...I don't know," Cynthia replied uneasily.

"I thought I saw someone, but now there's nothing there."

"Shouldn't we check?" Colin asked, clearly frightened, but not wanting to admit it.

"Probably," Cynthia said with reluctance. Leaving the key in the ignition, she put the Cougar in park. Since she had neither a scarf nor a raincoat, there was no way to avoid getting wet. Gritting her teeth, she shoved the car door open and got out.

Cynthia winced as the rain hit her. She slammed the door so that at least her seat wouldn't get soaked. She was quickly drenched as she circled to the front of the car. Cynthia frowned as the water ran down her face and into her eyes. Her hair was a sodden mess...

There was nothing...or no one on the road in front of her car. The car wasn't damaged; that would've been the last thing she needed. Thank God, it was still drivable! Still, what the hell had she hit?

Cynthia heard a growl before she saw from where it had come. The sound froze her in shock. It suggested a dog; a very, very big one that was close by. Primed by Colin's story, she feared it was something far worse than any dog.

Colin had heard it, too. He gestured wildly for her to get back into the car. Off to one side, she saw a pair of blazing green eyes amidst blackness deeper than the night surrounding it. The thing rose to its full height, well over six feet. It looked enormous to her. Even the headlights failed to reveal much detail, save that it stood on two feet and wore the ragged remains of what might've been a human's clothes.

Whatever it was, it definitely wasn't human. Colin's beast! It was real after all! Its torso and limbs were too manlike to be either an ape or a bear; despite its size and the wet black fur that covered it. Water streamed off it, dripping from its legs and arms. The nightmarish face was bestial, yet not simian.

The eyes were sunken beneath heavy browns, the snout vaguely canine. Its pointed ears were too high up on its head for it to be a man, and its jaws were lined with viscous-looking fangs. Talon-like claws tipped each finger and toe.

Part of her brain screamed that it had to be makeup or a costume, but it looked too convincing. Besides, could either make-up or a costume stand up under the pouring rain? It was so big, so powerfully built. How could that be if it was just a man in a costume? Colin had been right all along.

Cynthia stared at the creature and it glowered down at her, each riveted in place for a moment. Then she screamed instinctively, hearing it before she consciously realized that she'd done it. That broke the spell. It snarled, baring its teeth and aiming a swipe of its gleaming claws at Cynthia. She ducked and screamed again, the paralysis of shock gone. The deadly claws barely missed her, passing through empty space mere inches above her head.

Heart pounding like it never had before, she ran, fumbling at the car door in her panic. After what felt like hours, the door opened and Cynthia jumped in. She pulled the door closed with a clanging thump, too frightened to put on her seat belt. She reached to take the Mercury out of park.

She moved too slowly. A furry, clawed hand smashed through the driver's side window. Glass shards burst across the interior.

Colins face was whiter than she'd ever seen before, his nightmare restored to full, vivid life. His eyes bulged in fear and he was unable to speak. One of the shards cut Cynthia's cheek, but she scarcely noticed.

Once more, she narrowly avoided being slashed by the thing's steely claws. Frustrated by two failed attacks, it howled angrily. Cynthia instinctively sought to fend it off by throwing her hands in front of her face. It grasped the door with both hands, and tore it from its hinges, with a painful screech of rending metal. The beast tossed the door away, and it landed several yards on the far side of the road. Neither she nor Colin heard it over the sound of the thunder, the rain, and the creature's growls.

The door no longer barred its way, so the thing bent inward, snapping viciously at her. Seeing this seemed to galvanize Colin; he reached into his shirt and pulled out the pendant, tears stinging his eyes. His aunt had died to save him. He couldn't sit and do nothing as it happened all over again with Cynthia.

She desperately tried to complete getting the car into gear. In the process of fending the beast away from her face with her left hand, it chomped down. Agony lanced through her and she cried out, on the verge of fainting from pain and fear, but she couldn't give in. If she did, both she and Colin were dead.

To her surprise, almost as soon as it bit her, the creature's jaws opened, releasing her hand. There was a hiss, like steam, and the odor of burning flesh. What caused it she didn't know, but she didn't care since it caused the thing to let go of her injured hand.

It drew back out of the car, with a sharp whine as though scalded. In that instant, Cynthia saw that Colin held the pentacle in one hand and had apparently pressed it to the beast's face or arm while it focused on her. The pendant had burned it, much as a cross to movie vampires.

Cynthia was profoundly grateful, yet had no time to think about it. At the same moment, the car slipped into gear and she slammed her foot on the accelerator. The engine revved, and the car lurched out of park to roar down the road. The tires squealed against the wet pavement. The car careened from side to side, just barely under

Cynthia's control. Her brain was on automatic.

The wind and rain whistled through the Mercury's interior as it raced down the road. Cynthia shuddered, her teeth chattering, her eyes wide and almost unblinking. Although she'd believed the boy's story was true in some way, she'd never let herself accept that it was literally true. Colin's pentagram had affected it. Hers should, too. Her sense of reality, already damaged, had just been torn to shreds.

But the night wasn't over yet. Colin was staring at the rearview mirror, terror in his eyes. "It's following us!" he just managed to gasp out.

"That's...impossible!" Cynthia's jaw dropped. A glance in the rearview mirror confirmed what Colin said. It was not something for which Cynthia wanted confirmation. The creature was running along the road behind the car, much as a dog might, but it was a lot bigger and deadlier than any dog, and quite a bit faster. It was not merely chasing them—it was catching up...

Cynthia's eyes fell onto her speedometer next. The needle had passed sixty, and was well on its way toward seventy miles per hour. Even a cheetah could only run sixty-eight miles an hour. Nothing on two feet was anywhere near that fast—except for this thing. How fast would she have to go to escape it?

Despite the increasing speed of the car, the creature kept getting closer and closer. Cynthia's heart rate went off the charts. She knew she was going to hyperventilate soon. She wasn't sure she could control the car much longer.

Then there was a popping clunk behind them. Cynthia couldn't risk looking back. She had to focus on the wheel and road ahead. The speedometer was passing eighty. Colin, however, turned to look "It's got hold of the trunk!" he yelled.

Checking the rearview mirror she saw that he was right again. It had grasped onto the trunk of the car, puncturing the metal with its claws in order to hold on. Even as she watched the mirror, the creature continued to climb the trunk on the way to the roof. What could she do now? How could she dislodge it? Neither speeding up nor slowing down would do any good.

Panic was cutting off Cynthia's ability to think. The creature disappeared from the rear- view mirror and back window, but they both heard it on the roof above them. The beast pounded on the Mercury's roof with one hand, holding on with the other, having punctured the metal there. Only the headliner hid the holes.

The grating sound of scratching on metal revealed what it was doing. The beast was tearing ragged gashes in the roof of the car with its claws, shredding it like cheap tin foil. This sis break through the headliner. Cynthia fought another scream, yet failed to hold it back. It would get through the roof of the Cougar, peeling it back as if it was the top of a can.

Colin held his pendant up above him, hoping to ward it off. Cynthia fumbled in her purse, searching for the canister she kept there. The creature swiped at them once it had peeled away enough of the roof. Once such slash left bloody cuts in Colin's forehead, and he slumped in his seat, dazed. He dropped the pendant onto the seat and it slid onto the floor of the car.

Having disposed of that danger, it leaned down into the opening it had just made. The beast chomped at her head. Saliva dripped onto her from its jaws. Cynthia's hand grabbed the mace, pulling it from her purse. Blood fell from the wound in her hand as she raised the canister and sprayed it at the face of the creature.

The spray struck it in the eyes. It blinked, then howled in pain and reared up. Instinctively, it brought its hand to its eyes, releasing its grasp on the car's roof. Seizing her chance, Cynthia stomped on the brakes, stopping with a zigzagging jolt.

The jolt threw the beast forward. It rolled onto her hood and from there onto the road. It continued to roll until it came to rest somewhere off the pavement. Cynthia didn't wait to see where it ended up. She'd made that mistake once. She wouldn't do it again.

Cynthia took her foot off the brakes then hit the accelerator, peeling away down the road. The car spit water behind it as she drove. Rain streamed in through the hole in the roof and the driver's side. She did her best to ignore it.

This time, she was under no illusion that it was dead or even unconscious. It would be on its feet and after them in minutes.

Maybe it already was. Cynthia couldn't afford to wait to find out. She'd half-forgotten where she was. It was somewhere near the estate, but how near?

Almost the second Cynthia got her bearings, an angry howl echoed behind them. Just as she'd guessed, it was still there. She went a little faster, though she was already going over eighty. She sighed with relief when she saw the wall of the estate, and the gates looming ahead of them. With some reluctance, she slowed down to turn into the entrance. She knew if she didn't, she'd probably crash into the gate piers.

Colin began to groan softly in the seat beside her. Cynthia's hand throbbed in pain, blood making the steering wheel sticky. Her left hand resembled raw meat. Her breathing was ragged and she was soaked to the bone. She probably resembled a drowned cat.

That was the last thing she cared about. She had to get Colin to a doctor, and the security at the gate was her best shot at doing that. She didn't even consider that it required more than some disinfectant and a bandage—maybe a good stiff drink, perhaps the whole bar.

Cynthia stopped short. The gates were closed! Why, of all possible nights, were they shut? That thing would show up at any moment. As angry as she was terrified, Cynthia pressed the call button hard. "This is Dr. Akers! Let us in! I've got Colin... Mr. Holderness' son is with me...he needs a doctor! Call Dr. Marsden!" She didn't even realize that she was shouting.

"Certainly, Doctor...right away. Dr. Marsden is already at the main house," answered a voice over the speaker The voice was calm and even, infuriating Cynthia even more. He had no right to be calm! No one did...not tonight! Before she could yell at the guard, the gates swung inward, and she drove through them as if the hounds of Hell were after her, because one of them was.

CHAPTER 23

BEAUTY AND THE BEAST
OCTOBER 3, 1982

Cynthia didn't bother to park in the garage. Instead, she slammed on the brakes, immediately switching off the ignition and tossing the key into her purse and throwing the strap over her shoulder. Then she hurried to the passenger side to get Colin. By then, a security guard was coming out of the other side of the garages, where their office had been set up.

His jaw dropped when he saw the car, and Cynthia helping Colin out of his seat. The guard was completely stunned, unable to imagine what could've happened. He was too startled to speak at first. "Call Dr. Marsden!" Cynthia cried out. "Hurry!"

That snapped him out of his initial shock. He lifted the radio and mumbled into it. Cynthia couldn't hear what he said, due to the staccato beat of the rain and booming of the thunder. Lighting still arched overhead, casting the scene in high relief.

"Mr. Seth...Dr. Marsden?" Aida came into the study, looking upset. "There's a call from the gate...something's happened to Mr. Colin and Dr. Akers. The guard said they needed you down there right away, Doctor."

"What's happened?" Richard responded with a worried expression. He stood and reached for his bag. Seth still appeared bored.

"I don't know, Doctor," the housekeeper answered. "But the guard sounded frantic. I hope they're all alright..."

"I'm coming. Let the guards know I'll be there as soon as I can," Marsden advised her. Aida nodded and headed for the kitchen.

"Don't get so excited, Richard," Seth drawled, heavy-lidded. "I'm sure it's nothing serious. After all, what could it be?" he raised a mocking eyebrow.

"Hopefully, you're right, Seth," Richard said through tight lips. "But we can't all take it for granted as easily as you do."

"I do try to remain a bastion of calm," Seth grinned sarcastically. "If you need me, I'll be in my rooms." Then he wheeled himself from the room, leaving Marsden to gawk for a moment. Shaking himself, Richard proceeded toward the front doors. Thankfully, he'd parked there rather than at the garage.

Relief flooded Cynthia when a second guard came out and moved to help her with Colin. They were finally safe. Yet, even as they all turned to head into the garage to wait for Dr. Marsden, a howl from behind froze her blood. She glanced over her shoulder. What she saw made her scream. She didn't want to believe it, but there was no denying the truth.

The beast had climbed over the wall, since Cynthia had convinced the guards to close the gates. It leapt from the top of the wall as if it was a single step on a staircase. Its green eyes glowed balefully through the night and the rain. There was no escaping it! If it could catch up to her car at sixty to seventy miles per hour, running was pointless.

Her scream alerted the two guards who, until then, had focused on Colin. She had to do something. Having no weapon, her only hope lay in the pendant Ian had given her. If Colin's had worked against it, maybe hers would, too. She withdrew it from her blouse, praying that she was right.

The creature gave her no more time to think. Once again, the guards were frozen into inaction by the sight of the beast. She, at least, had heard it described before and been somewhat forewarned, if too slow to act. For them, it was totally new and unexpected. When hired, they had not been told to keep their eye out for stray werewolves...nor would they have taken the warning seriously if they had been.

One guard held onto Colin, who was semiconscious. The other drew his revolver and shakily aimed at the oncoming beast. His eyes were wide, incredulous. "Stop! Stay where you are or I'll shoot!" If he could still think at all, he must've assumed it to be a man in costume. Nothing else was possible.

The beast ignored the guard's order. Unaware of its incredible speed, he waited too long to fire. Cynthia held on tightly to her pendant, displaying it in front of her. The creature avoided the glint of its reflection, lunging instead at the guard who stood several yards away.

It seemed to fly through the air, fangs bared, claws extended. The thing was upon him before he could react. It pummeled him to the wet cobblestone pavement. The pistol flew from his startled grip.

Letting Colin drop gently to the ground, the other guard began to reach for his own revolver. Cynthia instinctively knew his partner would be dead before he could fire. She didn't know whether she could do any better, but she had to try, or they were all doomed.

Cynthia had been a good shot once, going to train at the firing range with Danny after he got out of the Marines. Her aim was actually better than his, though he had a firmer grip and reacted less to the recoil.

She knew what the guards didn't; that the thing was almost certainly a werewolf and it was adversely affected by silver. More to the point, their guns were loaded with silver bullets, though they were unaware of it. That gave her a slim hope. Yet, it might prove their only one.

Cynthia saw where the fallen guard's gun landed. Without thinking further, she managed to scoop it up and regain her balance, despite the wet cobblestones. She heard the other guard fire as she braced her right wrist with her left hand to steady it.

The beast continued to snarl and snap, yet was temporarily distracted from the fallen guard, though his partner's shot missed its mark. Not wanting to see the pentagram, it ignored Cynthia. The creature's attention was now focused upon the guard with the revolver, who was preparing to fire again.

Cynthia realized she would probably only get one shot in before it came after her, so she had to make it count. The beast moved swiftly, disarming the standing guard and slashing him across the chest. He staggered back, and cried out in pain and surprise.

Steeling herself, Cynthia aimed and fired. There was a flash of light, and the acrid smell of smoke. Only then came the bang and recoil. Time seemed to have slowed down. She expected it to move fast, so she'd aimed at where she estimated it would be when she squeezed the trigger.

The beast yelped as the bullet struck its right shoulder. It went rigid, grasping at its upper arm in surprise and burning pain. Its eyes flared. Its lunge toward the second wounded guard ceased as its gaze fell on Cynthia.

She'd hit it, but not in a vital spot. Knowing it would go after her now, Cynthia fired again. This time it was hit in the chest. The thing yipped and reeled back, stunned, but it didn't collapse as she'd expected and hoped. Had Ian been wrong about the silver bullets? Or was it just that her aim was off? With the creature still on its feet, there was no way to be certain which it was. Maybe not all the guns were loaded with silver bullets...

The beast stood still for a brief moment, swaying slightly, unsteadily. It glared at her, infuriated, but it made no move to attack her. The creature gritted its teeth in pain, considering what to do next. The thing shuddered with agony and emotion.

Suddenly, its decision made, it grasped at its bleeding chest, reared its head and howled, the rain drenching it. Then it loped off into the night and the storm, splashing as it went. Despite its wounds, it somehow made it back over the wall once more.

Cynthia knew she ought to have shot again. She didn't want to waste bullets she wasn't sure would do any good. In the time that it took to think about it, it was already too late. The beast was beyond her hearing and sight. Why had she hesitated?

Still, at least it was gone...for now, but now she could not deny that it was real. While she couldn't definitely say it was truly a werewolf, the torn clothes, sensitivity to silver and the pentagram suggested that it was. It was a full moon tonight, as well, but if it was one, who was it?

Physically and emotionally exhausted, Cynthia let the gun drop to her side; the moment of action was past. The adrenaline rush subsided. She felt weak and limp....so tired. Dr. Marsden arrived then. He came up beside her, and wordlessly offered to let her lean on him until he could get her to a place in the garage to sit down.

Richard surveyed the scene, and realized he required help. He would do what he could in the meantime, but collectively they needed more than he could give them. After he called for paramedics, he phoned the local sheriff's office. There was no way to avoid notifying them. So, he deemed it best to get it out of the way immediately. None of those involved would be up to answering questions, unless it was done quickly or put off until tomorrow...

The creature staggered through the woods, periodically doubling over and bracing itself against trees for support. Every so often, it fell to its knees, even onto all fours.

The first bullet had deeply grazed its shoulder, searing like fire. The second bullet remained lodged in its chest. While it hadn't hit the beast's heart, it was far too close. The thing had lost a lot of blood in its effort to escape. Yet, it had no choice, save to flee.

Instinct told it to avoid places where his prey dwelled, whenever it was wounded or injured. It needed to find a place to hide...to rest. It always healed, though sometimes faster than other times. To do that, however, it required time and solitude. For when it was weakened, the prey became its hunters. The beast could not afford to be cornered by them.

Finally, it spied a rise in the ground amidst the trees. It groped its way to the top to look around. The top of the rise was flat... and cold, like stone. The creature looked down. In the light of the full moon, visible due to a break in the clouds, the rain having temporarily let up, it saw that the mound was the remains of a building—its foundation. .

The creature sensed that its prey no longer dwelt here. There was an opening in the platform, with steps leading down to a dark doorway. A weathered wooden door hung half off its hinges there. The thing limped down the steps, dripping blood as it went, seeking the cool darkness beyond the door. It entered, collapsed onto the cold ground...and knew nothing more.

CHAPTER 24

THE MORNING AFTER
OCTOBER 4, 1982

"Is she up tuh bein' questioned yet, Doctor?" asked Sheriff Fitch. "I don't wanna be a pest, but we really need a deposition from Miss Akers. She's the only witness who remained conscious throughout the whole incident. The two guards have already given their depositions. We're just waitin' on Dr. Akers and the Holderness boy."

Amos Fitch had been a cop for twelve years, but had only become sheriff two years before when his predecessor, Harry Sampson, retired. Though born locally he'd begun his police career in the city. He'd become a cop only after fifteen years in the army, including a tour in Vietnam. At forty-five his dark skin was weathered like old leather, his short hair, gun- metal gray. He had a lean, yet sturdy, build and a kindly face.

"She's still resting, Sheriff," Richard answered guardedly. "She's been through a traumatic experience. I gave her a sedative to help her rest last night; Colin, too. They should be awake before long, but it can't be rushed."

"I understand," Amos nodded sympathetically. "Just let me know when they're ready. I won't badger them. I feel sorry for what the boy's been through, and I admire Dr. Akers. Whatever that thing was might've killed them all, if not for her."

"That's true," Richard agreed. His tone was tightly controlled, his expression unreadable. "She's very brave."

"Though she didn't kill it, we're lucky her aim was good," Fitch commented. "But I wanna know what the hell that thing was…and where it is now."

"I…I imagine so," Marsden nodded, his face a bit pale. "It must be very frustrating."

"That thing's still out there somewhere, alive or dead. Hopefully we'll find it out in the woods dead, but I doubt we're that lucky."

"No," Richard shook his head sadly. "I doubt we are."

"Well I gotta be goin' now. We still haven't found Mr. Holderness yet. His bike was off the road not far from here, but no sign of him. There was another accident close to where Holderness's turned up. It belongs to an acquaintance of mine—Carl Foster. He crashed off the road, but someone or…something broke through the back window of the truck's cab," Fitch mused in bafflement. "His shirt was all bloody, and torn around the neck and shoulder, but when the blood was cleaned away all they found was an old scar. We're tryin tuh figure out whose blood it was."

"I'm quite worried about Ian," Richard said, gazing out the window distractedly. "I can't imagine where he can be. You'd think he would've been near his motorcycle."

"You would." Amos put his hat back on, turning towards the door. "But maybe he was dazed...wandered off intuh the woods or lookin' for help. With all that rain and it bein' night, he could'a got lost—disoriented. It wouldn't' a been hard last night. Hopefully, he didn't meet up with that thing out there. Either way, we'll keep looking until we find him. He'll turn up."

"I hope so," Marsden sighed. "I really do."

Ian's eyes gradually fluttered open, though they felt almost glued shut. His mouth tasted like mud. His head ached. He felt too weak and dizzy to even sit up. His shoulder and chest were searing agony. Examining them with one hand, he noted a warm, sticky substance—blood. He must've been shot...he would've healed already, unless...the bullets were silver.

That meant the guards....glancing around, he saw where he was. The light was very dim, but Ian recognized the place. It was the cellar of the estate's original mansion. He must have crawled there after being wounded the previous night. He prayed that he hadn't hurt anyone. Yet, he realized how improbable that was. He dreaded discovering what havoc he'd caused.

He had been such a fool to take the risk of going to the picnic. He'd cut it too close. He had failed to take...delays into account, and was paying the price for it now. The question upper- most in his mind was if anyone else had paid for his mistake. How much further guilt was to be piled atop what he already drowned in?

Ian had to get to Richard somehow, so that he could remove the bullets. In a way, he wished that the shots had proved fatal, but Colin needed him now. He couldn't afford to take the easy way out. He had tried and failed once before. Ian could no longer seek release that way.

Groaning, he forced himself to sit up, bracing against the moldy brick wall of the cellar. He gritted his teeth against the pain. With immense effort, he struggled to his feet. He felt off balance, his legs wobbly, but he had to make his way out of the basement of the ruined mansion. Step by agonizing step, he climbed the stairs.

He dared not go directly to the house in his current condition. That left only the garage, and the tunnel to the safe room. He could call Richard from the waiting area. At least he could lie down there again—if he made it. Wounded as he was, that was a very big if.

"How are you feeling?" Marsden asked, his concern evident.

"I'm fine," Cynthia replied, rubbing her eyes and fighting a yawn. "Is Colin alright? Are those guards okay?"

"Colin's still asleep," Richard answered. "Cleaned the cuts on his forehead, and bandaged them. He's got a mild concussion. He should recover fine. As for the psychological impact, it's too soon to say, but you doubtless know that as well as I."

Noticing the bandage on her hand, Cynthia frowned, recalling now it had been injured. "I'm surprised that this thing doesn't hurt more than it does. It hurt like hell last night. I thought that thing's bite might've crippled it. I hope it didn't have rabies..."

"What do you mean?" Marsden perked up. "Are you saying it bit you? There was some blood there, but I just assumed it was cuts from the glass, though I didn't see any sign the skin was broken—only an old scar."

"You're kidding!" Cynthia looked at him in disbelief. "I felt its teeth puncture my hand...the pressure from its jaws. I saw the wounds. Now you're telling me they're not there? That doesn't make sense! I know I didn't imagine it."

"I'll show you," Marsden responded, confused. "There were a few scars, but they looked over a month old—nearly healed..." Richard eyed her skeptically. He walked over and carefully removed the bandage on her left hand. Cynthia watched him closely. When all the bandages had come off, she glanced at her hand and gasped. There were a few ragged pinkish-white scars that could've been puncture wounds, but Marsden was right. They looked as though they'd healed weeks or even month before.

"I...I don't get it!" Cynthia exclaimed, incredulous. She shook her head, frowning. "I'm not crazy! I'm not! It happened. Look at my car! Could a fantasy tear off the door or rip open the roof?"

"I believe you," Richard responded. "Ian told me of your conversation a few days ago. I can admit to you now that I saw it that night seven years ago and shot at it. Colin saw it then, and again last night. So did those guards. It's only the part about your being bitten I don't understand. I'm willing to accept what you say happened, since you have no reason to lie or imagine it, but why the wounds healed so quickly is beyond me."

Cynthia was flabbergasted. What could the answer be? Then something occurred to her. The thing looked and acted like a movie werewolf. Ian and Seth were both fans of those films, and they owned copies of them as well as scripts. Maybe the answer lay in one of them.

"That thing acts like a werewolf from the old movies," Cynthia observed. "So, what do the movies say about the bite of a werewolf? My brother knows horror movies better than I do. I avoided them because of my nightmares, but every child knows that survivors of a werewolf's bite become werewolves themselves, much like anyone who dies of a vampire's bite. What about the wounds themselves? We need to check."

"In this case, we don't," Richard noted quietly. "It didn't occur to me before, because I didn't know you'd been bitten until just now. Ian was a fan of the films; you're right. Seth was, too. I do recall now some of what Ian told me about them. One detail he mentioned is that the victim's bite wound healed very quickly, within hours. That was a point, because people doubted they'd been bitten."

"Does...that mean what I think it does?" Cynthia paled, bringing her hand up to her mouth in shock.

"I don't know," Richard answered. "But we'll know tonight. Ian told me the cycle always lasted three nights, the full moon and the ones before and after it. So, there's one more night left to go. Hopefully, nothing will happen; but I can sedate you, if you begin to feel anything tonight. To be safe, there's a room in the cellar where we can go ...it's isolated if need be. It's a vault where they once hid booze during Prohibition. The wine racks are gone now, but it's secret and strongly built—just in case."

"I pray that won't be necessary," Cynthia half-whispered. "But let's go down there near nightfall just to be safe. I don't want to take any chances."

"Ian is still missing," Richard added, visibly worried. "The sheriff's men are looking for him..."

"What happened?" Cynthia temporarily forgot her own troubles, previously unaware Ian was missing.

"He never arrived home last night. He'd asked me to meet him here before going to the sanitarium. That's why I was here when you got home. The deputies found Ian's bike abandoned beside the road a mile or so from here. Carl Foster's truck was crashed a few hundred yards away. They suspect Foster might've knocked Ian's bike off the road before crashing himself. Foster's in the hospital, still unconscious, but they haven't located Ian yet."

"That's terrible!" Cynthia gasped. "He might've been hurt...what if that thing found him when he was injured?"

"I'm more troubled about the crash," Richard commented. "He knows how to handle the beast. Besides, it got here relatively soon after sunset. Since it was shot, it may not have been capable of hunting as it normally would have."

"God, I hope you're right," Cynthia said fervently. "He's got to be alright."

"Dr. Marsden?" Ida called out as Richard descended the main stairs. "There's a call for you. The gentleman says it's urgent."

"Did he say who he is?" Marsden asked distractedly.

"No," the housekeeper answered "But he doesn't sound well, whoever it is."

Marsden continued down the stairs and strode over to take the receiver from Aida. Once he had it, she turned and left the foyer without a further word. "Hello? Can I help you?" Richard asked, his tone slightly annoyed because he didn't appreciate the interruption.

"I need …your…help…Richard…" It was Ian.

"Where are you?" Richard almost shouted before he regained control.

"Down…stairs…I've…been…shot…" he rasped out.

"I know," Marsden replied in a near whisper. "I'll be there as fast as I can."

"What ….did…I do?" Ian asked, his voice barely a dry croak.

"I'll tell you when I get there. It…It's complicated," Richard responded with understatement. "But at least no one died…"

"Hey, you okay, buddy?" Eddie asked, visibly worried. "Yuh scared the fuckin' shit outta me, man! What the hell happened?" Hastings eyed his friend expectantly.

Carl was confused. He didn't know where he was or how he got there. A quick glance around revealed that it was a hospital room, but even that didn't tell him where it was or why he was there. He'd been in his truck, watching Holderness's estate…gradually, the memories returned, though they remained disjointed and difficult to assemble in the correct order.

That thing—that monster—it couldn't be real! It had to be in his head. Nothing like that horror could actually exist…

"What am I doin' here?" Carl asked haltingly, his gaze darting about uneasily.

"You're askin' me?" Eddie chuckled nervously. "You were there, buddy. I wasn't. The cops found yer truck smacked into a tree off the side of the road. What were you doin' there? How'd yuh crash?"

"Uh….it was …that nutcase…Holderness," Foster began to concoct his excuse. "He….he came right at me, on that bike o' his, in the fuckin' rain. Tried to play chicken with me…I swerved tuh get past 'im and slid off the damn road. It…was too slick …I couldn't stop…musta hit the tree."

"Fucker!" Hastings hissed between tight lips. "You gotta tell the sheriff. Creep coulda got you killed."

"Where's he?" Carl wondered aloud, trying to hide his reason for asking.

"Holderness?" Eddie asked, baffled. "Nobody knows. They found his bike beside the road, too...not that far from your truck, but the rain washed away any footprints or scent for the dogs."

"Damn!" Carl frowned deeply. "Fucker got away again."

"Maybe, maybe not," Hasting responded. "The sheriff's been pretty busy. Somethin' attacked that bitch o' his n' his kid. They were drivin' home n'whatever it was jumped 'em—tore off one o' the doors on her car, tore open the roof, an' raked the kid's head. Deputies're lookin' fer the thing. It took down a coupla the Brit's guards, too. The bitch drove it off with one o'their guns after the rent-a-cop dropped it."

Tough little cunt," Carl grumbled. "I'll give'r that."

"What about this—whatever the hell it was? Anybody else see it?" Carl inquired, trying to sound conversational.

"Nobody knows what it is or where it came from. Got people scared shitless," Eddie answered, not fully understanding what his friend asked.

"Then it's real!" Foster breathed, hardly paying attention to Eddie.

"Why, Carl?" Hastings couldn't comprehend what difference the beast made to anything. "Did you see it?"

"I maybe ...Eddie. I...ain't sure. It's all pretty hazy, but it sounds...familiar. I ...saw something. I'm not sure what it was or if I was dreamin'. I was ...kinda shook up at the time," Carl answered as honestly as he dared to. "I sorta hope it wasn't real."

Moira arrived at the estate, with Lisa and Mat. They knew only that Ian had not yet gotten home when they were called the previous night. All three were shocked to see the sheriff's deputies alongside the security guards, as well as the condition of Cynthia's car. By the time Hunter had parked the van in the garage, Ian's motorcycle was being towed in.

"What the heck happened?" Mat watched what was going on.

"I hope Dr. Akers and Colin are okay," Lisa peered around his shoulder, concern battling curiosity. "I wonder if they were in the car when that happened."

"Hopefully not," Moira commented, eying the Mercury warily.

"That looks nasty. I hate to think what could've caused that damage."

"Me, neither," shuddered Lisa. "What could rip off the door and pull up the roof that way?"

"And what happened tuh Mr. Holderness—if the cops're bringin' his bike back like that?"

"I guess we'll find out soon enough," Moira noted. "Maybe we can ask one of the deputies or security guards."

And so they did. They were shocked at the answer. Lisa went pale, and Mat was incredulous. Moira was equally surprised, but she recalled her conversation with Cynthia only a few days before. It put a sort of period to it. Based upon what they saw of the car and heard about what had occurred, it would seem that their recent speculations had become reality.

Despite what she guessed, Moira held her tongue, not wanting to end up in an asylum. They didn't know when or where would that creature show up next, for the moon would still appear full tonight. It might well be far from over yet.

CHAPTER 25

MOON RISE
MONDAY OCT 4, 1982

The sun sank toward the horizon, washing the sky in pink, orange, and lavender. Few clouds were visible. Cynthia gazed out the window of her room, her nerves frayed. Each tick of the clock brought her closer to sunset...and moonrise. What was she going to do? There seemed to be no way to tell how the moonrise would affect her.

Was it going to be like any other night, or would she endure a transformation she'd have deemed impossible only days before? Cynthia had no experience to draw on that could answer her questions, or reveal how best to handle it. To make matters worse, Ian was still missing. What has become of him? Was he alive?

What would it be like if she did change? How would it happen and how would it feel? She couldn't even imagine it. What might she conceivably do if she became a creature like the one that had attacked her? Dr. Marsden had promised to do what he could but, realistically, what could he possibly do?

"How are you holding up, Dr. Akers?" Richard inquired with gentle concern as he came into her room.

"About as well as can be expected," Cynthia sighed, slumping into a chair. "I keep wondering how long we—I—have...how high does the moon have to get? How low does the sun have to go down? The definitions of sunset and moonrise vary by hours. How does the change begin? How long does it take?"

"Well, I...I can't tell you for certain, but we know the beast appeared despite the storm. That suggests the change doesn't require direct exposure to moonlight. It attacked you and Colin at what—8:00pm?" Marsden surmised.

"I'm not quite sure," Cynthia admitted wearily. "I don't think it was later than 7:30."

"That indicates the change doesn't wait until full dark. It could be as early as 5:30, at the onset of dusk, but it's probably in between then and, say, 7:30. The moon rises a bit later tonight than last night, but not by much. How long it takes...who can say?" Marsden hypothesized.

"What do I do then?" Cynthia rubbed her forehead, her eyes closed. "If...I do change, I don't want to hurt anyone. There has to be a way to keep me from escaping and doing who knows what."

"I've brought a gun with silver bullets, though I pray I won't need to use it," Richard said guiltily. "I brought a sedative in the hopes that we can keep you unconscious for the night. It...It's the strongest one I have. I also have some manacles at the sanitarium for the most violent cases. Thankfully, we don't have to use them often. I could go and get them. It's 3:30 now. I should be back well before sunset, or you could go there with me, to the isolation ward there. It's up to you."

"How would we explain my going, if I didn't go this morning?" Cynthia asked almost rhetorically. "If you can bring them here, I'll go to that vault you mentioned in the basement. You can give me the drug. I...I'm not sure I'm comfortable with the manacles, but have them ready."

"I will." Richard avoided her eyes. She didn't notice, preoccupied as she was.

Colin was in the foyer when Cynthia and Dr. Marsden came down the stairs. "Where you goin?" he asked, his expression both suspicious and worried. "The moon'll still be full tonight. It's not safe to go out!"

"It's because of the moon I have to go, Colin. Although you drove it off with your pendant, it was already too late. It bit me. You know what that could mean. If I'm lucky, nothing will happen, but we can't afford to take chances."

"But they haven't found Dad yet," Colin objected, though he could see that it was futile.

"I know," Cynthia replied sadly. "I'm worried, too. I wish I had another option, but I don't. I refuse to potentially endanger you or the others. I'd rather look stupid if we're wrong. Either way, we'll know after tonight."

"That's not fair," Colin said dejectedly. "You finally believe me, but it might be too late."

"No, it's not fair," Cynthia nodded with a wry smile. "This is just a precaution. We don't know anything will happen, but I'd never forgive myself if something went wrong and I hadn't done all I could to prevent it."

"You won't change your mind?" Colin made one final try.

"I…I can't," Cynthia answered, trying to sound strong, though she didn't feel that way. "I'm going to the…sanitarium," she fibbed, not wanting to explain in greater detail and risk him coming down to 'check' on her. There's an….isolation room there I can use, but don't tell anyone else. I…don't want to try to explain. They'd think I was nuts…" she chuckled nervously.

"I get it. I won't tell," Colin rolled his eyes knowingly. OK…see you…tomorrow," he added a wave and a forced smile.

Cynthia waved back at him. Then she and Marsden were gone. It was going to be a long night…for everyone.

Carl lay in the hospital bed. He was restless. Eddie had been visiting him most of the day, but the nurses hustled Hastings out around 4:00 pm and brought Foster his dinner, such as it was. The food was bland, due to a lack of spices. It tasted like paste or unsweetened baby food to him, adding to his frustration. He was anxious to get out of this place.

Foster didn't like hospitals. He hated the dull décor and foul smells half-hidden by antiseptic cleaning solutions. The hushed rooms, periodically broken by cries or other odd noises, got on his nerves. The food was awful.

Carl could not stand being at the mercy of doctors and nurses. They could wake him whenever they chose, or force him to take any drug he was prescribed. Going to the damn bathroom was turned into a major production. They could push and prod him or stick him with needles whenever they wanted to, and he couldn't do anything about it. Besides, with Eddie gone and dinner eaten, it was boring and lonely. There wasn't much on TV, except the news, but he was desperate enough even for that. So, he picked up the remote and clicked it, aiming at the screen.

The remote's light flickered briefly, and the television screen brightened. It took a moment for the picture to become clear. He began to impatiently go through the channels, hoping to find something that might distract him until Eddie could return in an hour or so.

Looking briefly out the window, he noted that it was beginning to get dark, though there was still plenty of orange and magenta in the western sky. The evening shadows, however, were already long and stark, impenetrable in places.

Carl felt anxious, though he couldn't explain why. It was more than just boredom or frustration—more even than worrying about the hospital bill…or getting his truck fixed. He was already strapped for cash and he had no health insurance.

Suddenly, there was a stabbing pain in his gut. Carl's veins turned to liquid fire. He doubled over, gritting his teeth. He'd never endured agony like this before. What could be causing it? His monitors began to beep and blink wildly as his breathing grew ragged, his heart rate going crazy. Perspiration covered him, dripping from his forehead, stinging his eyes.

Foster cried out, clawing in futile desperation at the air. He rolled out of bed as he writhed, since the railings were not up. It was as if his entire body was being ripped apart from the inside. The sound of nurses and orderlies running down the hall toward his room was barely audible to Carl through the veil of pain.

By the time the nurses arrived, they found the room empty. The window was broken, yet there was no glass on the floor inside. Whatever shattered it came from within. The curtains billowed. The bed was a crumpled mess, the mattress soaked in sweat, the shredded cover mostly on the floor…

There was nothing else to be done now except call the police. Carl Foster was missing. In the east, the moon rose…

Cynthia and Richard walked down the hall towards the kitchen. Marsden checked carefully to be sure no one else was about, and then he reached up and pressed one of the carved rosettes in the paneling. A sliver of darkness opened up before them.

"A secret door!" Cynthia said in mild surprise. "I suppose I should've expected it."

"Every old manor needs at least one, right?" Richard winked, temporarily breaking the tension. He gestured for her to follow him into the passage, which she did. Once inside, he flipped a switch and a dull yellow bulb, encased in a metal cage, came on. Its illumination was dim, but just enough to see by. Turning, Richard pushed a small lever on the wall, closing the door behind them.

Before them, lay a stairwell going down into the darkness. At its base was a riveted steel door with a small window at eye-level that could be shut off by a metal sleeve. Since it was closed, it omitted no light from the other side. The air smelled musty and there was dust on the steps, as well as cobwebs along the walls in places, but there were footsteps disturbing the dust, so the stairs had not gone completely unused.

Marsden descended the steps first, Cynthia not far behind. Lost in their own thoughts, they didn't speak. He stopped before the door, and inserted the key into the lock and turned it. They both heard the click of the tumblers as the antique door unlocked. Richard pushed the door inward, and entered the room beyond. Cynthia held her breath a second then followed him.

Cynthia heard a thump and a slight outcry. There was a swish of air and a ...snarl...an all too familiar snarl. It was back! How could it be here? Even before she saw it she screamed....

· · · · · · · · · · · · · · · · · ·

"Are you sayin' Carl just jumped out that window?" Amos asked the nurse incredulously. "He was hurt—he'd still be on the ground if he did. He's not there. So, where'd he go? How?"

"How should I know?" the nurse snapped. "We responded to the monitors, but found it like this. He's not in the room, and that window was burst outward. There were no visitors. If he didn't jump out himself, you tell me what happened!"

"This don't make no sense," Fitch shook his head in disbelief. "But you got me. I can't figure out what happened here. If he did jump, he cant'a got far...in his condition. He shouldn't be hard to find..."

· · · · · · · · · · · · · · · · · ·

Carl ran faster than he ever had in his life. There was no pain anymore. The cool night felt glorious—freedom. It was difficult to concentrate, but he didn't care. Strength surged through every nerve and sinew. It was as if he could do anything. He couldn't for words yet he had no need for them. Words were the futile bleatings of his prey. He could smell their blood and sweat on the wind, hear their hearts beat—their blood course through their veins...

His vision was different, too. Everything was shades of red, brown, gray, or black. It was sort of like a negative or heat-seeking image. Carl ought to have been totally confused, stumbling around bumping into things, but he wasn't. He adjusted perfectly, as if he'd always seen things that way.

Foster reared his head and howled. It felt great. So, he howled again. Where should he go? What should he do? First, he wanted to get out of the place where the weak ones lived. It was too noisy—the myriad smells were bad. While he was tempted to hunt some prey, he wanted to reach the woods where he belonged...cars beeped as he ran across the road. He paid them no heed. He snarled and growled instead, eying them angrily.

If they got too close, Carl snapped at them or raked them with his claws. They tore through the metal easily. Several vehicles careened off the road at the sight of him, or due to the damage he'd done. It was a mess.

Surrounded by cars, Carl stood at bay, clawed feet braced wide. That was where the sheriff's deputies found him. By then, Foster's impatience and frustration had turned to blind rage. He clenched and unclenched his hands; iron-like claws clicking, they stared at him, uncomprehending in disbelief. At first they thought him to be a kook in a costume...

Infuriated, he roared, then chose a direction and leapt at the squad cars that barred his way there. The deputies aimed at the beast, but he was upon them before they could fire He landed atop the hood of one of the squad cars, crushing it in like cheap tin foil. The glass of the windshield cracked due to the impact. Steam rose from the ruptured radiator like the cloud from an active volcano.

The startled deputies shot at him, to no avail. Carl shrugged off their bullets effortlessly. He immediately bounded away from the wreck of the police car. The deputies attempted to prevent his escape, but Carl swatted them aside with ease. They landed a few feet away, moaning, yet unable to get up. The other officers hung back, uncertain what to do.

Then, a handful of officers rushed Carl with their batons. He snapped one in his right hand, and two broke upon striking him, as if they were made of balsa wood. Foster grasped a deputy and raised him high overhead, defying their bullets with impunity. He threw the struggling deputy over the roofs of more than one of the cars. The man crashed into one of the windshields, shattering it, before rolling off onto the pavement. He lay there, unmoving.

Beyond the men who'd rushed him, another fired at Carl from behind the door. Foster shoved the door closed on the deputy, who screamed as his ribs caved in. Then Carl pulled on it the opposite way, wrenching it from its hinges.

Grasping it with both hands, Foster flung the heavy car door like a massive misshapen Frisbee. It grazed one deputy in the head, knocking him out. The door virtually cut another of the deputies in half when it hit him in the gut.

One final car maintained the cordon. Baring his fangs, Carl lunged at it, shoving it over on its side, then toppling it, pushing the vehicle out of his path. At last he was beyond the police, though they continued to fire at him in anger and futile desperation. It did no good. In minutes, he'd disappeared into the night.

CHAPTER 26

CREATURES ON THE LOOSE
OCTOBER 4, 1982

Cynthia screamed again. The beast looked at her and growled. Dr. Marsden lay crumpled, unconscious upon the concrete floor of the room. Behind it was the open door to a smaller, cell-like room. The door was inches of thick polished steel...the thing was just as she recalled it, perhaps worse because she could see it more clearly in the brighter light.

It seemed even more gigantic than it had the previous night. Its lower limbs bend backwards, so that it was half-way in a shape between that of a man and a wolf. Its wicked claws glinted like polished black iron, its fangs like ivory, saliva dripping from them. The green eyes glowed unnaturally beneath overhanging, bushy brows. It glared at her intently, ignoring Marsden.

Cynthia stumbled back in shock, brushing against the door to the stairwell, partially closing it. That largely cut off her escape in that direction. There was another door opposite that to the cell, but it, too, was closed and the beast stood between it and Cynthia. She was trapped, unable to even make it to the cell and close the door before the beast reached her.

Aside from that, there was Dr. Marsden. While he might be dead already, she couldn't be sure of that. He might just be unconscious. She could not leave him to his fate, though she had questions as to why the beast would be here. Did that cell mean it was kept here on a regular basis?

She had little time for such questions. The creature was much stronger and faster than she, and Cynthia had no place to run—no weapon with which to defend herself, but her life was not the sole issue. If it escaped this room, it wasn't merely she and Dr. Marsden who could die. The thing might slaughter the entire household, with no way to stop it. This must be the doom she'd been warned about!

To make matters worse, she'd been feeling queasy and feverish since before they reached the hidden stairway. She'd thought it was only nerves. Now, she wasn't sure. Sweat beaded her face and arms. Her head hurt and her joints ached. Was it...happening to her, too?

The screams broke the spell, which temporarily held the creature where it stood over Dr. Marsden. It stalked toward her. She fell back further, soon finding herself against the wall. The beast savored its prey. It realized that she could not escape, as she did as well. There was no need to rush...

It lunged at her, pinning her against the wall's cheap paneling. The pressure on her shoulder was a crushing weight. She thought that it would pulverize her very bones. She could feel its hot, rank breath on her face. Cynthia closed her eyes and turned away from it, though she knew that it was a futile gesture.

She was doomed. Cynthia was certain of it. Nobody except Dr. Marsden knew where she was. Bullets, even silver ones, had failed to stop it. Only the pendant! She'd largely forgotten it. The pentacle might at least give her breathing space...

She reached into her blouse, withdrawing the pendant Ian had given her, but initially she still kept her eyes closed. She would be trapped even if it worked. Still, it was better than nothing. At any moment, Cynthia expected to feel the beast swipe her with its claws or to chomp down, tearing her flesh and crunching her bones.

She was amazed when it didn't. Fearfully, Cynthia opened her eyes. The beast continued to pin her to the wall with one clawed hand, but it hovered at a distance, staring at the pendant she held before her indecisively. It snarled from deep within its muscular chest, but it refrained from biting her or raking her with its talon-like claws. The pentacle froze it in its tracks.

She was alive, for the moment, but what could she do now? She still couldn't escape its grip. At that moment, Cynthia heard the creak of hinges. The door on the far wall began to open by itself. The beast heard it, too. It turned its shaggy head to look in the direction of the sound.

When the door was fully opened, a tunnel came into view, lit by the same sorts of bulbs as she'd seen above the stairs. It was dark compared to the brightly-lit cell and the room she was in, which was furnished like a cheap doctor's office. A slight figure now stood in the doorway.

It was Jennifer Blackthorne, but this time she was not pale, soaked, and bedraggled, but as she had been in life. She looked as solid as the beast or Dr. Marsden. Yet, Cynthia's mind told her that was impossible. It had to be some sort of illusion.

The beast acted as though it saw her too, though it sniffed at the air suspiciously and seemed baffled by the conflict between its two senses. It could see her, yet evidently not smell her.

Jennifer beckoned to it, pointing to the tunnel before which she stood. "The woods are waiting." the apparition said softly. "Don't hurt her. You know deep down that you don't want to. I know part of you is still there. You must fight the beast…" And then, as always, she was gone, with no sign she'd ever been there.

The beast glanced back and forth between Cynthia and the doorway to the tunnel. If such a creature could have a quizzical expression, it did. It was deciding whether its desire to rend her limb from limb was greater than that to run free in the woods.

Although it felt interminable, it came to its decision in seconds. The silver pendant, or one much like it, had burned the beast before. It did not like pain. That was what it inflicted upon the prey. The draw of the woods was strong…a pull that was difficult for the beast to fight. It hated giving up prey. To be free, to escape this prison where it had spent so many nights, was a lure too powerful to resist.

Releasing her shoulder, the thing turned away from Cynthia. She was too weak to move once freed, save to slump to the floor, breathing hard. Ignoring her, the creature loped purposefully to the doorway then onwards into the tunnel. After it had gone several yards along the tunnel, the heavy steel door closed of its own accord, just as it had opened.

That was how Richard found her when he came to, though her breathing had become more regular by then. Checking his watch, he realized that it was well past moonrise. The blow that felled him the moment he came through the door must've come from the beast. Glancing at the cell, he saw the silver-plated chains hanging limply, empty. That told him all he needed to know, save how the manacles had been unlocked, with their key still in his coat pocket….

It answered another question, too. Cynthia had not changed, though she theoretically should have. Why not? He was grateful that she hadn't, but it made no sense. How was she—how were they still alive? Ian should've torn them to bloody shreds by now. Mysteries upon mysteries. Where was he going to find the answers?

· · · · · · · · · · · · · · · · · ·

Theodore "Ted" Robeson pulled into his driveway. He put his pick-up into park and switched off the engine. Then he flicked off the truck's headlights. It had been a long day at the worksite, and he was exhausted. Work was behind schedule, because was shorthanded—and not for the first time either.

Most of the fault lay with that hulking idiot, Carl Foster, and his sniveling bootlicker, Eddie Hastings. Foster had been coming in late and leaving early every fucking day for the last week, and dragging his ass uselessly half the time when he was there. Carl was good at what he did, but he was temperamental and didn't take orders well, but the company was Ted's—Robeson Contracting, Inc.

It was hard enough to get work in or near Corchester. Ted could ill afford to anger his customers by being late to finish or doing half-assed jobs. Now Foster had ended up in a crash that put him in the hospital. The bum had probably been drunk behind the wheel, though the weather had been awful that night. Still, what he was doing out there at all was a mystery. With Carl in the hospital, Hastings hadn't come in today either. Ted ought to fire them both!

Shaking his head in annoyance at the thought, he got out of his truck, and closed its door. Hopefully, his wife had kept dinner warm for him, since he should've been home more than an hour before. Martha wasn't going to be happy he was late. It was getting to be a habit...one he wanted to break as soon as possible.

Although he wasn't sure she'd have the door locked, Ted fumbled through the keys on his ring, just in case. It wasn't so late that she would've gone to bed, but he didn't see any lights through the front windows. That was odd. Normally, he'd see the glow from the living room television and lamps at least...could she have gotten fed up waiting and gone out?

Ted checked the front door and found it unlocked. Stuffing his key ring into his pocket, he went in. The entire house was dark. His boot crunched on what sounded like glass or broken ceramic. Reaching for the light switch, he was shocked to see the room in shambles. He'd stepped on the remains of a shattered and toppled lamp. Cushions were knocked off the couch and shredded. A chair and table were thrown over, a mirror that had hung on the wall lay broken on the floor…what could've happened? Had a thief broken in?

"Martha?" he called out. "Where are you? What's goin' on here?"

She didn't answer. Ted grew worried. What if she was hurt, or worse? He began to search the house frantically. The back door was smashed in, little more than kindling left of it. Damage was everywhere. The door to the master bedroom and its bathroom were both smashed beyond repair.

Martha, or what was left of her, lay huddled in the shower, blood splattered all over the tile. Ted collapsed to his knees, crying and retching at the same time. Who…could've done something like this? Why? Martha could be a bit sharp-tongued at times, but nothing merited this! In a daze, he stood on unsteady feet, bracing himself to avoid collapsing again. He had to contact the police.

He never made it to the phone. A massive, dark shape awaited him near the end of the hallway. Details were hard to make out but, despite standing erect on two legs, it was not human. Its eyes glowed unnaturally amidst its dark fur. It blocked his way to the only exit. Thankfully, Ted kept a pistol in the bedroom nightstand for protection. He reached for it. With shaking hands, he tore open the drawer and grabbed for it. He wrapped his fingers around the handle, pulling it from the drawer.

The creature charged down the hall at him with amazing speed. Ted did his best to aim, squeezing the trigger almost instantaneously. He thought the bullet hit its target, but the beast did not slow down. Ted fired again, and then again, until the gun was empty. Smoke rose lazily from the heated barrel. The beast kept coming.

Ted's eye bulged in terror and disbelief, his mouth wide in a scream, but it didn't last long. Neither did Ted's life…

. . . .

"Are you alright, Doctor Akers?" Richard sat up, rubbing his head and side ruefully.

"I…could ask you the same," Cynthia tried to smile. "What just happened?"

"He…it was waiting for me as soon as I walked in…" Richard replied guardedly.

"I figured that part out," Cynthia became more serious. "What the hell was it doing down here? You said this place was used during Prohibition. The stairway we came down fits with that, but this room was recently furnished. The paneling is modern, so is the linoleum on the floor and the furniture. The magazines on the table can't be more than a few years old, and some are current. Why is it all here?" She gazed at him in a mixture of confusion and accusation. "You've been keeping it down here, haven't you? Ian hasn't been hunting it. He's been...keeping it imprisoned down here...hasn't he?"

"Yes," Richard closed his eyes as if in pain, his voice weary and resigned. "We both have. It was the only way."

"Why didn't you kill it, after all it's done? Why are you protecting it? It can be killed, can't it?" Cynthia asked, her indignation rising.

"It can die," Richard answered with almost a groan. "Silver bullets will do it, if the wound is fatal. Silver shuts off its ability to heal as it would normally do. It...heals very fast. Aconite can poison it. I use small amounts to render it unconscious, combined with colloidal silver. Regular sedatives don't work. Sunlight—ultraviolet light—suppresses the change. Fire might work, but I had no way to test it; the same for asphyxiation."

"Then why didn't you do it?" Cynthia asked, genuinely baffled.

"Because I couldn't do it, Doctor Akers...not to him." Marsden shook his head, sadly embarrassed.

"Oh, God!" Cynthia put her hand to her face in shock, the realization dawning. It all made dreadful sense to her now: Ian's monthly seclusion, the cell beneath his house, the pendants and silver bullets, the intense guilt. She'd been right all along much as she didn't want to be. Except, Ian wasn't just a psychopath. He physically transformed into that...that monstrosity. "When...when did this start? How?"

"Eight years ago," Richard sighed, unable to face her gaze. "He... changed for the first time shortly after Thanksgiving in 1974. We don't know why. It's physically impossible in scientific terms, but as you've seen, it happens. There is a medical...marker, you might call it. It's an unusual blood cell mutated by a virus as it reproduces.

For want of a better term, I call it the Lycan virus. I've never found evidence of it elsewhere. Yet, how it works I don't know. Neither a virus nor a blood cell explains a transformation like this. Nothing relational does."

"He...killed all those people?" Cynthia asked in a small voice, feeling sick.

"As far as I ...we know," Richard answered sadly. "He has no memory of doing any of it. He'd wake up in the morning, caked in dirt and blood, not knowing whose it was. He'd learn of what occurred the previous night. We presume he—the beast—did it. All the deaths and disappearances took place in the first few months, before we knew what was happening to him. He realized the clues before I did, but was understandably reluctant to believe it was true. In time, we restrained him. I filmed the transformation. Later, I did that many times and put them on video tape. We discovered that ordinary tranquilizers were useless, and that straps or normal chains couldn't hold him. It required silver-plated manacles to do it. He figured out the silver bullets and pentagrams. We did what we could, Doctor Akers. He's my godson. He ...wanted to die after what happened here seven years ago. He...tried to do it. I stopped him—restrained him for weeks; convinced him we could keep it in check. Until two nights ago, we did."

"And...I got him to...break his routine to go to the picnic," Cynthia felt a sudden wave of guilt.

"It wasn't just you, Doctor Akers. The others did, too. None of you knew the truth. He knew, but he wanted to be ...normal for a day. It had been so long. I warned him of the danger. He thought he could get back in time. If not for Foster, he would have."

"Foster ran him off the road, then?" Cynthia wanted to confirm her theory.

"Yes," Richard nodded. "Please believe me, Doctor Akers; he has no control over what he does in that form. I know I'm not a psychologist or psychiatrist, but I hypnotized him to determine what, if anything, he remembered. I could never break through whatever blocks his memory."

"If...if you're right, it proves he has no conscious control, but subconsciously it's harder to say. Lord! I'm talking about it like it's some normal case—he's a ....monster! He's slaughtered people—a child—his own family!" She put her head in her hands. "How do I process this? I...I like Ian, but how can I excuse this? He nearly killed me twice...and Colin, too. Yet, I know he did his best to protect us. He did. We'd be dead now, if not for these pendants and the silver bullets. Part of me wants to make excuses for him, but I...I don't know if I should."

"I understand the dilemma, Doctor Akers," Marsden sympathized. "I share it."

"More importantly, what do we do now? He's out there. We have to deal with that somehow. Nobody knows the danger. It's up to us." Cynthia locked eyes with Marsden.

"I have a gun that shoots drugged darts. We could take one loaded with silver bullets...just in case. The manacles are in the cell there," Richard responded dully, emotionally drained.

"What about me?" Cynthia wondered aloud. "What does that bite mean?"

"I don't know," Richard admitted honestly. "I wish I did. If you were going to change, you already would have; beyond that, it's all speculation. That cell is in your blood. I checked one of the samples I took this afternoon. That means the virus is there, too. Why you didn't change, I don't understand. You're younger than Ian, but not by enough that is should matter. You're similar enough in ethnicity. I can't see that explaining it, though some diseases affect certain ages or ethnicities more than others. Without a more detailed medical record to compare, only two differences stand out—blood type and gender. Given the creature's increase in muscular bulk and its violence, it could relate to testosterone levels in some way, but it will require a lot of experimentation to find out."

"Can I ...pass this thing on to anyone else?" Cynthia asked nervously.

"It's too soon to say," Richard responded, rubbing his bearded chin. "I presume the only way the virus could spread is via the beast's saliva. Unless you bite someone, it shouldn't spread it. I wouldn't give blood, though. That ought to result in direct transmission. It could be passed on to any children you have. Yet, that's a possibility rather than a certainty. I would guess that if your saliva got into an open wound, it might spread, but that's conjecture."

"That's …a lot to think about," Cynthia frowned. "We don't have time for it right now. He's …got a pretty good head start and he's a lot faster than we are. We've got to get going or we'll never catch him."

"You're right," Richard agreed, standing unsteadily, and then helping Cynthia to her feet. "But there…there's something else you need to know, Doctor Akers."

"What's that?" she inquired warily.

"I locked him in those manacles before I went up to your room. They're not broken nor are the chains. Someone let him loose."

CHAPTER 27

A HOWLING IN THE WOODS
OCTOBER 4, 1982

"What the hell was that friggin' thing?" gasped Deputy Harry Donaldson surveying the scene of carnage, his eyes wide and staring. "Our bullets didn't do a goddamn thing to it!"

"Can't say as I know, Harry," answered Amos, still in a state of shock himself. "I never saw nothing like it before. Don't know as I want to again either, but we gotta find it; can't let a thing like that run loose."

"What the hell do we do when we catch up to it?" Donaldson was visibly shaken by what he'd just seen. "Nothing seemed to phase it."

"I don' know. We gotta find a way—try something new; maybe stun guns, tranq darts, steel nets, gas. There has to be a way and it's up to us to find it. This must be what attacked that lady doc n' the kid last night. Might a' caused Carl's crash, too. She drove it off somehow. Why did she succeed, when we didn't? Gotta be a reason." Fitch had a faraway gleam in his eyes as he spoke.

"I wanna girl like that," Donaldson laughed nervously, incredulous. "When do we sign 'er up? How'd she do it?"

"She used the gun of one of the guard's, that'd been dropped. She's a brave one alright. What I wanna know is why it ran from her but tossed us around like chumps. I intend to take a close look at that gun. Somethin' must'a been different, but what?" Amos asked himself aloud, more than he spoke to Donaldson.

"I don't care what the thing is, but if I ever see it again it's too soon for me," Donaldson whispered under his breath. Distracted though he was, Fitch heard him.

"You might not, son," frowned Amos. "But I do. I wanna see the damned thing dead at my feet."

. . . .

"Who could've done that?" Cynthia gawked at Marsden. "Why would they?"

"I don't know," Richard gritted his teeth in frustration. "Ian insisted I chain him. As far as I know, the only key is in my pocket. I suppose any lock can be picked if you know how, but I don't know anyone who's good at picking locks. Even if I did, how did they know about this place? Aside from Ian and me, you're the only other person who knows. You didn't hear about it until this morning. Why anybody would do it is another mystery. Then there's the question of where they are. Anyone fool enough to free it ought to be dead, or at least unconsciousness in the cell."

"I hate to say it, but the motive was probably for Ian to kill us. I don't know whether that's because we represent a threat, or to torment him with more guilt; maybe both," Cynthia theorized...

"It still doesn't tell us either who or how." Marsden grabbed his medical bag, into which he placed the dart gun. He loaded some darts with the sedative he kept in vials in a refrigerator in the 'waiting room'.

"No, I suppose it doesn't," Cynthia acknowledged. "I wounded Ian the other night. The bullets were silver. Why is he still alive?"

"He almost wasn't," Marsden admitted. "He barely managed to make it here this morning. He called me, using the phone here. The two wounds hurt him—weakened him. But they didn't hit his heart or brain or cause enough bleeding for him to pass out. I ...removed the bullet. Then I chained him and used the moon lamps in the cell to speed up his healing."

"Well, at least that means the silver bullets have the...desired effect," Cynthia concluded. "Let's pray we don't have to use them."

. . . .

Amos could barely prevent himself from throwing up. The scene at the Robesons' house was....indescribable. He wished it was also invisible. Fitch doubted he would ever forget what he'd just seen. He wanted to forget it. The nearest approach to this was the incidents back in the mid '70s, but this was even worse than that.

It had to be the work of that thing. No human could've done what he found. Martha Robeson was severely gashed all over. Although her husband, Ted, had emptied his pistol, it didn't save him. He wasn't even in one piece when the police arrived after a neighbor called about the gunshots and screams.

And that horror was still out there! How many more victims were there going to be? The situation was out of hand, but what could he do about it? It wasn't as if he could tell the State Police or the FBI that he needed help to hunt a werewolf.

Mat and Lisa stood in the garage, at the foot of the stairs to the second floor. It was time for her to head back to the main house, and Mat had insisted on accompanying her there. After the events of the previous night, he wasn't willing to take anything for granted. Even the walk up the main drive wasn't necessarily safe. Nothing was going to happen to Lisa if he could do anything about it.

Just as they strode out onto the drive, he was grateful he did insist. Their blood was chilled by an echoing howl. They looked around for the source of the sound. Before they could locate it, a giant, dark shape hurtled out of the shadows behind the garage. Although it landed on the opposite side of the drive, whatever it was clipped Mat in its lunge.

Hunter was thrown helplessly to the cold cobblestones, and Lisa sent reeling when he was forced to release her hand. The breath exploded from Mat's lungs as he struck the pavement. Lisa steadied herself with difficulty, whirling to see if Mat was alright. Beyond him she saw the beast rising to its feet, eyes glowing in the darkness. A scream ripped from her lungs, her eyes widening in fear.

Lisa went rigid in shock, unable to look away as the creature loped toward her and Mat. Neither had a weapon with which to fend it off, but her scream and the howl caused the dogs to bark, and drew the attention of the security guards. They rushed to assist Mat and Lisa. Hunter attempted to stand, but he was bruised and still catching his breath. He'd never make it in time.

The guards drew their revolvers, but they had to be careful. The beast was between them and Mat and Lisa. They risked hitting the pair if they fired at the beast. Yet, if they did nothing, the pair was doomed. The dogs came running at the creature, snapping and barking at it.

They circled it and jumped up, chomping at the beast's legs. Angrily, the thing growled back at them. It swiped at the dogs. Most managed to avoid its savage blows, but it sent one of them yipping and flying through the air. When the dog landed, it lay quiet and still. The beast raked another, which ran off whimpering.

Mat finally made it to his feet, moving protectively to Lisa's side. She still couldn't get herself to move. Hunter knew that he could do little if the creature attacked them, but he could try to get Lisa away and out of the guard's line of fire. "Move, Leese!" he yelled. "Duck!" Grabbing her, he shoved her toward the trees on the opposite side of the drive. She gasped in surprise, but allowed herself to be carried along by him. It was not a moment too soon, as the guards let loose a barrage of gunfire. They failed to hit the beast, which moved with incredible speed, tossing a third dog to one side. Yelping angrily, it turned and charged the guards. They were so stunned at its change of direction that their aim went sideways. The creature toppled one guard, and easily threw another several yards away.

After that, it raced through the open gates. The guards' bullets pinged into the iron of the gates, and struck the piers to either side, but before any of them could fire again, it was beyond the gates and the access road, and into the woods on the far side of it. Once more, it has escaped. Two of the guards and three of the dogs were injured, but luckily no one was dead. How much longer would that luck hold?

"You think this'll work, Sheriff?" Donaldson asked, clearly skeptical. "If bullets didn't stop it, why would nets or stun sticks?"

"They're all we've got left tuh try shorta bombin' the damn thing. We don't have no jets or attack copters. The stun sticks are just tuh hurt it a bit. Our best chance of takin' it down is the gas. Make sure yuh get that mask on. I just pray that net'll hold it, once the gas knocks it out," Amos explained.

"Even if it works, where do we take it?" Donaldson looked baffled.

"We're usin' one o' the county's transport trucks. There's nobody at the jail now so, we'll put it in the cell until we can figure out what tuh do with it," Fitch answered, his expression determined.

"How do we find it, though?" Donaldson asked. "We lost its trail…"

"We've got tracking dogs on the way, but I'm headed out to the Holderness's estate. The thing just showed up there again," Amos replied.

"How the hell'd it get that far?" Donaldson blinked.

"I got no idea, but somehow it did," Fitch responded. "An' if it's there, so am I."

"He's gone into the woods," Cynthia observed in a whisper. "How do we track him, without him turning on us or at least getting lost? Neither of us is a hunter. We're running out of time. The sheriff's already on his way here. We want to catch him before he hurts anyone else."

"I'm not sure," Richard answered thoughtfully. "We've got to stop back at my car to get my flashlight or we'll be stumbling around in the dark."

"I should've thought to get one myself," Cynthia agreed.

"One will have to suffice," Richard concluded. "Are you sure you're up to this? I've done it before, if not often or recently. You don't have to come with me."

"No...I guess I don't," she acknowledged. "But I will anyway. The fact that the pendant he gave me and the silver bullets he provided saved my life, might be canceled out by the fact that it was he who endangered Colin and me. But if I'm willing to accept that he can't control this, then it isn't his fault. Foster prevented him from getting to you in time and someone unlocked his chains. Most of all, Colin needs a father. For now, I'll...set aside my...other concerns."

"You're not tempted to tell the sheriff when he gets here?" Marsden raised an eyebrow, watching Cynthia closely.

"Why? So he can lock me up in the drunk tank or the nearest asylum? How will that help Colin—or me for that matter? I'd lose my job here...get a reputation as a nut. Revenge might feel good for a few minutes, but it won't help any of us in the long term," Cynthia answered. She wasn't happy about it, but she had to help Marsden, even though Ian was a killer. She wanted to believe that it wasn't his fault.

From a certain perceptive, did it matter? Ian was a danger as long as he lived. His guilt or innocence consciously did not entirely absolve him of what the beast had done. At the most, it might affect which type of murder charge he was guilty of. She set the questions on the back burner, because she couldn't settle the moral debate.

"I'm sorry you've been dragged into all this, Doctor Akers,"

Marsden said apologetically. "We thought we had it under control."

"Oh well," Cynthia sighed. "The best laid plans of doctors and werewolves…"

"It's been sighted!" yelled one of the deputies. "Get the net and the gas ready!" The dogs barked and yelped behind him. Red and blue lights flashed all around. A howl echoed in the woods, growing nearer. It was headed for the clearing. It would be there any moment.

Amos waited impatiently. It wouldn't be long before he knew if his plan was going to work. It had better, because he had no backup plan. If this failed, what then?

CHAPTER 28

THE BEAST MUST DIE!
OCTOBER 4, 1982

Shots rang out in the night air. Yells and cries mingled with growls, snarls and howls. The creature swung wildly at the stun sticks, yipping if it touched them. More than one was snapped off or torn from the deputy's hands, but it didn't break their cordon. It chomped at them viciously. Several who got to close were thrown aside like helpless children.

In seconds, the creature was enveloped in clouds of gas. The lights of the squad cars became freakishly diffused by the chemical fog. The thing's nose sniffed the air, and it growled raggedly in displeasure. At first it appeared the gas was having little effect, but then the thing started to stagger almost drunkenly, coughing and spitting like a giant cat with a hairball. It pawed futilely at the smoke, fighting its inability to breathe.

"The net!" Fitch called out urgently. "Release the net!" His order was followed. The net arched into the night sky above the beast. It swirled about. Then its weighted edges dropped towards the ground, draping over and around the creature. It fought the net wildly, infuriated, but the steel mesh resisted its claws and fangs. That only angered it more.

Despite its best efforts, the beast had breathed in the gas. Even it needed air. The staggering grew worse, becoming ever more unsteady. Finally, it collapsed to its knees. Shortly after that it, fell over on its side. Before long, it ceased to even twitch.

Gradually, the gas dissipated. The creature lay still beneath the net. No one approached it immediately, distrustful that it wasn't faking. They'd all seen what it was capable of doing. Nobody was anxious to risk those claws and fangs, but they couldn't just leave it where it was.

"Well, don't just look at it!" Amos exclaimed. "It's out. Get in there and put it into the truck. We don't know how long we have till it wakes up." It required four deputies to lift it after the net was removed. They carried it with difficulty, and nearly stumbled trying to load it into the truck.

"God, that fuckin' thing's heavy!!" Donaldson huffed and puffed, even after it was loaded in the back of the truck. "Must weigh a damn ton..."

The doors of the truck were slammed shut and locked, the deputies sighing with relief. "Now that we've got it, we've gotta find out what the hell it is," Fitch concluded. "Where'd it come from? There are still a lot of questions to be answered. I want 'em answered—soon."

Watching from amongst the trees, Cynthia and Marsden saw the capture of the beast. Though tempted to, neither spoke. What could they do now? Dare they do anything? When Ian changed back, what would they do then? Would it result in the first werewolf trial since the 17th century? Or might the government swoop in, to take Ian to be experimented upon? The options were not pleasant to contemplate.

"We should go back to the house," she whispered. "I don't think we can do anything here. We've got no way to free him and, while he's ...like that, we shouldn't even try."

"I know you're right, Doctor Akers," Richard responded, eyes glued to the truck. "This is hard for me—leaving him to his fate. I've been protecting him for so long, it's second nature to me, but I don't see any way to help him escape. I'm not a spy or a lock smith. Assuming we could get to the truck unseen, I don't know how to get those doors unlocked before they notice us."

"And it won't be any better than the local jail, where they're taking him," Cynthia shook her head in disappointment. "I'm afraid we've lost. It's over."

"Unfortunately, I think you're right," Marsden acknowledged with reluctance. "Let's go. I can't watch any more of this."

October 5, 1982

The truck bearing the beast clattered along the estate's access road towards town. For the time being, the town's jail would have to do. It was currently empty and it was nearby. That gave it an advantage over any other potential option. Amos wouldn't feel better until it was behind thick, steel bars.

It was still a couple of hours until dawn. Fitch wondered what it really was. It was as big as a bear, yet more man-like, and it wore the tattered remnants of clothes. Could it actually be a werewolf as old Sheriff Sampson had theorized? Or was it some weird lab experiment?

Within the truck, the beast's eyes opened, the effects of the gas quickly wearing off. It growled deeply at finding itself meshed in the steel net in the back of the moving truck. It had no intention of remaining there.

It began to struggle against the net. Without the weakening distraction of the gas, the net failed to hold the beast for long. Its claw cut through the net; the thing's immense strength pulled it apart as if it were string. Then it rose to its clawed feet...and hurled itself at the double doors of the police "wagon".

Seated in a squad car behind the wagon, Amos heard the ominous pounding from inside. His driver, Henry Ormond, heard it, too. The metal of the doors began to dent, buckling outward, echoing in the night. Finally, its locks strained too far, the doors burst open...and the beast leapt out.

Amos had to know if his hunch was correct. How could it be that Dr. Akers was able to drive it off, when nothing else worked? He needed to check the ammunition that the security guards at the Holderness estate had used. Still, even that hadn't brought the beast down and it always sought to escape them. So was the incident with Dr. Akers just a fluke?

"Good mornin'," Fitch smiled wanly. "I hate to be botherin' you at this hour. I wish I had better news. We caught the thing—gassed it and drugged it, but it came to and escaped; tore the damn doors of the truck right off."

"That's quite alright, Sheriff," Seth yawned. "It's good of you to come out in person to let us know. So, your men are hunting it again?"

"Ain't got no choice," Amos answered, embarrassed. "Can't let that thing run loose."

"No, I wouldn't think so," Seth nodded. "I'll have the guards stay extra alert, for all the good it'll probably do."

"I'll talk to 'em on my way out, Mr. Blackthorne I want to get a few more details 'bout what happened earlier, anyhow." Fitch tipped his hat as he left the foyer.

"They're at your service, Sheriff." Seth gave a brief wave just before the outer doors closed.

Down at the garage, Amos asked the guards a few questions, but they didn't know much, since the shift had changed after the incident took place. Although Mat Hunter and the secretary, Miss Ramirez, had been present, both were in bed now, exhausted by what happened. The Ramirez girl had been so upset, that Dr. Marsden gave her a sedative in order to rest. Fitch decided he could talk to them tomorrow...or was that later today? It had been a long night.

Pretending that he was just checking on the caliber the guards were using, Amos examined one of their revolvers and a box of bullets they had stored in the guardhouse. Secretly, he pocketed one. To him, they did look like they could be silver, but he wanted to make sure. That purloined bullet would give him the answers he sought.

If he was right, why were the guards armed with them? They did not seem aware of it, but somebody was; presumably Holderness, who was still missing. That might mean Holderness knew about it and prepared for it. The question was how he knew and why nobody else did. Of course, old Sheriff Sampson had theorized it was a werewolf after all conventional avenues proved fruitless. Everyone thought he'd gone nuts in the end, from all the pressure. Now, unfortunately, Fitch knew better. Sampson had been right.

The creature staggered through the woods, periodically doubling over and bracing itself for support. Every so often, it fell to its knees; even onto all fours. The injuries he had sustained the previous night had still not fully healed.

The graze wound on its shoulder, though knitting fast, still seared like fire, the nerve endings raw. The chest wound hurt even more, if that was possible. While it hadn't hit the beast's heart, it came close. The thing felt that the bullet was gone. Yet, just enough of its casing remained in the wound to slow down the healing process, which was normally almost instantaneous.

The beast had lost quite a bit of blood, too, which weakened it. Though grateful to escape its prison, it was in no shape to hunt tonight. The local prey was getting used to its presence—prepared for it. That was not good. Once it healed, it was time to seek newer hunting grounds...less dangerous ones.

Instinct told it to avoid the dwelling places of the prey, until it was strong again. When it was weak, the prey became the hunters. The beast could not afford to be cornered by them. Finally, it came to a building; a ruin. It sensed the prey did not frequent this place. Entering, it collapsed to the floor and knew no more.

CHAPTER 29

AWAKENINGS
TUESDAY OCTOBER 5, 1982

Ian came to with a groan. He ached all over, but his chest still hurt. His eyes stuck together as if they'd been glued. His mouth tasted like a swamp. On top of everything else, he was starving, and thirsty enough to drink the river dry. It had happened again. He wasn't in the safe room. How had he gotten out?

Then flashes of hazy memory came back to him. Richard had locked the manacles before he went up to escort Cynthia to the cell. They had debated whether or not to do it, but ultimately both agreed that she had a right to know now that she was infected. Yet, after Richard left, the cell grew icy cold and he was surrounded by a black fog that smelled of stale flowers. Before he blacked out, he heard the lock on the manacles click open. By then it was too late to relock them and Richard had the key...

What had he done last night—and to whom? At a certain level, Ian didn't want to know. The truth was never good. Sometimes it was too terrible to contemplate, like seven years ago. If only he had the strength to end it all, but there was Colin to think about. On the other hand, could he ever be a real father to the boy as he was? Where was he this time? Ian attempted to sit up, but was too dizzy. He was on a wooden floor, not the open ground. He was in some sort of building. The floor was dusty and dirty, not well maintained. The sunlight was greatly diffused by the grime on the windows. Ian fought a sneeze.

Gazing upward, he saw shadowed wooden rafters; cobwebs obscuring some of them. Brighter light lanced through a broken window. The place was familiar somehow, though at the moment he wasn't sure where or what it was. Ian racked his foggy brain for an answer.

Then, at last, it came to him. He recognized where he was. It was the old abandoned train depot that once served the estate. It had been built in the 1860s and fallen into disuse in the early 1930s. It was around a mile from the house, a bit less from the edge of the estate, but what would he find when he returned there?

Ian prayed he hadn't killed anyone last night. The question was what to do now. He was roughly an equal distance between the sanitarium and the estate. To which should he go? If he couldn't sit up, the point was moot. How was he going to explain his condition—and where he'd been the last two days?

Gritting his teeth against the pain, Ian forced himself to sit up and eventually to stand. He decided to head for the estate. He'd just have to tell them he collapsed at the old depot, after having wondered semiconscious from the site of the accident with Foster's truck. Richard and Cynthia would know the truth, but neither was liable to contradict him.

It was a long walk, especially in rags and bare feet, but it wouldn't get any shorter by waiting. How he hated this; though it was the least of his troubles. The only good thing about it was that he had a little while before he discovered what horrors he'd committed last night. That was always fun....

Carl's eyes fluttered open. He felt horrible...hungry, thirsty, every muscle and joint throbbed. His skin felt like it had been scrubbed with sandpaper. His mouth tasted like partially-dried paste. Foster's head pounded in his ears, and the morning light hurt his eyes. Despite how hungry he was, he was afraid he'd throw up if he ate anything.

He must really have tied one on last night...He couldn't remember where he'd been. Looking around, Foster saw that he was at home. It was messier than usual. Carl vaguely acknowledged that he was no Neatnik, but he didn't normally leave his windows wide open or track mud across the floor, and topple his furniture.

Then, he realized that his window was not open. It had been smashed in; pieces of broken wood and shattered glass lay everywhere. What the hell? Why the heck wasn't he wearing anything? It wasn't uncommon for him to pass out at the end of the night, but he was always in whatever clothes he'd worn the previous night.

Only then did Carl notice that his feet were muddy and grass-stained. That didn't make any sense. He never walked outside barefoot; even to pick up the morning paper. Finally, his memories began to flood back...the accident...the hospital...the pain...then there was running, leaping; cool night air, a thousand sights, sounds, smells, gunshots, and cops…was any of it real, though? Or was it all just a really weird dream?

Carl wasn't sure he wanted to know which it was. He got up and headed to the bathroom to take a shower. What day was it? He saw almost 9:00am…fuck! He was late for work! Ted will dock him for sure; if he was even just five or ten minutes late, the fucker would dock him the whole hour. One day that creep'd get his…

After he finished his shower and dressed, Carl went into the kitchen to get something to eat. He opened the refrigerator, hurriedly searching for something—anything to eat or drink. He was ravenously hungry and so thirsty. He considered a sandwich, but that would take too long. He needed food now, not in five minutes.

He grabbed some cold cuts, pulling out several slices at a time. He stuffed them into his mouth, barely chewing them before he swallowed them. Foster quickly went through all of his cold cuts. He very nearly choked, trying to swallow so much so fast. It wasn't enough. He needed more.

Returning to the fridge, Carl took out a two-pound package of ground beef that he'd intended to use that weekend, when his boy, Andy, was over. Foster tore into the chilled burger. He almost inhaled it, pushing hands-full of meat into his mouth, until no more would fit. He almost choked again, but didn't stop until it was all gone.

Then Carl rushed to the faucet of his kitchen sink, desperate for water. His throat was so dry it was painful. He guzzled frantically. Two hours later, his hunger and thirst began to subside.

Carl considered calling into work, but he chickened out. It was way too late now. He tried phoning Eddie, but Hastings didn't answer. He was probably at work. Where else would he be near noon on a Tuesday?

Plopping down into his well-worn recliner, he picked up the remote and pressed the power button. It took a while for the old Zenith to warm up. It brightened and finally popped on, the picture gradually growing clearer. Nothing much was on at this hour but the noon news. Carl reluctantly settled for that.

The promo for the local news came on first. "Stay tuned for local news. Police report the brutal murders of Theodore Robeson and his wife, Martha. Robeson was a local contractor; details after these commercials..."

"Somebody offed Ted?" Carl's jaw dropped in surprise. "Guess he won't be dockin' me today," he chuckled sarcastically. "Might as well sit back and relax. Wonder how he kicked the bucket."

Almost half an hour passed before the advertised story was broadcast. According to the report, an unknown assailant broke into Robesons' home on the outskirts of Corchester. Windows were broken and the door bashed in. Robeson and his wife were found in their bedroom. The manner of death has not been released, since the autopsy had yet to be performed.

As he watched the story, Carl saw repeated flashes in his mind. They were distorted, disconnected images that grew increasingly troubling, even for Carl. They all involved Ted's house. Were they real or imagined?

It was night. Foster battered at the door and broke one of the windows, then splintered the door. Ted's wife, Martha, ran into the living room, drawn by the sound. She held a fiberglass baseball bat in both hands. She was yelling, but there was terror in her eyes.

Carl easily disposed of the baseball bat, bending it until it snapped in two, one of her arms with it. She screamed in agony. She ran, ending up in the bathroom. The bedroom and bathroom doors proved minimal obstacles. He raked her. Long bloody gashes scored her from throat to groin.

Then Foster heard the truck pull into the driveway. More prey! Ted came into the house, unaware that Carl was there. By the time Ted realized Carl was there, Ted was in the bedroom. He shot at Carl. The bullets whizzed past, grazing him. Foster lunged for Ted's exposed shoulder and throat, biting them like a wild animal would, nearly decapitating Robeson in the process.

Carl's teeth tore through flesh and muscle, crunching bone. He drank the blood gushing from the wound, greedily, without a trace of guilt or hesitation. He chewed and gnawed on the skin and sinew beneath. By then, Robeson was dead. Before the body cooled, Carl ripped out the liver and ate it, busting the ribs to get at Ted's now-stilled heart...

It was a nightmare; just an hallucination induced by the story on the news and the shock about it. His imagination was just a little morbid and way too vivid. That was all. That's all it could be. Not even Carl was capable of such an abhorrent act. He might be strong—but not that strong. It couldn't be real—it couldn't...but what if it was?

October 5, 1982 Tuesday

Cynthia sat on a bench on the terrace, gazing out at the garden below. The flower beds were empty until spring. The trees were less green and full than in summer. She shivered slightly in the breeze. She'd put on a sweater, but it didn't help much.

Lost in thought, Cynthia was largely oblivious to her surroundings, save for the cold. Her mind was in turmoil. How should she react? Ian had hidden the truth about himself, even when the subject of the beast came up. It was understandable that he would try to hide it. Until she saw that creature, she was unlikely to have believed him. It would've sounded like a bad joke or a delusion, but Cynthia wasn't laughing.

Once she did experience it, she had good reason to fear him. After all, he'd attacked and infected her, though the result of the latter remained to be seen. Who wouldn't be upset? Most people would have run screaming by now. That's what Danny would tell her.

So why was she still sitting here? Was it just dedication to Colin? Was it the money? Was it because she'd been infected? Cynthia had not transformed. Maybe she never would, but the virus would always be there inside her, and she could potentially spread it.

Life held no guarantees. Still, Ian and Dr. Marsden knew more about this condition than anyone else she was ever liable to encounter. Nobody else would understand better than they would, and yet not having changed meant that she could only partially understand Ian and what he'd gone through.

Ian had caused the deaths of his mother, his stepfather, half-sister and friend. He'd traumatized his own son, and presumably killed those victims mentioned in the articles collected by Colin. What could possibly excise all that? How could she wrap her head around it? Since he'd lied to her, too, why should she believe anything that he could conceivable tell her?

What was a mildly flirtatious physical attraction compared to all those objections? Yet, Cynthia remained here, actually considering talking to him. Was she utterly insane? It annoyed her that she kept asking that.

Maybe she was crazy. Despite all the logical objections, she wanted to hear what Ian had to say. She needed to. She could probably guess the majority of it. Doubtless, he would give a self-serving version of events, but in his voice, gazing into his eyes.

She wasn't stupid, but she acknowledged to herself that his charm might win her over. Cynthia could believe him because she wanted to...because it was easier than admitting that she'd been totally fooled. Romantic that she was, Cynthia was reluctant to give up the rosy fairytale she had begun to let herself hope for.

The handsome prince turned out not merely to be a beast, but also a deadly one, a nightmarish serial killer. His "kiss", as it were, had doomed her to the possibility that she would become one, too. That potential might never be realized, of course, but as long as she lived she could never be entirely sure it wouldn't be. Worse still, she wouldn't know unless and until it occurred. How could she ever forgive Ian for the "gift" he'd saddled her with?

Dare she risk that his good looks and charm would sway her? That her own bias towards him would pave the way? On the other hand, were she to leave now, Cynthia could never have children of her own without the risk of passing on the virus in her blood. Nor could she explain why to anyone else. They'd think she was mad.

Was it transmissible by means other than a bite? Would she have to become celibate? There was no danger of infecting Ian, but they couldn't have children either. With the virus affecting both parents, any child was nearly certain to end up with it. It was a lot to give up in one fell swoop.

Cynthia's options were limited. There was no turning back now. She had to deal with the situation, as it was not as she wished it to be; part of that included giving Ian a chance to explain himself. If she didn't, she'd always wonder what he would've said…

The only potential excuse was that he had no control as the beast. Dr. Marsden had told her that, and she could figure it out for herself, but it wasn't an automatic get-out-of-jail-free card. But it was the only explanation that even partially expunged his guilt. Yet, it was only a partial excuse even then.

It paralleled excuses made to the courts based upon psychological conditions, like multiple personality syndrome, but that was only valid if Ian really didn't have conscious control over what he did. How could she ever be sure?

Cynthia hissed in disgust. She could debate with herself endlessly and never resolve the questions. She couldn't even turn Ian in. Nobody would believe her. So, it boiled down to her reaction to him. Could she live with what he'd done, under the circumstances? If so, what were they?

Could she turn her back on Ian and the life that they might've shared? Could she walk away, knowing what she did and what he might do? If not, was she up to destroying Ian to prevent what he might do? The last question included dealing with Carl Foster, too, and herself if the need arose. It had probably been Foster in town last night.

Enough! It was time that she faced Ian. Standing, Cynthia turned to go inside. It couldn't be put off any longer…

"They found him!" Colin came close to shouting when he saw Cynthia come into the house. "Did you hear?"

"Yes," Cynthia replied as neutrally as she could. "Dr. Marsden told me a little while ago. It's …wonderful news." She tried to hide her ambivalence. Colin wouldn't understand it.

"He says he was dazed after the accident and wandered into the woods—then woke up at the old train depot!" Colin exclaimed excitedly.

"I'm so happy …for you that he's alright. I know how worried you were," Cynthia responded. "Thankfully, we all made it through."

"You're ok, too, now aren't you, Doc?" Colin asked with genuine concern. "I was scared for you, when you said you got bitten…"

"I'm fine, Colin," Cynthia lied. "Since I didn't change, maybe I did just imagine that part…"

CHAPTER 30

TRUTH OR CONSEQUENCES
TUESDAY OCTOBER 5, 1982

A knock sounded upon the door of Ian's room. He sat near his window, trying to figure out what to say to Cynthia. Glancing up, he tensed instinctively. "Yes? Who is it?"

"It's Cynthia," she replied. "May I come in?"

"You don't have to ask, but are you sure you even want to?" Ian responded warily.

"No, I'm not certain," she answered. "But what I want and what I need to do are not necessarily the same. We need to talk. I don't think we can afford to wait."

"I agree," Ian stated nervously. Cynthia pushed the door inward and entered. "This isn't easy for me."

"Me neither," Ian said. He wanted to look away, afraid to meet her eyes, yet knowing that he dared not to do it. Whatever happened next he had to face. Cowardice was tempting, but there seemed no way out here. He owed it to her to explain—to face her—even if she renounced him and vowed his destruction. It was what he deserved. He'd almost killed her twice! Worse still, he'd sentenced her to a life of uncertainty and denial. All life involved uncertainty, but this was a peculiar sort that he had caused.

"I gather you know now," Ian stated, as pronouncing a death sentence on him. "What I don't know is how you can stand to be in the same room with me."

"Because I have to be here," Cynthia looked down, her palms sweaty, as uneasy as he was. "I...I've got to know, to hear the truth from you...to see you in person when you do."

"Will you believe anything I say?" Ian asked skeptically. "I'm not sure I would if it were me." He fidgeted, reminding her of a guilty child about to be scolded by his parents.

"I don't know yet," Cynthia admitted. "I've never been in a situation like this before."

"Neither have I," Ian tried to sound neutral. "I don't really know what to tell you."

"When did it begin? How?" Cynthia queried. "I guess I've got to start somewhere."

"I've never known what caused it..." Ian hesitated awkwardly. "I can backtrack to the first night I changed, November 27th, 1974 and the two nights after that. I didn't realize what was happening then. It took a few months for me to put it all together and several more before I accepted the truth. It's always been three nights in a row, the full moon and the night before and after it. The only exception was seven years ago, when the moon wasn't full and I didn't change the next two nights. It begins with abdominal cramps, quickening heart rate, a headache and joint aches, a sudden, severe sweat…then the convulsions, followed by blacking out, but then the visible change already started. I saw it, but I didn't want to believe what I saw. Given the pain of the convulsions, I initially thought the changes I saw were hallucinations or a bad dream. But they weren't. I'd seen the movies. There were no conclusions in the old Universal films due to the nature of the special effects they used. But most other movies include them, I don't know why I go through them, if it's derived from those movies. It took me a while to admit to myself that it was real. Once I change, I have no control over what I do. I don't even remember it. I have to piece it together after the fact. Sometimes I can't; there's not enough to go on …" his tone was wistful, guilty.

"I assumed you'd say that, that you couldn't control it. I wasn't sure about the memory thing. Why should I believe you? If you wanted me to be sympathetic what else could you say? 'I'm a serial killer and I enjoy it'? There's nobody I can ask for advice. No one would believe me if I told them. I want to believe you, because if I don't, it means I was totally wrong about you-completely taken in. For someone in my profession, that's not particularly flattering to admit. We're paid to 'read' people—evaluate their honesty and intentions, but I can't let all that sway me. It's got to be the truth; not just what I want to hear."

"I don't know what to tell you," Ian answered sadly. "What I told you is the truth. I can have Richard show you tapes of the change, but it won't get you inside my head. If you don't believe me, there's nothing more I can tell you to convince you. I understand why you'd be reluctant to trust me after what I did the last couple of days. You're right, Cynthia. I have to say I can't control it, but that doesn't mean it's true. I suppose you could hook me up to a lie detector machine, or try hypnosis or sodium pentothal. That's all I can offer. I don't want to be what I am, but there's no cure. Believe me, we've searched. I've done the best I can to avoid getting loose…yet I still did twice in a row. It's my own fault. I shouldn't have agreed to go to the picnic, or I should've left sooner, but it's too late for what-ifs. I did what I did. I can't call it back no matter how much I want to." He sounded sincere.

"I've been wondering something," Cynthia temporarily changed the subject. "When you were leaving the picnic, you seemed suddenly upset by something. What was it?"

"I …see the pentagram on my potential victims—just like in the movies. I saw it on you then, and it scared the hell out of me."

"So, that's what it was," Cynthia perked up, fascinated by the revelation. She'd been right. He had seen something.

"It's one reason I got my family those pendants, though I was too slow in giving them out. I'd never transformed without a full moon before. I thought it was safe to hold that party. When I realized I was wrong, it was way too late. My mom was scared when I went into convulsions. I couldn't break away to go to the safe room in time. She didn't understand what was happening. I couldn't explain. There wasn't time. I still have no idea why I changed that night. It's never happened that way again since."

"That must be why you had Irv make all those silver bullets," Cynthia theorized. "It wasn't to hunt the beast. It was so the security guards could kill you, or drive you away if you got free."

"Right again," Ian gave her a weary, self-deprecating smile. "By the way, thank you for saving Colin and those guards the other night. I'm grateful to you for that."

"You're glad I shot you?" she eyed him skeptically. "I might've killed you."

"Definitely," Ian was empathic. "It had to be done. I'm glad someone was there to do it, though I'm sorry it had to be you. It was unfortunate you were put in that position. I'm grateful that you were up to it. I wish none of it happened, of course, but Colin and those guards are alive because of you."

"You're …welcome." Cynthia didn't know how to react to that. "I think..."

"Try to understand something about me, Cynthia; I...miss my family. You can't imagine how much. I grieve for them every day. I'll never stop blaming myself. I couldn't control what I did, but I should never have endangered them as I did, no matter what that meant for me. I ...failed to protect them...from me. I can never forget that or forgive myself for it. I was...selfish, afraid to be found out...to pay for what I'd already done. Foolishly, I kept hoping for a cure—a way to return to my old life again, but there is no going back. I crossed that line a long time ago. I've killed people, Cynthia; killed them horribly. It took that night—losing my family and Paul—to teach me a lesson. I can't ever go back now. I don't deserve a cure, even if one is ever found. I can't bring back my victims. My life...my happiness is not worth their lives. I should be dead, not them."

"Dr. Marsden, he...he said you tried to commit suicide once—after that night—that he stopped you..."

"He did," Ian reflected. "It was right after the funerals in November '75. He sensed what I had planned and prevented me from doing it. He kept me restrained for days—weeks. Sometimes I wished that he'd let me do it. At least it would've been over for me. I couldn't do any more harm, but ...it wasn't meant to be, I guess. It was too easy a way out. I hadn't paid enough for what I did. Maybe I never can. I don't even know how many people I've killed. I doubt I ever will. I guess I'm weak too—cowardly. There's no easy way to do it. A silver bullet in a vital spot, the correct amount of wolfs bane, decapitation, maybe asphyxiation. I haven't had the courage to do it. Although it would've hurt Colin, I wish you'd succeeded. I'd be at peace now."

"Suicide should never be the answer," Cynthia said haltingly. "We're supposed to confront our problems, overcome them; not run from them. Suicide is the ultimate cowardice. It's giving up, but what do I know? I'm just babbling. You can't correct what you've already done, but maybe you can partially make up for it."

"I would if I could," Ian sighed, "but how? What could possibly even things out?"

"Perhaps you can't," Cynthia sounded uncertain, "but you've got to at least try, whether you ever succeed or not...if you're not lying to me."

"I'm not," Ian insisted. "I promised you."

"Then, for now, I'll try to give you the benefit of the doubt. No rational person would believe this unless there was no way to deny it. Your death might save others in the future, but it won't bring back those you've already killed. Nothing will. It's a cliché, but all you can do is try to see to it that they didn't die for nothing, that no good came afterwards. I'm not saying you can give their deaths meaning just by performing good deeds. Still, whatever good you do somewhat mitigates your continued existence. I'm being selfish, too. I want to believe that my assessment of your character wasn't entirely wrong. Multiple personality patients often do not know of their other selves, and have no control over them. I could be naive to equate your condition with multiple personality disorder, but it's the closest analogy I can think of. I ...I don't want to be alone in this. Then there's Colin. He needs a father. Losing you now...I'm not sure what it would do to him."

"You're not going to turn me in—or leave?" Ian seemed surprised.

"Who would I turn you in to? The sheriff? He'd think I was nuts. Even if he didn't, he would probably kill you. Then where would Colin be? The media would never admit the truth. They would label you a serial killer. Your son's life would be destroyed. I can't just leave. Colin needs help. I think we're beginning to make progress. If I left suddenly, without a good explanation, I'm afraid he'd suffer a setback. I don't want to risk Colin finding out the truth after I left, and having to deal with it alone. That's too much for anyone, let alone a fourteen-year-old. I still need this job, too, crazy as that sounds. How could I explain my sudden departure, after only two weeks, to anyone else?"

"Then you're staying solely for Colin's sake?" Ian inquired almost hopefully.

"No...not just that," Cynthia struggled to give a coherent answer. "But it's a major reason. I already told you I don't want to face this alone. I might never transform, but I will never be sure of it. If you're looking for forgiveness, I'm sorry, Ian; it's too soon. I'm not certain how long it'll take me to sort it out. Instinct tells me to run. Don't make me regret that I didn't. That's the best I can do right now. You're the first...werewolf I've ever met before. God! Did I just say that out loud?" she shook her head in self-mockery. "I'll get back to you."

October 7, 1982

Breakfast had just been cleared away. Sunlight streamed in through the glass in the solarium. They sat around the oval table, no one speaking. Ian was at the head of the table. Moira had not arrived at the house yet, and Lisa had already finished and was busy. Mat was doing the lawn.

"Did anybody watch the morning news?" Seth broke the ice.

"No, Seth," Ian replied distractedly.

"There was a particularly unpleasant murder two nights ago—a local building contractor and his wife. Someone forced their way into his home. The reporters were circumspect, but it sounds quite gruesome." Seth's eyes were alight, and he rubbed his hands gleefully.

"Seth, we just had breakfast," Ian rolled his eyes in annoyance.

"I just thought you might be interested," Seth shrugged indifferently. "Your ...friend, Mr. Foster, is evidently a suspect. He disappeared from his hospital room the same night. He used to work for the victim and had no alibi. They were known to have argued..."

"They've accused Carl Foster?" Ian suddenly looked up in surprise, his expression troubled. "He just walked out of the hospital without being seen?"

"Not quite," Seth yawned. "The nurses were alerted by the monitors going wild and went to investigate, but Foster was gone. The window was broken from the inside."

Cynthia and Colin's eyes grew wide. Ian paled. 'Interesting," he commented, trying to sound conversational.

"Foster was listed as missing, but he turned up at his home, though he hadn't contacted the hospital. He also didn't go to work, as if he knew his employer wouldn't be there...still, for now, they're calling him a 'person of interest'. He hasn't been arrested."

"It…doesn't seem to be his day," Ian observed. "Didn't he crash his truck near here a few days ago?" he added innocently.

"I believe that's why he was in the hospital," Seth replied, already seeming bored.

"I knew something would happen," Colin said earnestly. "It must've bitten him. Nobody will admit it, but it had to have. When a werewolf bites you, if you live, you become one."

"I thought that was vampires," smirked Seth with a sardonic twinkle in his eyes.

"Them, too," Colin agreed. "Except that their victims die first and it might take several bites to do it. With werewolves, it only requires one bite. With zombies, it's one bite but the victim dies before they change. It was a full moon the last two nights."

"My, you do know your monster lore," Seth chuckled. "I'd forgotten a lot of that. I used to watch those movies all the time, but I haven't for a few years now. So, they create zombies by bite, now, do they? What happened to a good old-fashioned voodoo ritual?"

"It's not just the movies," Colin insisted, his expression serious. "I don't know about zombies or vampires, but werewolves are real. I've seen one twice. Dr. Akers saw it, too, the other night."

"Really?" Seth cocked an eyebrow. "Do tell, Doctor. How did your little meeting go?"

"I'd rather not talk about it," Cynthia frowned at Seth. "It wasn't pleasant. It severely damaged my car. Colin was very brave. I plan to visit the injured guards this afternoon. It came back two nights ago, as well, and attacked Mat and Lisa, injured more guards, and some of the dogs."

"I knew there'd been some kind of ruckus from what the sheriff said, but a werewolf? Really?" Seth rolled his eyes mockingly.

"Believe what you like, Mr. Blackthorne. I saw it; so did Colin and the guards." Cynthia didn't retreat from his sarcasm.

"You should've seen her!" Colin gushed with uncharacteristic enthusiasm. "When the guard dropped his gun, she dived for it and shot the werewolf twice. That's what made it leave. It would've killed us, if not for her."

"Don't exaggerate, Colin. I didn't do that much," Cynthia blushed slightly. "Anybody would've done it."

"Don't be so modest my dear," Seth said appreciatively. "It seems we owe you a debt of gratitude. Perhaps we should've hired you as a bodyguard instead of a doctor."

"Don't embarrass her, Seth," Ian admonished him. "I'm grateful she was there."

"I wasn't trying to embarrass her," Seth denied his stepbrother's claim. "It's too bad she didn't kill the ruddy thing. Then we could all sleep safely in our beds again."

"She did hit it," Colin interjected.

"She couldn't have or it would be dead," Seth disagreed.

"Colin is right, Seth!" Ian defended his son and Cynthia's marksmanship. "The security guards confirmed that she did. It just must not have been in a vital spot, but it drove the thing away—that's what matters."

"Well, it seems I was wrong." Seth threw her a tight artificial smile.

Ian gave Seth a stern glance but said nothing. Cynthia watched the exchange. She wondered how much Seth knew. Had Blackthorne figured out the truth? For all his sarcasm, Seth was highly observant and far from stupid. Despite what he'd said, he knew those films and was unlikely to have forgotten them. So it was entirely possible that he'd guessed. Cynthia decided she ought to keep an eye on him.

He could not be as naive about the recent incidents as he had pretended. Doubtless his skepticism had been to rankle Ian, mock her, and upset Colin by questioning his veracity again. Blackthorne always liked to keep the pot well stirred...

Later, Cynthia met up with Colin on the stairs. "I wanted to ask you a favor."

"Sure Doc, what?" Colin turned towards her.

"Don't tell anyone I was bitten—especially your uncle. He'd just rib me endlessly about it."

"Whatever you say, Doc," Colin agreed. "It's between us."

CONTINUED IN...

BOOK 2

ALL HALLOWS' EVE

THE MAN IN THE MIRROR